THE PAWNSHOP DOOR BLEW OPEN IN A BALL OF FIRE . . .

The floor of the tunnel where Garry hid shuddered with the force of the explosion. Static filled the computer screen, then cleared to show the intruder, taking something from beneath his jacket. Another explosion. Garry's father jumped back from the window. Sudden blinding flash.

The last thing the computer showed was his father hurtling backward, one hand—the place where a hand had *been*—spraying a bright arc of red.

Garry bit down on a nauseating sense of loss—and he fought against other, more crimson emotions that threatened to sweep him back into the certain death of the pawnshop. After a moment he took a deep, shuddering breath, held it, then let it out. There were things to do.

He went . . .

YESTERDAY'S PAWN

W. T. Quick

A SIGNET BOOK

NEW AMERICAN LIBRARY

A DIVISION OF PENGUIN BOOKS USA INC., NEW YORK

NAL BOOKS ARE AVAILABLE AT QUANTITY DISCOUNTS WHEN
USED TO PROMOTE PRODUCTS OR SERVICES. FOR INFORMA-
TION PLEASE WRITE TO PREMIUM MARKETING DIVISION,
NEW AMERICAN LIBRARY, 1633 BROADWAY, NEW YORK,
NEW YORK 10019.

SIGNET TRADEMARK REG. U.S. PAT. OFF. AND FOREIGN COUNTRIES
REGISTERED TRADEMARK—MARCA REGISTRADA
HECHO EN DRESDEN, TN. USA

SIGNET, SIGNET CLASSIC, MENTOR, ONYX, PLUME, MERIDIAN
and NAL BOOKS are published by New American Library,
a division of Penguin Books USA Inc.,
1633 Broadway, New York, New York 10019

First Printing, July, 1989

1   2   3   4   5   6   7   8   9

PRINTED IN THE UNITED STATES OF AMERICA

Chapter One

Customer.

He looked scared to death, which wasn't usually a good sign in a pawnshop. Nor did what he pulled behind him on a small dolly look very promising, and Garry's dad was famous for making crazy loans. Once he'd loaned money on a man's memory, which wasn't really what it sounded like. That guy had been a professional mnemonic, with enough stuff hard-wired inside his skull to hold half the secrets of H'hogoth. How his dad got those chips out of the man's skull and into his safe was worth a story in itself.

It was his dad's day off, however, and Garry was minding the store. He'd been doing it for almost a year, ever since he'd started college. His dad said he would pay for education, but Garry had to pay for fun himself. The salary was pretty good, and working the loan desk at the most famous—or notorious—pawnshop on the entire planet of H'hogoth was almost an education in itself.

One of the things he'd learned was that frightened people weren't good risks. Quite often they were only out to make enough money to run from whatever had them all shook up. This customer filled that bill too well. Short, with thin black greasy hair combed pitifully over a bald spot the size of a child's hand, he weighed maybe sixty kilos dripping wet. Which he was. His threadbare coverall, a couple of sizes too large for his emaciated frame, was soaked. Either he'd just taken a bath fully clothed—and Garry's nose sensed that to be improbable —or he was sweating up a storm. Garry stared at the man's eyes as he huffed the final few steps up to his window. They were a wan yellow, like gold plate almost rubbed off a cheap watch, laced with jagged red tracer-

ies, and surrounded by livid, purplish-orange coronas.
When the guy turned the other cheek, somebody had
popped him again.

Would I loan money to this man? Garry wondered.
Maybe . . .

"Hi, pal. What you got there?"

The man stood a moment, his scrawny chest heaving,
and Garry enjoyed the view of a pair of lips that looked
like strips of liver flapping in the breeze.

Finally, between gasps, he said, "You the pawnbroker?
You look awful young."

Garry sighed. It was a problem. He knew what this
bedraggled would-be customer saw—a thin, wiry body
topped with the kind of face a mother loves. Bright green
eyes, a thick, curly mop of black hair, and a slightly
hooked nose that Garry thought gave him just a touch of
dash to offset all that sweetness. The overall effect was
even younger than his true seventeen years. He knew
how to handle it, though.

He grinned most professionally. "Yeah? Well, you're
probably right. So you don't want me to loan money on
whatever you're dragging there. Maybe you should come
back in a few years when I'm mature, huh?"

"Hey, don't take no offense. I expected somebody
older, is all. I mean, you're pretty famous. The Golden
Ball, I heard of it years ago." He thought about this for a
second. "Are you sure . . . ?"

Garry decided that if he heard this man's nasty, nasal
voice on his phone, he'd hang up and change his number
immediately.

"It's my dad," he said.

"What?"

"Forget it. I'm just jerking you a little bit. My dad
owns the Golden Ball . . . but it's okay. I'm licensed too.
And I'm in charge today, so why don't you show me that
gizmo there?"

The man turned around—the sudden nervous movement made Garry think of a rat darting for a hole—
stared at the thing for a second, then shrugged. "You got
to come out to look at it. I ain't hauling it any farther."

Garry checked the guy out some more. It wouldn't be
the first time somebody tried to stick up a pawnshop.
Behind the monomole reinforced armorglass of his window he was fairly safe from anything smaller than an

attack vehicle, but outside, things might be different. Finally, he decided the guy didn't look much like an armed robber, and even out of the cage, the store sported a few gimmicks that weren't altogether orthodox. Besides, the readouts said the man wasn't carrying anything obviously dangerous.

"Sure. Just give me a second." He keyed in certain telltales, strapped a short-barreled .44 under his armpit, and ordered Hal, the House AI to keep an eye on him. Then he let himself out, went down a short hallway, and stepped onto the main floor.

"Okay, let's see what you got here."

Ratface didn't say anything, just moved aside so Garry could examine his treasure firsthand. Garry found himself staring at a silvery-gray cube about half a meter on a side. What appeared to be faint scratches marred the top surface. Two standard heavy-duty power outlets protruded from one face; something about them didn't look quite right. Also on the top surface was a small hole that he estimated at maybe a centimeter in diameter.

Whatever it was, the cube was heavy. The thick steel bars of the dolly sagged slightly beneath its weight, and the dolly's four hard rubber wheels pushed almost an inch into the carpet.

"Hal?" he subvocalized. He and his dad both had Hal implants embedded beneath their right ears so they could communicate with the house AI at any time.

"The power outlets are not normal to the artifact," Hal said. "They've been added sometime after its manufacture. And the engraving or incising on the top surface isn't accidental. It shows patterns typical of intelligent thought."

Now he began to understand why Ratface was sweating. He felt a few beads begin to form on his own forehead. Somehow, the vast, cluttered room had grown oppressively hot. There was something about that cube that was familiar, that conjured up a sick, hungry feeling deep in his gut. "Hal, what is it?"

"If you mean, what does it do, I don't know. But what it *is* is a Kurs'ggtha artifact."

"Oh, jeezus," he muttered silently.

He knew he should throw Ratface and his mysterious cube right back out on the street, but of course, he didn't.

* * *

Garry didn't expect the deal to take very much time, and it didn't. Ratface was in such a hurry to get rid of his alien cube, grab his getaway money, and run that he almost forgot to take his pawnchip with him. It didn't take much brains to know the chances of his ever redeeming the loan were about as high as him having come by the cube honestly in the first place.

Garry sighed and hauled the cube into the back and wrestled it onto the floor in the main vault. "What do you think, Hal? Is it likely to blow up?"

The dry voice of the computer answered from an overhead speaker. "There is some slight radiation, X rays mostly, but not enough to be dangerous. I don't think it's an explosive device."

"We have to hold on to it for six months," he mused slowly. "That's the law."

Hal made no comment; he knew all there was to know about laws dealing with loans, pawned goods, and pawnshops. Garry'd named him in a whimsical moment years before, because his voice reminded him of an antique video to which he'd been addicted at the time. But now he had a problem. To the best of his knowledge, less than a dozen Kurs'ggtha artifacts had ever been found in all of H'hogoth Confederacy space. So it didn't much matter what this thing was, or even whether it worked. He'd given Ratface one kilocredit for it after a few moments of haggling—maybe the rodent even believed him when he told him he had another one just like it. He clearly didn't know what he was selling. Estimated conservatively, if the cube was genuine, it had to be worth a thousand times the loan. Which led to other problems, like where Ratface had gotten the artifact, how he had gotten it, who had it before, and who was looking for it now. The last question seemed the most imperative. Ratface hadn't struck him as being real intelligent, and Garry suspected his backtrail was easy enough to read.

His dad had once promised he'd never get on him for making a decision, even a bad one, but that he'd whale his hide for not making one at all. Now Garry wondered what he'd say when he saw the ominous fruit of his maxim resting on the floor of his main storage vault.

His dad was named Garth Hamersmidt, and so was he,

although he bore the unlikable diminutive Junior. He preferred to be called Garry, however, despite his father's preference for Garth. That pretty well summed up their different points of view. Garry, for instance, regarded himself as young and rather dashing, while Garth favored the phrase "wet-behind-the-ears whippersnapper."

One of Garth's better stories dealt with how he established himself and the Golden Ball from the proceeds of a seven-week poker game involving two ship captains, a slow virus pirate, a bootleg AI dealer, and Hilgren, a High H'hogoth who still—by human standards they lived practically forever—swung a lot of weight in Goth, the capital city. Garry recalled this as a comforting example of the kind of contacts Garth could call on if necessary, for as he waited for his father to return home that night, it seemed to him they might need all the clout Garth could swing. The more he thought about the enigmatic cube in the strong room, the more worried he got. It was worth a thousand times what he'd paid for it? Who knew? Maybe a million times . . . and people had been nerve-knifed in Great Goth for the price of a stymshow.

When Garry finally heard heavy footsteps at the door, he was jumpy enough to forget he still clutched the .44 in aching fingers.

"Hi, Dad."

Garth stared at him. "Parricide, Garry?" he shook his head. "And so young too. Me, I mean." He shook his head again and shambled toward the kitchen. "No, wait," he said. "'For this, I want a beer." He paused and looked at Garry's face. "Two beers."

Shakily, Garry replaced the pistol in its shoulder holster. Garth was back in a few seconds, a great, bearded, bearlike man holding a Budweiser in each paw.

"Two beers. One for you." He handed it to his son, then settled himself in his favorite armchair and switched on the vibrator. He closed his black eyes, raised the bottle to his lips, and chugged it in a pair of long swallows. "Ah. Okay. So you want to tell me why you greet your papa with a big ugly gun in your hand?"

In less than half an hour they were back at the pawnshop.

In certain circles—thieves, pickpockets, bankrupts, fences of all races and species, and not a few of the nobility—the Golden Ball was a respected, maybe even revered institution. In the information universe there are those who still prefer their business done silently, and in cash. Garth was a loanmaker, true, but also a banker for those who didn't wish either H'hogoth or Confederate snoops to be privy to their transactions. They lived in Great Goth itself, capital of the H'hogoth Nest, which some found strange, although it made perfect sense. The Human Confederacy was most definitely the more recent and more junior of the two vast political structures which made Goth the principal city of both races. Like all such cities, Goth seethed with commerce of the kind that made the Golden Ball prosperous. Besides, Garth had once told him there'd been a bit of trouble on Terra, and while he might like to visit his homeworld again sometime, prudence dictated a cooling-off period—say a couple of centuries. Garry didn't mind. He was a H'hogothan native, holding dual citizenship by virtue of birth and parentage, and the green hills of Terra were but a dusty rumor to him. Besides, he loved the action in the ancient, sprawling city of warm-blooded saurians who'd sold man the drive in the first place, thereby allowing the Confederacy to exist at all.

Garth had a jeweler's loupe in his right eye as he bent over the cube. "These scratches look regular, like writing of some kind," he said. His deep, rumbling voice was thoughtful.

"That's what Hal says too."

"'Oh, he does, does he?" They both believed in anthropomorphism as far as Artificial Intelligences went. How else could you talk to the damn things comfortably?

Almost on cue, Hal's flat voice buzzed from the ceiling speaker. "There is potential hostile activity around our perimeters."

Immediately, Garth stood up. "More, please."

"At least ten people, all of them armed, are surrounding the Golden Ball. The pattern they are setting up is a classic attack enclosure."

"Humans?" Garth said tersely.

"There are six Humans and four H'hogotha."

Garth paused a moment, chewing lightly on his lower lip. "Okay. Call the police."

"Which police?" Hal asked.

"Confederate."

YESTERDAY'S PAWN

Garry thought about Human status on H'hogoth. The
Golden Ball was located on the edge of, but still well
within the boundaries of the Sector. As a consequence of
the original treaties between the two races, each ceded to
the other a substantial piece of territory in their respec-
tive capital cities. There was ground in Brasilia, on Terra,
that was legally H'hogothan as well. Each side adminis-
tered its own area, so in theory, the Sector did its own
policing. In fact, of course, the Sector swarmed with
covert agents, industrial spies, and traitors of both races,
as did the H'hogothan Sector on Terra. Not to mention
the fact that the legitimate authorities had so riddled
each other's communication systems and data banks that
speaking to one was the same as speaking to both.

Someone hammered on the front door of the pawnshop. The sound boomed in the dusty shadows.

"We're closed. Go away," Garth called.

Hal patched through the reply from the front intercom.
"I have a pawnchip to redeem. The law says you have to
open up."

"Video," Garth said shortly. On the wall in front of
them a screen lit up. Outlined in a pool of patchy blue
light before the front door was a tall, very well-dressed
man who held in his right hand a tiny pawnchip.

"Right," Garth said. His voice sounded suddenly
strained. His ruddy face paled. Garry thought it looked
as if he'd seen a ghost. "Insert the chip for verification."

He was stalling. Garry recognized the distinctive gold
tag, and the man on the doorstep seemed to know that
while the Golden Ball usually closed during night hours,
legally they had to redeem legitimate loans at any time—
indeed, crawling out of bed to go down to the shop at
some god-awful hour was a fairly usual occurrence.

While the visitor fumbled with the chipslot, Garth
glanced at Garry. "Hal, go to max red on defense," he
said. "Do we have a confirm on the police call?"

"Yes, Garth. Eight minutes on their ETA."

"Eight? That's too long."

"The chip is legitimate," Hal said.

"Data, please," Garth replied.

The screen immediately flashed a picture of Ratface,
followed quickly by a picture of the cube. Garth sighed.
"I figured as much," he said. He turned to Garry. "Is
that the man who pawned the cube?"

"Yes."

The visitor said, "May I enter now?"

"You aren't the man who pawned that item," Garth replied.

"It doesn't matter. The law says the legal possessor of a chip may redeem it."

Which was also true, Garry reflected.

"Seven minutes," Hal said.

"You," Garth said to Garry. "You I want out of here. Use the tunnel." He stopped. "Will that take him beyond their perimeter?"

"Yes," Hal replied.

"Okay." He walked over to the gun rack and unlocked it. Garry'd never seen him handle a heavy blaster before, but he seemed quite familiar with the stubby, massive laser.

"Dad, I'm not going anywhere."

"Yes, you are. Now get going." His ragged black eyebrows drew together. "Listen, you little puppy, if something happens here, I want one of us out of it and able to do something about it. You understand me?"

Garry shrugged. "If that's the case, I should stay. You've got more competence in those areas than I do."

"I do?" Garth grinned suddenly. "True, but I never thought I'd hear you admit it."

"So do I stay?"

"Nope. You leave. Trust my competence, okay?" He reached out and patted his son's cheek gently. "I'll be all right."

Garry realized suddenly that his dad was worried about protecting him in a firefight. And knew it was true. He'd only slow Garth down.

"Okay, Dad," he said. He stuck out his hand. "Good luck."

Garth's big fingers squeezed his gently, and then, without warning, the big man folded Garry in a massive, smothering hug. "Take care of yourself, son," he said. "And don't worry about me."

Garry nodded, turned, and punched the hidden pressure patch for the back door. A spot in the armored wall slid open, and he stepped into the tunnel. Behind him, he heard the door roll shut with a soft, metallic crunch. He walked on down the tunnel. He was leaving, but going no farther than he had to.

*   *   *

There was a small comm-unit on the wall next to the exit door. Garry knew the door led out into a long unused sewer passage; from there he could go almost anywhere in the Sector, even out of it, as long as he didn't mind the stench. He tapped a code onto the touchpad of the unit and waited a few moments for the screen to light up.

"Hal."

"Yes, Garry."

"I want a split overview."

Obediently, the screen began to cycle back and forth between the front door, the interior of the shop, the vault, and a view of the shadowy figures who had ringed the Golden Ball.

"Close-ups, please."

One by one, starting with the man at the front door, Garry stared at head-and-shoulder shots of the intruders. He recognized none of them. Not that the H'hogotha are easy for humans to individualize—right-brain intuitional recognition systems aren't built that way.

"Okay, back to split."

Garth had activated all the defense reflexes. Now he moved to the loan window and said, "All right, Hal, open it up."

The night visitor smiled as he stepped into the shop, still holding out the pawnchip like some kind of talisman.

He didn't look like a thug, Garry decided. His suit was from one of the Potential Worlds, and had cost considerably more than the kilocredit he'd given Ratface. He had a high forehead, a big nose, a wide, white smile, and short, carefully groomed blond hair. Hal placed him at just under two meters tall, and exactly ninety kilos. His blue eyes snapped over his too-white smile. He looked about thirty Terran years old, although with the newest thymal diffusion techniques—and he looked like he could afford them—he might be any age.

He moved to the window in a slow, gliding shuffle that made Garry shiver suddenly, and presented his chip. He didn't seem to notice that the front door had closed softly behind him. "My name is Hyarl Thomas, and I swear that I am the legal owner of this pawnchip. I have come to redeem my property."

He knows the law, Garry thought coldly.

Garth grunted noncommittally. "I know you, Thomas. Do you have a notarized transfer?"

Thomas smiled even more brightly and produced a grubby sheet of paper on which were scrawled a few words. He slid the paper across.

"Analysis?" Garth said.

Hal replied, "The notarization is genuine. The thumbprint is genuine. The transfer is legally acceptable."

"And so it is," Thomas said cheerfully. Now he produced a creditchip. "Withdraw one kilocee. May I take my property now?"

"Not so fast," Garth said. "You seem to know the law very well, so you will understand when I tell you I have reason to believe the item in pawn may be stolen. Therefore, I must inform you that the authorities have been notified. You will have to satisfy them on this matter as well as me." His voice had gone stiff and formal.

Garry hoped it would be enough to short-circuit this whole mess, but Thomas only grinned more widely. Hal whispered from the comm-unit, "The attack enclosure is collapsing."

Misty, shaded figures moved closer in the night. Two of them wrestled with something bulky in front of the Golden Ball's locked door.

"The authorities?" Thomas said. "But the authorities aren't here at the moment. Isn't that a shame?"

The front door blew open in a ball of fire. The floor of the tunnel shuddered at the force of the explosion. Static filled the screen. It cleared in short bursts, and Garry watched a strobelike vision of Thomas taking something from beneath his perfectly tailored jacket. Another explosion. Garth jumped back from the window. Sudden blinding flash.

Figures moved like swift ghosts.

"Gas," Hal's voice announced.

The last thing the screen showed was Garth hurtling backward from the inner door, one hand—the place where a hand had *been*—spraying a bright arc of red.

"*Go*, Garry!"

Garry wondered what effort those last warning words had cost. He bit down hard on a nauseating sense of loss, realizing only then just how much he loved Garth Hamersmidt—and he fought against other, more crimson emotions that threatened to sweep him back into the certain death of the pawnshop. After a moment he was able to see again. He took a deep, shuddering breath, held it, and then let it out. His face felt cold. There were things to do.

He went.

Chapter Two

Garry made three turns and went four blocks before he dared to stick his nose out. The corroded manhole—H'hogothhole?—cover was heavier than ancient sin and it took him a couple of minutes to slide it open, as quietly as he could.

He peered carefully around. The street, dim and swaddled with tendrils of fog, appeared deserted. His shoulders screamed as he heaved himself out of the hole and scurried toward a narrow alleyway between two darkened warehouses.

The night air smelled of damp and rust. Far down the block a street lamp fought a losing halogen battle against the night. He froze. Not far away, sirens played an eerie symphony, woop-wooping up and down the scale. He knew where those sirens were converging, and the sense of loss slammed him in the gut all over again. Garth's injury wasn't likely to be fatal in itself. They could grow him a new hand, if they got to him in time and if he didn't get hurt any further. Neither seemed likely. He doubted if Hyarl Thomas intended to leave witnesses to his evening's work.

Some of the sirens wailed in the distinctive tones of fire equipment. No doubt Thomas had also tried to destroy the Golden Ball itself, in hopes of taking out the AI he knew had to be there. If so, Garry decided it might be his first mistake. Perhaps he had, or would, make others. That was his job, then: to find those mistakes and use them. He had no doubt at all that Thomas would discover there'd been another witness. Perhaps he already knew. Sooner or later, somebody would come along to tie up loose ends. Maybe Thomas himself. The thought

18

made Garry's lips creak upward in something that was almost a smile.

He patted the .44 under his left armpit, wiped his nose—had he been crying? He didn't remember—and retreated silently into the alley, cradling the thought like an ember.

Maybe Thomas would think a seventeen-year-old college boy was easy game. Maybe he would come himself.

Goth, as a city, was at least twelve hundred years old. The H'hogotha, not particularly interested in archaeology, conceded that much. Garry ruminated on that as he crept through the darkened streets, keeping close to the damp, forbidding walls of stone that sealed off the inner buildings of the Sector from the public paths. It made for an interesting city. The Human Sector had been ceded, buildings and all, to the new Confederacy, but it had not meant a wholesale rebuilding. The Embassy Center neighborhood was new, a cluster of characteristically human towers—even now, he thought, we like to remember the trees in which we once lived—but the rest was simply a matter of moving in and taking over. The H'hogotha, true to their slower, more dreamlike reptilian heritage, built low, and built to last. The Sector had been a newer part of Goth, considered by the natives less desirable—and the H'hogotha shared at least one trait with man: they enjoyed selling swamp to ignorant immigrants as much as the next lizard. Even so, Garry knew of buildings, squat, hump-shouldered monsters of dark granite, that were well over six millennia old.

He shivered suddenly against the slow cooling of the night breeze, his shirt and pants clammy against his skin. The thin jacket he wore was little help. He'd selected it as concealment for the .44 rather than for any real protection. The momentary ague jerked him into the present, and he stopped as the overwhelming danger of his predicament sank in, triggered by the realization that the clothes he wore were about all he had at the moment. He couldn't go back to the shop, or the comfortable house that perched on a low rise above it. If those places still existed, someone would be waiting there. Someone like Hyarl Thomas or, worse, a H'hogotha mercenary assassin. He had his creditchip, but ceechips could be traced. And if the enemy was powerful enough, credit balances

could be erased entirely. His haunts and habits would
be on file somewhere as well. Garth Hamersmidt was
crucial enough in certain circles that files would be
maintained on his minor acquaintances, let alone his only
son. Kidnapping, blackmail, and murder were ancient
and well-accepted H'hogothan business practices. So
he was essentially alone. Turning to friends would only
endanger them.

No friends, no money, no secure roof for his head. It
left one thing. He looked up, surprised to see where his
wanderings had taken him. Perhaps the right side of his
neocortex had already worked it out. At any rate, without realizing it, he'd come within a block of the blazing
lights of Starport, and all around him, bustling, laughing,
singing, drinking, fighting even at this late hour, stretched
the twisted underworld anarchy of Reef City.

"Hey, yobbo," muttered a half-strangled voice. "Move
your ass."

Garry jumped sideways, his right hand sliding toward
his jacket, but it was only a scarred, shoulder-twisted
drunk trying to tack past him toward a door that mumbled softly the raucous tunes behind it.

The drunk slammed a fist that was all knuckles on the
pitted iron. After a few seconds a peephole opened,
emitting a narrow ray of yellow, and a voice even more
evil than that of the would-be visitor.

"Yeah?"

"It's me, asshole. Open up."

"You got money, Frego?"

"My wallet's none of your business, pin-brain, but I
got money. And there's no law says I gotta spend it in
your dive, either."

With a rusty crash the door slammed open. Garry got a
quick glimpse of a head like a hairless football perched
on the shoulders of a giant, and then he was inside,
scuttling along with the drunk as if they were a pair.

It was a Human bar—drifting overhead a few glo-globes
cast a wan yellow light over the scene. The lizards preferred a harder, more actinic light, and shop owners who
wished a certain racial clientele often used this difference, just as others used music, to accomplish their de-
sires without open segregation. Garry glanced back at the
giant guarding the door and decided the illumination was
an effect of the customers rather than cause. The door-

man looked perfectly capable of segregation, even if he probably couldn't spell the word.

On a low stage against one side wall pooted and tootled and thumped a trio whose one virtue seemed to be an ability to make itself heard above the surrounding din. Several couples of various sexes and combinations lurched and staggered around the handkerchief-sized dance floor. Garry stepped away from his juiced entry ticket and moved slowly toward the opposite, darker corner. He suspected haste of any kind in this place would draw a quick and violent response.

Two walls were lined with narrow booths. Only one was empty. He slid as far across the torn imitation leather of its seat as he could, scrunched himself against the inner wall, and began to search his pockets.

Normal citizens carried ceechips, needing no other form of money, but at the pawnshop Garry dealt with folk decidedly abnormal every day, and had gotten into the habit of keeping some hard currency on his person. The small bits of gold and silver made good conversation openers at school. Girls, in particular, seemed impressed by the bizarre stories he wove about the small nuggets of metal, and impressing girls seemed to have become one of his paramount interests in recent years.

Carefully, he spread out eight pieces of cash on the scarred Formica tabletop. Two gold, six silver. About a hundred credits. He wasn't entirely broke, although the sum wouldn't rent a room for long, or buy the help he might need in the upcoming trials. At least he could afford a beer, which meant he could pay the tariff on this booth for a while. He stared at a squashed plastic bottle of catsup clustered with a lidless mustard jar, a greasy pair of salt-and-peppers—for some reason, both were filled with salt—and made an idle bet with himself as to whether the cockroach scaling the side of the catsup bottle would go on to the top or scurry for the safety of the table if he slapped his hand on the wall.

A waiter who reminded him of Ratface ambled slowly to his table. He wore an apron tied under his armpits, from which Garry could read, in stain language, the menu for the last week.

"What you want, kid?"

"Budweiser," Garry said.

The waiter's eyebrows moved like something greeting

morning from a hole in the ground. "That's import shit, kid. You got money?"

Garry slid one silver cash onto the table.

The waiter nodded and the glittery bit disappeared. "Back in a sec."

Several minutes later another waiter, no less sanitary, pushed a familiar red and silver can across the tabletop. Garry looked up. "Where's my change?"

"What change?"

"I got change coming from the other waiter."

"Joey? Joey left. Shift change, y'know."

Garry stared at the beer he'd just paid the price of a six-pack for. "That's nice."

Silence. The waiter hovered.

"Something you need?" Garry asked.

"Where's my tip?"

Garry grinned suddenly. "With Joey. Wherever he is. You see him, tell him he owes you half."

The waiter's yellow teeth appeared, but Garry didn't think it was a smile. "Real cute."

Garry tasted his beer. "Real good. Cold and everything."

"I oughta kick your ass, kid."

Garry turned just a bit sideways so that his jacket opened up enough for the heavy wooden handle of the .44 to be visible.

The waiter's eyes bulged. It wasn't a pretty sight. He backed up one small step. "I'll talk to Joey," he said.

"You do that," Garry replied.

He sipped slowly at his beer and tried to arrange things rationally. The events of the night kept slithering and slipping away from him. He knew he would have to sleep soon, and knew also that coffee would be better for him than beer. But if he ordered coffee in a place like this, looking as young as he did, he would only attract unwelcome attention from the management.

Slowly, an agenda of sorts began to form. Priority one was to establish himself safely somehow. That meant money, cash money. Already, glancing around the bar, he had some ideas about that. Next he needed a place to stay, a secure base of operations. Money would make that simpler. Once he had these two things, he could move on to the next phase. Garth Hamersmidt. Was he alive or dead? He knew he couldn't simply call up all the

hospitals and ask. Public comm-lines were exactly that—
public. But there were other ways.

Finally, there was the mystery of Ratface, the cube,
and Hyarl Thomas and friends. Common sense dictated
that he ignore the whole problem and concentrate on
keeping his skin in one piece. But he knew that unless
that conundrum was finally solved, he would never be
entirely safe. *Someone* must know that he'd originally
written the loan on the artifact. And if those people were
as insanely ready to kill as they seemed to be, they would
never stop until anyone who could point a finger at them,
or even testify to the existence of the Kurs'ggtha relic,
was but a bloody memory.

And why had the police taken so long to respond? The
probable answer to that question sent chilly little claws
scuttling up and down his spine. To manipulate Confederate cops like that took clout. Lots of it. And who held
more clout on H'hogoth than the lizard government itself? The more he thought about it, the more likely it
seemed. Even the officials of the Nest itself would be
extremely interested in something like the cube. Yet the
raiding party had been biracial. Something about that
smelled like week-old *rink* fruit.

Both states publicly paid homage to the great depth
and breadth of their eternal friendship, but Garry had
studied history. He knew it had made him cynical, but
suspected that cynicism itself was probably a survival
trait. Anyway, the chances of either government cheerfully sharing a Kurs'ggtha find with the other were remote. Perhaps circumstances had dictated some kind of
arrangement, or maybe even a third group was involved,
one made up of both races, and obviously carrying a lot
of weight in each camp.

It was not a warming prospect. He mentally backed
away from the whole problem and began to watch the
small group of men gathered around a low table a few
meters away.

If he was going to do it, he'd better get started before
he got too tired to make it work.

There were five men gathered around the low chessboard. Two were playing as the other three bet on various aspects of the game—the outcome itself, the moves
of the players, and potential board positions several moves

out. Garry drifted up as quietly as possible and watched
for a few minutes. Finally he took one of his silver coins
and laid it next to a relatively well-dressed gambler, a
man with manicured fingernails, a dark brown suit, and a
wickedly healed slash running redly from his forehead to
his chin.

The man looked up. "What's that for?"

"Him," Garry said. He nodded at the far player, a
short, thick man who reminded him of a potato farmer
with a streak of violence. "He takes the other guy's rook,
no more than three moves."

The gambler scanned the board, his eyes deeply
squinted. Lines wrinkled the skin above the bridge of his
nose. "Yeah?" he whispered. "I don't think so." A piece
of silver matching Garry's bit of cash appeared magically
beside it. Two moves later, Garry scooped up both pieces.

Within an hour he'd won almost a thousand credits,
and half the bar was gathered around the chessboard.

"That's it," he said finally, picking up the winnings
from his last bet. The first gambler had disappeared
some time before, after losing almost all of his stake, and
Garry was nervously expecting his reappearance. The .44
was a nice piece of protection, but using it would attract
all kinds of unnecessary—and undesired—attention.

"Maybe not," a thin voice said.

Garry turned slowly, thinking ruefully that greed never
paid off in the end. He should have stopped at two or
three hundred credits, but the winning fever had swept
him on, heedless. Now there was trouble.

His first victim had returned. For a moment, as Garry
stared at the man's companion, he felt relieved. The
second man was no thug, at least not one of the usual
variety. He was short, frail, and seemed to have trouble
breathing. Thick lenses covered his eyes, giving him a
sullen, opaque appearance. Garry noticed that the lenses
were surgically inset into the man's face, and wondered
what kind of eyes were hidden behind the thick polymer
sheets.

"You gamble pretty good," the sportsman said.

"Thanks."

"You wanna make another bet?"

"On another day," Garry replied. "I'm leaving now."

"I doubt that too."

The doorman had moved up behind the gambler, grinning nastily. Slowly, in tune with a rhythm only he could hear, he tapped an ugly-looking sap in the palm of his left hand.

Garry looked at the sap—it had ominous rusty blotches on it—then at the gambler. "What's the bet?"

"Him." The gambler jerked a thumb at his glassy-eyed companion. "You play a game of chess with him. For"—he glanced at the cluster of gold in Garry's hand—"for about a kilocee. How's that sound?" He smiled brightly.

"What if I don't know how to play?"

"That'll be okay too, kid. You know what I mean?"

Garry sat down. "Good thing I know how, isn't it?"

His opponent opened with a tricky variation on a classic Alekhine ploy, and Garry settled back. The few real aficionados in the crowd murmured softly at the opening, and Garry pondered the strange twists that led to championship-caliber chess being a staple in spaceport bars.

Back in pre-Exchange days, when the Soviets and the Americans were battling each other for superiority, the Russians, due to immense labor on their part and virtual abdication by the United States, had moved far ahead in the race for space. When the Exchange had finally freed man from the confines of his own solar system, it had been the sons of the commissars who'd first fueled the Expansion, and with them they took their habits and hobbies. So it was that when the kids from Missouri finally arrived on freshly settled new worlds, they learned chess rather than poker. Card gambling wasn't unknown, by any means, but the dusty American vision of John Wayne on Mars had never truly come to pass.

He tried to keep his mind on the game, but it was hard. His eyelids kept sliding down. He was ashamed to note it took him almost twenty minutes to beat the local champion. Hal, his partner, instructor, and opponent for almost fifteen years, would give him hell when he heard about it. Of course, Hal had an almost permanent hammerlock on the H'hogothan AI trophy and tended to be sniffy about human competition anyway.

He stood up and stretched. "You want to give me that money now?"

The gambler, his scar a livid thread of rage, glared bleakly at him out of a face the color of fish bellies. "I suppose you think it works just like that? That easy, kid?"

"I certainly hope so. I'd hate to have to mention you to my father. On Mephisto."

The effect was every bit of what he hoped for. The outraged gambler went even paler than he already was. His scar bleached out until it was nearly invisible, and a bunch of nerves on his cheek began to misfire, jerking skin into a jittery little gavotte.

The man inhaled sharply. "Beg pardon, then, mister," he said. "I didn't know."

Big, gristled, ugly men were doing their best to look invisible as they melted away. Garry felt a steady breeze from the constant opening of the front door, where the doorman spoke softly and rapidly into a wristmike.

"You thought," Garry said as he let his facial muscles go slack, "that perhaps I was a child?" He knew what effect his new appearance was having on the sickened gambler in front of him. In the first waves of the Expansion of man had gone the crazies, the dreamers, the madmen who would carve strange new societies from the stars. Old Terra, bound in the straightjacket of its own flesh, hidebound and slow, had no place for the magic men, the edge sciencers, the saucer believers, the mystics. But they found their homes in what became the Potential Worlds, and on some of those worlds, between genetic crapshoots and frenzied revelation, odd and appalling abilities began to flourish. None odder or more appalling than on Mephisto, where athanasia technology was second to none, where tastes were violent, and the words "talent" and "lethal" had much the same meaning. One-on-one, Mephisto produced the greatest killers in the H'hogoth Confederacy and due to a particular quirk, they never sent their children off planet. Many had learned this to their sorrow—but off Mephisto, youth and innocence were only another cloak for death and destruction.

"Here's your money, sir," the gambler said, and held out the pile of gleaming metal with shaking hands.

"Thank you." Garry put the cash into his jacket pocket, once again revealing the brutish, businesslike grip of the .44 Magnum.

"You may go," he said gently.

The gambler nodded slightly, turned carefully, and

didn't begin running until he was actually outside the bar. Credit for that, at least, Garry thought.

As he followed the terrified man out into the thin gray drizzle of dawn, he paused a moment by the doorman. "Nice evening," he said. "I enjoyed it. Maybe I'll be back."

The doorman just stared at him, but once Garry was outside, the strength with which he slammed the heavy iron door gave testimony to his real feelings on the matter.

Something light and dizzy bubbled between his ears. In a few minutes it would be morning. He stared at the fading lamps of the Port, wondering what to do next.

So he didn't hear a thing when the thick human arm draped itself across his shoulders and a faintly familiar voice rasped, "Nice bluff in there, kid. You'd think people like that would know all the Mephistan scum have castemarks tattooed in that little fold of skin between their left thumb and forefinger. Maybe they just didn't notice. But that's okay—you get to come with me anyway."

He might have tried to run, but the point of the knife drawing a tiny bead of blood just beneath his right ear kept him absolutely still.

Chapter Three

"I should have remembered that," Garry said.

He sat in a comfortable armchair across from his captor. The window at their side looked out over the Port, but despite the general shabbiness of the area, the apartment in which they sat was neat and clean. The rising sun picked out small details: two ancient lithographs, each of a Terran tree, one oak, one maple. A Lhyrran rug, bright as a pile of emeralds and rubies. Several glowing oil paintings, each signed with flamboyant black strokes.

A cat, fat and complacent, purred softly to itself on a pillow-piled sofa. A horn-handled knife, its blade open and gleaming, lay on the low table between the two men, tipped with a tiny dot of dried blood.

"Who are you?" Garry said. "I heard the doorman call you Frego."

It was the drunk who'd brushed past Garry and who he'd then used as an entry ticket into the spaceman's bar. But the man's previous appearance was much modified. Instead of the tattered poly jacket he'd worn earlier, he was dressed in a neat, cheerful plaid robe. He'd evidently shed the strange shoulder deformity with the jacket. Frego's round, cherry-colored face was still scarred, but in the light the damage wasn't as bad as it had first appeared. His eyes glittered in the dawn shadows with the color of ripples across a broad river, a bottomless green flecked with shards of amber. Dragon's eyes.

Garry remembered the walk to this apartment, Frego's arm companionably about his shoulders, the concealed knife still pricking its warning message into the flesh next to his carotid artery. He'd gone with the man numbly, cracked and exhausted by the events of the previous hours.

"'I don't give a shit, really," he'd told him then, his voice a soft rasp of surrender.

"Sure you do," Frego replied. "Or you will. In a while."

Even Frego's voice changed once he entered the apartment, rising from a phlegm-choked guttural grumble to a pleasant, even tenor. Now his face was almost inviting, with a squat, battered nose centered beneath a hairline receded almost to the crown of his skull. The longish fringe of hair around the bald area was the umber color and texture of a mink's pelt.

"Frego?" the man said. "Yeah, that's my name. One of them. Your dad knows a few others."

Garry's eyes snapped wide. "My dad?"

"Uh-huh. Garth Hamersmidt. He's your dad. Old friend of mine. In fact, Garry, when you were a baby, I used to bounce you on my knee."

Garry forced himself to breathe softly, recalling lessons he'd learned at the hand of a tiny Japanese emigrant from Terra. Shi-tzsu had taught him many things, but breathing had always been the first. Another lesson dealt with treachery, Garry reminded himself. Anybody could claim friendship with Garth Hamersmidt. Many did. Sometimes it was even true.

"I don't know what you're talking about," he said flatly. "What do you want with me? Why am I here?"

Frego stared at him calmly. Finally he sighed and slapped his broken-knuckled hands on his knees. "You're here because your dad got busted up bad several hours back, because the Golden Ball was gutted by what the casters are calling a fire of mysterious origin, and because you, my young friend, are mixed up in something that's way over your head."

Outside on the street, early-morning workers drifted like aimless puffballs toward the Port entrance across the street, intersecting the paths of bleary-eyed refugees from the night shift in lazy pinball arcs. The tall fence around the perimeter gleamed in the morning sun like a frozen waterfall.

"What you're saying, anybody could say. Anybody could find out." The deep scream that had been pushing at the door of his throat threatened to blaze forth then, but he managed to hold it.

Was Garth alive? Who was this man? A friend? An enemy? Something else?

Frego nodded slowly. "Yeah, you're right. Anybody could. But not everybody could say, ' 'Bye, baby bunting, Daddy's gone a hunting. . . .' "

Unbidden, Garry's right hand reached up to swipe sudden moisture from the corners of his eyes. He knew there were many things about him that weren't ordinary, but for one instant he felt like any other kid who, tired, frightened, and alone, had finally come into a place of warmth and safety.

"Oh," he said softly. "Then you can help me."

Frego leaned forward and placed his broken hands gently on Garry's thin shoulders, moving his fingers as if he was soothing some small animal. "Of course I can," he said. "Of course I can."

He was flying. It was like swimming, except he didn't have to move his legs. He cut through the star-scattered night with slow, easy movements of his arms and shoulders, his eyes on the clotted shadows below.

Light. A tiny spark at first, faint and red, then turning yellow and hard. He willed himself lower, his arms moving in powerful strokes, pulling himself through the air.

The Golden Ball twisted and turned like a melting rose, opening slowly and revealing within its burning heart his father.

Garth raised his massive hands, his lips moving soundlessly, but Garry heard the silent words in his very bones.

He tried to dive, to break through the yielding, invisible barrier, and as he did so, his father's face changed— and the silent, unseeing knife came down in a splash of red.

"Dad!" he screamed, but he couldn't push the word past his lips. And then something vast and soft began to press down on his face, choking him—

Garry twisted bolt upright, his hands clawing at his cheeks, covers slithering away like shed snakeskins. The cat that had sought a place of warmth on his chest *m'rowled* once and fled. His eyes bulged in the darkness of the room and after a moment adjusted to the faint light flooding from the windows, painting everyday shapes silvery and magical.

He realized he was sweating like a pig. "Only dreams," he whispered. "It's only a dream."

He checked the glowing readout on his nailtale. O-six-hundred hours. That seemed odd. Had he only slept a half hour, then? Despite the nightmare, he felt refreshed.

The fat cat prowled and nattered as it wound itself around his bare feet. "C'mere, cat," he said. The honey-colored animal stared at him unblinking. Its eyes seemed to gather all the light in the room and focus it on him. Where had he seen eyes like that before?

"Up here, kitty," he said again. Obediently, the cat nodded, licked one paw, then daintily made its way to his chest. He wrapped his arms around the furry bundle and lay back down, but his own emerald eyes remained open.

As the cat made sounds like a tiny fairy trying to start a car on his chest, the bloody vision of his dream kept drifting up, like a soap bubble from hell. Finally, in desperation, he tried to push the image away with other thoughts. Something humdrum. Schoolwork. He thought about dragons, and why a Budweiser was so expensive on H'hogoth.

Mr. Deilworthy's voice drifted nasally onto the foam of his awareness. Mr. D taught interspecies anthro with a passion that Garry found amazing.

"Man is an accident!" Mr. D said often.

So true, Garry thought. He numbered the facts. Three centuries before, an American scientist named Stephen Dole made a study of the criteria needed for habitable planets and concluded that the Human galaxy might contain as many as a hundred and eighty thousand planets capable of bearing intelligent life. His calculations, based on the limited sampling made in H'hogothan-Human space, seemed correct, but what everybody had missed was the much smaller chance of such life being mammalian. On earth, man owed his existence as an intelligent being to an incredibly arcane bit of chance—an event that occurred about fifty million years before, which scientists called the Great Dying. Earth had a silent partner in its system, an invisible companion star that had turned to clinkers and ash. Once every twenty-eight million years this older brother swept near enough to disrupt the Oort cloud of comets, sending millions of the icy balls into the heart of the solar system, splattering earth with frozen detritus in the process. It just so happened that such an event killed off the great lizards on earth at just about the time that a spindly, big-skulled reptile named *Sauror-nithoides* was walking about on its hind legs and using its four-fingered hands to eat eggs, among other things. The ostrichlike lizard died with the rest, and the mammals that would lead to man won the evolutionary race by default.

And by chance, Garry reflected. The odds of such a thing happening at such a time were vanishingly small, and of the seven other intelligent or near-intelligent races known to man, all were reptilian. . . .

Mr. D called it the cosmic joke.

Nonetheless, the H'hogotha, undisturbed on Goth by any similar catastrophe, traced their heritage back to something quite similar to the Terran four-fingered ostrich-lizard, and, though evolving slower than mammals, had discovered the shield drive while man was still deciding whether the eventual survivors of *Ramapithecus* would have tall or low foreheads. By the time *Homo sapiens* had resolved the issue and begun to build pyramids, the H'hogotha had colonized almost a hundred planets over an area perhaps sixty light-years square. But there was a catch.

Humans figured out, starting from the scratch of stone axes and fire, the principles of the H'hogothan shield drive in less than ten thousand years. The H'hogoth had taken one hundred eighty times as long. The Humans called the principle the Einstein-Rosen path, or "the Wormhole Drive." The concept of the drive, as far as Humanity had developed it prior to the Exchange, was simply a shield that allowed a ship to penetrate into a black hole without being destroyed by either gravity or tidal forces. The H'hogotha had also discovered how to exit the wormhole path between a black hole and a quasar at any chosen point, which allowed for great accu-racy in point-to-point travel.

It was the testing of the shield, involving as it did the twisting of the very fabric of space-time, that alerted the H'hogotha to mankind's existence, and led directly to the Exchange, where the lizards had given man the perfected drive, as well as one more invention—something human-ity came to call the "timeband."

Mankind had not "exchanged" anything material for

the use of the saurian shield drive. Rather, they had guaranteed to never use the drive without also submitting to the timeband.

Matter compressed into a black hole can squeeze out elsewhere, sometimes very far away, in a short period of time. The payoff, the balancing of the scales for cheating relativity of its light-speed limit, is that the matter reappears one year in the past for every light-year of distance. The saurians discovered this early—but their greatest scientific triumph was a consequence of this early work. Time travel had been a laboratory mystery till the Exchange, when the H'hogotha showed how it could be done—provided one traveled forward from the *past*. It was something that could not have been discovered without the wormholes, for neither man nor lizard knew how to travel backward without the black-hole pathways. Nor was there any way to travel forward from realtime present. The timeband only functioned in the special circumstance of being initiated in the past, and it was a one-way trip to current realtime, rather like a rubber band "snapping back." Once the timeband was turned on, a ship immediately came forward to the present, but in the spatial coordinates of its past-time position.

The essence of the Exchange was that mankind must guarantee to use the timeband drive on each of its ships, or face destruction at the hands of the H'hogotha, who politely explained they couldn't allow anyone access to their own past.

The net result was that you arrived at about the same time you left, if the computers did their job correctly.

And it did make Budweiser expensive on H'hogotha.

Mankind naturally regarded the entire process as inelegant and unwieldy, and so the search went on for a true faster-than-light drive. So far there had been no success, but one of the very interesting things about some of the Kurs'ggtha artifacts was that they seemed to indicate the mysteriously vanished race might have possessed the secret. . . .

Which thought brought him to the cube, the Golden Ball, and his father, and Hyarl Thomas.

"I am in deep shit," he told the cat softly. The cat *murped* at him. "But that can change too."

*   *   *

"Bathroom's through there," Frego said briskly. "You feel better? You slept the whole day round."

"I did?" Garry wrapped the blanket around himself and stood up from the couch. "No wonder. Yeah, I feel a lot better."

"Good. Get yourself cleaned up while I fix up some breakfast. Then we talk. You like eggs?"

"Sure."

"Good. Eggs we got."

Garry knuckled his eyes with one fist and dragged himself and his blanket toward the washroom. Inside, he dropped the blanket and stared at himself in the mirror.

Somehow he'd expected to look different, be physically changed by recent events, but familiar eyes stared back at him with bright green certainty. He sighed. His face still held a dusting of freckles across the nose he privately felt was much too big, although a girl once said it gave him a hawklike cast. Above the nose a thick mass of curly black hair dropped to a crest, although for some reason his faint beard was blond.

He stepped on the scales. Still fifty-nine kilos, and he doubted he'd grown beyond the hundred seventy-five centimeters he'd been in gym class two weeks before.

Not big, he thought, but his muscles were hard and wiry, and he knew his wrists were much thicker than other boys his age and size. Thanks to Shi-tzsu, and that would probably come in handy too.

The hard, hot spray of the fresher soon brought him completely awake, and he luxuriated afterward in warm blasts of drying air. A quick depil, some fast work with comb and toothspray, and he felt ready to face the world again.

The smell of eggs frying and coffee perking led him by the nose to the small kitchenette off the main living room. While Frego set out plates, he folded blankets and straightened out the sofa.

"You look real chipper," Frego said, sipping his second cup of coffee.

"This stuff's from Terra," Garry replied. "How do you afford import coffee?"

Frego's dragon gaze flickered. "You mustn't let appearances deceive, Garry. Your dad never did. Just because I live in a poor neighborhood doesn't mean I'm broke. You understand?"

"I understand you're not what you seem. But I don't understand what you really are. Some kind of spook, I guess. But I don't remember you. What'd you say, bounced me on your knee? I don't remember that."

"You were very young." Frego's round face took on a reminiscent glow. "We were all younger then."

Garry let that pass. "Okay, so you know the help code my dad gave me years ago—that if I ever got into trouble and for some reason he couldn't help me, there would be somebody with that code, and I should trust them."

"Uh-huh, that's right. Two other people besides me have the code, Garry. Did you know that?"

Garry shook his head slowly. "I thought it was some kind of game. I never thought I'd have to use it."

"That's what your dad was good at, kid. Looking ahead."

"So why you?" Garry sipped his coffee. "How come you're the one? Who are the others, by the way?"

Frego shook his head. Morning sunlight gleamed off his shiny skull. "I don't know. Garth never told me. That way, I can't tell anybody else. Maybe the other two aren't even around anymore. Garry, maybe you should know. Your dad wasn't everything he seemed to be."

Garry nodded. "That's kinda obvious, isn't it? But what was he, then? And who are you?" He kept his voice soft and level, but an indiscriminate kind of pain was rambling around in his gut—Garth had kept secrets from him, still had them, and Garry needed to know.

"Frego, what's going on? It's that cube, isn't it? Somehow, Dad's mixed up with it, isn't he?"

Frego's eyes slid toward the window. He didn't look at Garry as he said, "No, not really. That the cube ended up at the Golden Ball was an accident. The man who brought it there didn't know where he was taking it. He was a nobody, a stupid fool, and he simply went to the best-known pawnshop in Goth to unload it."

"You're lying," Garry said.

The dragon eyes snapped back, now narrowed to muddy green slits. "Of course I am. Garry, my responsibility to you is to keep you safe. In fact, that responsibility is to Garth, not you, and I don't think I serve either one by telling you a lot of stuff you don't need to know."

Garry kept his voice level. "Frego, how do you know what I need? I'm not a little kid anymore. That .44 you took off me isn't a baby rattle. You claim to know my dad. Okay, you think he'd raise me to be helpless at seventeen?"

"I took that hog leg off you pretty easy, if you're as good as you think you are."

Garry's cheeks flamed. "Yeah, you did. You want to give it back and try again?"

"Not really. And you're missing the point. The first time is all it takes, Garry. You don't get second chances in my world."

Garry raised his coffee cup again. He knew the point. He was a little, skinny, baby-faced kid. Nobody could take him seriously.

Okay, fine. Take *that* and use it, then.

He set down the cup. "You win," he said flatly. "So you tell me what you feel like. What do you plan to do with me?"

"What do you think?"

"Well," Garry said, "there's a Kurs'ggtha artifact involved. And a bunch of spooks, Human, H'hogothan, and otherwise. Somebody's after me, for sure. I'm the only outsider that knows about the cube. Except you, of course—but you're not an outsider either, are you?"

Frego shook his big head slowly.

Garry exhaled. "Your best bet is to get me off-planet, I guess. The problem is here. But if really heavy people are involved, it might be hard getting me on a ship. The Port will be covered like a rug."

Now Frego's face split into a wide grin. "You let me worry about the Port, kiddo. It might be easier than you think. But yeah, you've got it about the same way I do. I think it's what your dad would want."

Garry nodded soberly. "Is there any way I could see him? Do you know where he is?"

"He's in Sector General Hospital, surrounded by Confederate cops, H'hogothan covert security, and some other people who don't fit any particular mold. You try to walk in there, all you do is sign your own warrant. Your dad's too."

"How about a message. To let him know I'm okay, and all?"

Frego's shoulders moved. "Maybe. Later. After you're out of it. You understand, somebody might have to risk a lot to get that message in? You want to take that chance?"

"I'll write something down and give it to you. Or maybe a chip or something?"

"A note's okay," Frego said, and Garry knew it didn't matter, because Frego had no intention of risking anything to deliver the message. He no longer doubted the other man's loyalty, but it was obvious that Garry's concerns were a low-priority item to him. Frego was a man with things on his mind, and all he wanted for Garry was to remove him from the equation of his other problems.

So many questions. . . . "I'll write the note," Garry said. "This is all pretty scary, you know."

Frego grinned, doing his best to look reassuring. "Don't worry, kid. I'll take care of you. I promised your dad, and I keep my promises."

I'll bet you do, Garry thought. "Can you tell me one thing?" he asked.

"Maybe."

"Just what is that artifact? Do you know?"

Frego paused for a long moment, then said, "What the hell. It can't hurt nothing." He drained the last of his coffee. "No, nobody knows for sure, kid. But some very good people think it might be the Kurs'ggtha stardrive."

Great, Garry thought. And doesn't *that* make things different?

Frego left on an errand, telling Garry not to leave the apartment. That was fine with him. He had no intention of going anywhere, not, at least, until he took care of some business of his own.

It was a matter of ten minutes to find Frego's safe, hidden behind a dresser in his bedroom. Twenty more minutes of delicate work went into cracking the surprisingly tough little box.

Inside, he found his .44, which he took out and strapped again under his armpit. He scrounged around until he found a small leather strap bag, which he filled with some other interesting items from the safe.

Last, and feeling just a bit guilty, he removed twenty big cartwheels, silvery on one side, bright gold on the other. Five hundred credit coins. It was only a part of Frego's stash, and Garry silently vowed to return the "loan" someday.

Quickly, he riffled through a bundle of papers and finally opened a small leather pouch. His eyes widened.

Inside, carefully wrapped, was a small, bright red chip. He recognized it instantly, of course—Imperial Terran Security Force ID. That was somewhat surprising, although not a lot, as riddled with spies as the Sector had always been. But what was his dad doing, involved with such a man? As far as he knew, Garth was still a wanted man on Terra.

Secrets. Again, secrets. And only one man had the answers he needed. Or perhaps one machine. Either way, he wasn't going to let himself be shepherded meekly off the planet until he had some answers. Somebody owed him that. Garth owed him that.

" 'Bye, cat," he said softly, and closed the door behind him.

What had Frego said? "If you're as good as you think you are?" He grinned slowly. He would just have to see.

Chapter Four

He felt naked and exposed as he wandered through the twisted back streets of Reef City. Had it been that good an idea to leave Frego's apartment? At least it was a safe place . . . or was it? Frego knew the code, sure, but how long ago had Garth set up that option? If it was something that had been dormant for years, what had brought Frego into the situation as quickly as he'd appeared?

Garry ran over the timetable slowly. It couldn't have been more than an hour between the time he'd left the Golden Ball and the moment Frego had literally bumped into him. Did that make sense? That good old Frego should be wandering around close enough to pick him up, just on the spur of the moment? And Frego had known all about the cube.

Something had triggered him. Either his dad expected something to happen, and Frego was aware of that, or—

What did Frego want? Garry thought a bit harder. If Frego had meant him harm, he could have carried out his intentions outside the bar the other night. It would have been quick and easy, and one more body in the Reef, more or less, would have raised few eyebrows.

If he'd meant to hold him captive, he sure hadn't done a very good job, although perhaps he felt that Garry, without money, his weapon, or any other resources, would be afraid to leave the apartment. Yet he hadn't made any extraordinary effort to keep him there, and as for the money part, Frego had to know that Garry had at least a kilocee on him, enough to support himself for several days.

So was he meant to do exactly what he'd done? Take the money and run?

For a moment he paused, dizzied by the ever-widening

ramifications of the evening. Permutations and possibilities began to seem infinite. He needed to narrow the field a bit, because at the moment, he had no idea what to do next.

There were too many secrets, too many players.

He glanced up at a forbidding brown building. A splash of bright neon picked out familiar words. It was a large store near the outer edge of the Reef. Not that far from the Golden Ball.

Not that far from—

Garry shifted the heavy weight of the revolver underneath his coat and drew in a long breath. Perhaps there was one player everybody had overlooked. It wouldn't take long to find out.

The computer center was almost empty. A single, feral-looking salesman eyed him hungrily as he entered.

"Yes, sir?"

"I'm just looking."

The salesman, dapper as a stiletto, looked at him carefully, taking in his evident age. "Oh. Well, go ahead, kid. Don't bust anything." His voice walked the narrow line between hope and disappointment. You never could tell with kids. Sometimes their parents had money.

Garry nodded. "This stuff all hooked up?"

"Uh-huh."

"How about that new IDM supermodem?"

"Sure. Hey, that's expensive equipment, you know."

"I'll be careful. You wanna watch?"

"Maybe I'd better," the salesman said.

It wasn't what Garry'd hoped for, but it would have to do.

He took a seat in front of the data terminal and looked up. "Universal access?"

"Anywhere. Like this," the salesman said.

Garry spent the next ten minutes accessing every boring data bank he could think of, until finally the salesman's eyes began to glaze over. "Listen, kid," the man said. "You call me if you need any more help, okay?"

Garry nodded without looking up. He waited until the man was on the other side of the room, and then he initiated a fast double cutout, to protect himself from casual snoops on the comm-lines. It was another instant's work to tap into the public com system and plug in the code for his own home.

The screen in front of him bleeped once, and a flat voice informed him he'd reached the Hamersmidt residence, but nobody was home. Would he care to leave a message?

Quickly, Garry coded an override and said, "Hal, shield this call from both ends."

"Done." A pause. "There are three datatraps on this line. I am feeding them all garbage. Where are you, Garry?"

"Never mind that. Where's Dad?"

As he spoke, he felt the tension slide out of his shoulders. If they'd gotten Hal, he would have been deeply out of luck. But Hal wasn't in the shop, or the house. Years before, Garth had buried the AI beneath a small apartment house almost a block away from either location. Destroying the Golden Ball had merely erased Hal's inputs and outputs there.

"Your father is at Sector General Hospital, in the intensive-care ward under heavy guard."

"Heavy guard? Why, Hal? Who are the guards?"

"They are a varied group, Garry. Some Confederacy people. Some from the Nest. A few local Sector cops. And a few others that aren't readily identifiable."

"Hal, what's going on? How is Dad?"

The AI's voice was flat as a silenced buzz saw. "Your father lost his right hand in the raid on the Golden Ball," he said. "He sustained lesser cuts and bruises and a few broken bones. His condition does not warrant intensive care, as far as I can find out. However, the IC ward is more easily sealed off from the general public. I suspect that is why he is still there."

Garry nodded slowly to himself. Of course. It was simply a ruse, to keep Garth a prisoner. But who was doing it, and why?

"I need to talk to him, Hal. Would you patch me through to him, please?"

"I can do that, Garry, but Garth can't hear you. They've been keeping him heavily sedated. I've tried to reach him on his implant, but there's no response. Just as I've been unable to reach you. Because of distance, I presume."

"Oh." He paused. If Garth wasn't badly injured, why keep him sedated? Unless they knew about the implant, or about Hal.

Damn! Always more questions, and still no answers.

"Hal, I really need to talk to him. I think somebody is trying to kill me—hell, I know somebody is. The same people that busted into the Golden Ball." He stopped for a moment. Then, "Uh, do you know anything about a guy named Frego?"

There was a long pause. Then Hal's flat voice took on an almost formal intonation. "Garth Hamersmidt, Junior. Do you state that your life is in danger and that you are unable to reach your father for help or advice?"

"Huh? What are you talking about, Hal?"

The AI simply repeated his question.

"This is really stupid, Hal, but I guess so."

"Answer yes or no, please."

He exhaled sharply in exasperation. "Yes, my life is in danger and I can't get through to Dad. Is that what you want?"

The screen in front of him suddenly flashed red, then cleared, and the face of Garth Hamersmidt appeared. He looked younger to Garry—maybe because Garry had never seen his father without a beard.

"Hello, Garry," his father said. "I'm sorry for all the rigmarole. This is a recording I started years ago, and I've updated it whenever it seemed necessary. Even Hal can't access this without you, and you alone, giving him permission. And he has to decide that you are in a life-or-death situation where I can't help. This is, by the way, an interactive program, so all you have to do is ask, and if I have anything that will help, I'll tell you."

Garry stared at the screen. He knew about AI submodules, but had never seen one in action. What his father had done was set up an expert system with special information files. In effect, within the limit of those files, he was talking to his father. And if the files were also updated from Hal's own data banks, the Garth system would be *very* knowledgeable.

Quickly, Garry filled in the Garth routine about the happenings at the Golden Ball.

"Dad, what's that cube? I mean, I know it has to be valuable, but why are people trying to kill you for it?" And me too, he wanted to add, but that was another question.

There was a pause. Since Hal's processing time was enormously fast, Garry could only imagine the complexity of the process he'd initiated.

"The cube is a Kurs'ggtha artifact, Garry. It must be. Have you ever wondered why I came to H'hogoth in the first place?"

"You told me, Dad. Some kind of trouble on Terra. You wanted to lie low."

"Not exactly the truth, son, I'm afraid. I was sent to H'hogoth."

"By who? Who sent you here? What for?"

"Garry, the Nest and the Confederacy have coexisted for a long time, but have you ever considered the fragility of that relationship? We are so very different as species. The lizards have a totally different outlook on things. They've had the drive for thousands of years, but their Nest only numbers a few hundred worlds. In less than two hundred years the Confederacy has colonized twice that number, and the rate of colonization is increasing. In the normal course of things, what would you expect the result to be?"

Garry thought about it. "Well, war, probably. Or no war, but cultural domination. We both can use the same planets. On Terra . . ." He stopped, trying to recall Mr. Deilworthy's example. "Like the Amerinds, I guess. Their culture would disintegrate."

Garth nodded. "Uh-huh. Why do you suppose nothing like that seems to be happening?"

"I dunno. I never thought about it."

"It's the drive, Garry. The drive is an unstoppable weapon."

"What?"

Garth's voice took on a lecturing tone. "Think about how the drive works. You go through a wormhole and pop out light-years away, and years in the past. Why bother to turn on the timeband in the first place?"

"Well, to come back to the present, I guess."

"There's no natural law that says you have to, son. But there is another kind of law—one that the Confederacy doesn't publicize at all. It's the central part of the Exchange. For instance, where do you think we get our drives?"

Garry ruminated for a moment. "Mmm. Two or three big companies build them. Uh, H'hogothan companies, come to think of it."

Garth nodded. "Right. Humanity buys the drives from the H'hogotha. And they are very special drives—we can't work on them. Any tampering results in a very large explosion. Our drives include an automatic timeband; we *can't* avoid returning to the present."

Garry still found a loophole. "Well, why don't we just build our own drives?"

"We could, except we never discovered the mechanism that would allow us to exit the wormhole at any point. Our own drives would only take us from one end to the other—black hole to quasar, willy-nilly. In other words, our drives are useless in any practical way. We have to use the lizard drives, and we therefore have to use the timeband."

"I get it. What it boils down to is the lizards control our interstellar transport system. But nothing limits them."

"What would happen if the Terran Confederacy were attacked by the Nest?"

Garry thought about it. We'd probably kick their asses," he said slowly.

"Okay. What if Terra was attacked two hundred years ago?"

"Oh." He finally grasped the implication of it. The drive was a time machine that worked both ways.

"Right," Garth said. "Now do you understand why the Human Confederacy searches so desperately for an alternative stardrive? At the moment, we are completely at the mercy of H'hogotha, completely dependent on their goodwill."

"Yeah. I see."

"Terran experts predicted the present situation fairly accurately—all they needed to do was compare our breeding rates to the H'hogotha to realize it was inevitable we'd outnumber them at some not very distant point. But numbers don't mean everything, not when the lizards have the weight of the wormhole drive—a time machine —on their side. So the Search was begun."

Garry began to feel overwhelmed, as if the sudden influx of data was causing synapses to short out in his skull. "What? The Search? What's that?"

"Terran scientists believe that the Kurs'ggtha had a true faster-than-light drive, one that operated in realtime. Of course our own people work constantly to develop such a thing, but at the same time, the Search for the Kuts'ggtha drive goes on. That's what I do—I look for something, some relic, some artifact, that will give us the information we need." Garth's image paused. "Well, my people do, at least."

"Wait a minute. You're telling me you're some kind of spy?"

"That's right," Garth said levelly. "Oh, you could call me an intelligence agent, or a covert operator, but yet, I'm a spy."

"The lizards are our allies."

"For now," his father said slowly.

He tried to soak it all in, make sense of it somehow, but the pieces wouldn't fit together. He inhaled slowly, then slumped in his seat, deep lines wrinkling his clear forehead.

"So what do I do now?" he said at last. "It's worse than I thought. I suppose every other spy on H'hogoth is after me now." Another thought struck him suddenly. "Dad? Do you know a man named Frego?"

His father nodded. "Yes. I've known Frego for a long time Why?"

He suddenly realized he hadn't explained about the stumpy little man, and without that input, the AI routine masquerading as his father couldn't give him any advice. Quickly he told Garth about his experiences of the night before.

"I don't understand why Frego was there. But then, Garry, I may have sent him myself. You have to understand, this program hasn't been updated for a couple of weeks, so I don't know what I've done since then."

"Would you have? Sent him, I mean? It was like he was waiting for me."

"He could have been. I just don't know. Frego is one of my people, of course. Without knowing what's been happening, my advice is to trust him, do what he says, at least until I'm—Garth—is able to advise you himself."

"That's not much help, Dad. People are trying to kill me. They have to be."

"Has anybody tried? Actually tried?"

Garry shook his head slowly, conscious of the silliness of it all—him talking with a computer program as if it were his own father. Yet it was all he had.

"No. Nobody's tried."

"So my advice stands. Trust Frego. As of two weeks ago, I had no reason not to."

"But what if something's changed? What about Hyarl Thomas?"

"Hyarl Thomas is a very dangerous man, Garry. Don't try to do anything about him. But make sure Frego understands who he is dealing with, and tell him that he must retrieve the cube, if he can. He must know this already, if he's done as much as you say, but tell him again. Then do what he says. You understand? Do exactly what Frego tells you to do, and you'll be okay."

"But what about—" For a moment Garry stopped, confused about talking with his father about his father, but then shook it off. "What about you in the hospital? Hal says you're under guard and drugged. Shouldn't I try to—"

Garth shook his head emphatically. "Other people will work on that end, Garry. I'm not without friends or influence. You just try to stay out of trouble. This trouble, in particular. There's nothing you can do. You understand me?"

Garry nodded. "Yeah, Dad. I'll try." He stared forlornly at the screen for a moment. "But I sure wish I could talk to *you*."

The face on the screen smiled. "And I'm sure I wish I could too, son. Be careful. I love you, Garry."

He felt something warm brim at the edges of his eyes. "Me too, Dad."

"Hey, kid, what are you doing?" The sudden voice of the salesman shocked him. Almost reflexively, he reached forward and shut down the data terminal.

"Who you been accessing? If you've charged anything to the store—"

"Not me, man," Garry said quickly. "It was just some dead files, theater stuff."

The salesman eyed him suspiciously. "Maybe you better let me get your credit code. Just in case."

Garry stood up slowly. The man was about his size, but maybe twenty years older, and looked soft. He grinned. "Sure, guy. Just a sec, here." He reached slowly into his jacket, then faked right, left and dodged for the door. He was through and into the street, running hard, before the outraged salesman could shout his first words.

"Where the hell have you been?" Frego was slumped on the sofa, an irritated-looking cat swishing its tail back and forth at his feet.

"I went out," Garry said. He paused, suddenly uncomfortable. After his headlong rush through the streets of Reef City, the apartment seemed cramped and stifling. "You mind if I open a window?" he said, staring across the room.

"No!" Frego's big hands were on the sash before Garry had even touched the glass. Garry filed the other man's liquid move under "Things about Frego I must not underestimate."

Frego faced him. "We got enough trouble, kid. No need to make it easier for anybody else."

"Easier for who? For what?"

Frego shrugged. "Maybe for whoever followed you back from wherever you went. You ever think about that, Garry? Where did you go? Back to the Golden Ball? Your house, maybe?"

Garry felt a wash of relief flow through him. Frego didn't seem to know about Hal. Or maybe he did, but didn't understand exactly how Garry could communicate with the AI.

"Maybe," Garry said.

Frego shook his head slowly. "Garry, Garry—didn't I tell you not to leave the apartment? You're gonna have to trust me on this. I'm an expert, and you aren't. You think your dad would have given me the code if he didn't want you to do what I tell you?"

Uncomfortably, Garry recalled the advice given him by his father's AI construct, buried deep in Hal's memory. "Frego, it's . . . it's hard, you know. So much has happened, so quick. Dad in the hospital, the cube, and you appear out of nowhere. I don't even know you!"

Frego dropped his hands from the winow, returned to the sofa, and brushed the cat back to the floor. The small animal let out a soft *yurp* of annoyance.

"Yeah," Frego said slowly, "it must be awful tough for you. But that's still not any excuse for you to steal from me. All I did was help you. You don't steal from friends, Garry."

It had been nagging him ever since he'd taken the handful of coins from Frego's safe, and now his humiliation and guilt painted his cheeks bright red. The ready excuses surged in his throat—but finally he had to admit the truth.

"I know," he said huskily, his gaze on the floor. "It

was wrong. It seemed necessary at the time, but you're right. It was stealing, plain and simple. And I shouldn't have." He fumbled in his pocket for the coins, began to take them out.

Frego waved one big palm back and forth. "No, you keep it. I was gonna give you some extra cash anyway. I think you're gonna need it." He leaned over and picked up the cat, placed it on his lap, and began to stroke its head. His touch was slow and gentle. "Garry, tell me the truth, now. Where did you go? And, uh, why did you come back?"

Garry watched Frego's twisted fingers move through the cat's fur as he tried to add it up. Finally he decided. He couldn't do it alone, not at this point, and his tenuous connection to Hal—suddenly he realized just how risky his jaunt had been—was not enough. He needed a friend. Frego seemed to be the only candidate. And you didn't lie to friends.

He exhaled heavily, sat down, and gave Frego the details of his excursion.

"Oh, yeah?" Frego said when he'd finished. "An AI subroutine? That's pretty slick—but then, your dad is one of the slickest customers I've ever known. So you know about the Search, then—that makes things a little easier. If Garth trusts you with stuff like that, then I've got a much freer hand."

Garry remained silent. A much freer hand than what?

Almost as if he'd read Garry's mind, Frego continued. "Even though you're Garth Hamersmidt's son, and even though he's explained a little about what he really does, I still can't tell you everything, Garry. Some things don't have any bearing on this situation, but the information might put others at risk. The less you know, the less you can tell."

"Uh-huh," Garry said. "But you are gonna make the decision, right?"

"I'm sorry, but yes. That's about it."

"Okay. So what is it about the cube? You say it might be the Kurs'ggtha FTL drive. Or maybe some kind of clue about it. Dad explained why that would be important. So who's got the cube now? Why did it come to the Golden Ball in the first place? Who was that rat-faced guy? And Hyarl Thomas." A quick, vivid flash of the tall, deadly man's lopsided smile played itself across the back of Garry's skull. "Who is Hyarl Thomas?"

Frego raised both hands, palms out. "Hang on a minute, kid. That's a lot of questions." He lowered his hands, leaned back, and chewed on his lower lip for a few seconds. Then he grunted softly.

"Let's take the last question first. Garth explained about the Search team, right? Well, it's not just Terra and the Nest, you know. There are others, in and out of the H'hogotha Confederacy, who have an interest too." His eyes grew muddy, fading from dark green to brown. "There are always outsiders. The Potential Worlds don't much like either side. But they'll work with anybody to achieve their own ends. And the fact that Thomas was once a Search team member makes him all the more dangerous. Of course, since the Nest is involved by now, he's probably kinda checkmated."

Garry stared at him in disbelief. "Wait a minute! You mean the H'hogotha know about the Search? They know what Terra is trying to do?"

" 'Course they do," Frego replied. "You couldn't keep a secret like that forever. Nobody really expected to, anyway."

"Well, why haven't they done something? The Nest, I mean?"

"They have. Unless you think it was coincidence that your dad is sewed up tighter than a Christmas goose."

"So what are you telling me? The lizards know, and they let things just go on?"

Frego raised his shoulders slightly, lowered them. "Why not? They have their own Search, have for thousands of years. But it's a big galaxy, Garry, and room for more than one team in the game. No, the lizards don't mind us playing—especially when they figure they can take anything we find just as quick as we find it. But the Potential Worlds—that's another story. People out there, some of them have gotten a little strange. Not Lizard, but not really Human anymore, either. We and the Nest understand each other. We've been playing the game for quite a while. These jumped-up supermen are a wild card. Us and the lizards both agree on that."

The more Garry thought, the harder it got to assimilate. Finally he said, "Well, how did the cube come to the Golden Ball in the first place? Was Ratface one of your buddies? Working for Dad, I mean?"

"Well, now, that's something else. I don't believe in

coincidence much, either, but one happened there. Believe it or not, our Search team didn't find that cube. Thomas—the Potential group—did. And your rat-faced friend—who didn't know a hell of a lot about what was going on—somehow found a way to steal the artifact. But he wasn't real bright, and pretty soon figured out he didn't have a chance of making any real money on the thing. So he took it to the first place he thought he could turn it for some fast cash. And that was the Golden Ball."

"Oh, jeez," Garry muttered. "Then it was all an accident."

"Uh-huh. When that guy pawned the cube to you, your dad was as surprised as anybody. Now, of course, we know the cube exists too. Probably the Nest as well. Still, Thomas has the cube now, and he'll try to keep it. But keep in mind all the factions involved—us, the Thomas people, the official Nest, and probably every free-lancer who picks up the rumors that are bound to start. You don't hijack a place like the Golden Ball and put Garth Hamersmidt in the hospital without starting a lot of smoke. But maybe it's better Thomas does have it, instead of the Nest—stealing something from the lizard government is almost impossible. And I think something else too."

"What's that?"

"The very first thing Hyarl Thomas will try to do is get the cube off-planet. Which is why you'll need the extra money. We're gonna take a little trip ourselves."

Garry's arms felt cold and achy. He rubbed them, hard. "Where are we going?" He thought he knew the answer, and he neglected to inform Frego that the Garth AI wanted his seventeen-year-old son to stay out of trouble.

He was right.

"If I can find out, we're going wherever the cube goes. It's the only way I can think to do both things Garth wants—get that cube and keep an eye on you. So I guess I gotta ask you a question too, Garry."

"Sure."

"Can I trust you?"

Chapter Five

Garry noticed spring was coming in early. High over the jumble of the Sector, fleecy clouds piled like great scoops of whipped cream floating in a bowl of watery blue ink. He'd never seen the arched firmament of Terra, so the H'hogothan sky, which was the color of royal sapphires rather than robin's eggs, didn't seem strange to him.

The morning was warm, He'd slung his jacket over his shoulders and held it there with the straps from his backpack. Frego had gone out early to a clothing store and picked up some things for him—now he enjoyed the soft feel of new jeans and a thick sweater, although the heavy boots Frego had purchased would need some time to get broken in.

All around him the rushing, chattering crowds of Reef City surged and ebbed, filling restaurants, shops, even the cheap, daytime bars where the spacers drank their breakfast to survive the leftover rigors of the night before.

He felt relatively safe. Frego had shown him how to bleach the black from his hair. Now it was curly and blond, almost the white-gold color of corn silk; the overall effect made him look older. To hide the distinctive emerald shade of his eyes he wore black sunglasses—although if he could find a place this morning he intended to get blue contact lenses.

"Come on, Garry, quit gawking. You aren't a tourist—you've seen Reef City before."

Frego walked a couple of paces in front of him. He'd told him to maintain that distance so that it wouldn't be readily apparent they were together. "More people know me," Frego had told him, "than are likely to recognize you. Especially in that getup."

Garry turned away from the H'hogothan beggar who

51

had painted himself bright orange—the lizard colors for the lowest caste—and who was singing an ancient Bob Dylan song from Terra. The lizard speech apparatus produced a surprisingly clear tenor, not at all the hissing sound one might have expected from a saurian. Lizards did not have darting tongues. Two sets of lips, one thick and narrow, the inner set long, thin, and facile, moderated their voices. The forgotten Terran troubadour was enjoying a revival among spacemen and the youth of many planets. The lizard's song was currently number one on the charts and Garry, who had listened to recordings of the original nasal versions by Dylan himself, thought the old master would have been pleased.

Without looking back, Frego ducked suddenly down a narrow alley between two buildings of heavy, dark stone. Garry paused a moment, smelling the myriad stenches and perfumes of the Reef: the burnt cinnamon smell of the lizards themselves, bacon frying, spilled beer, a hint of green from the greater city beyond, a taste of ozone from the early-morning thunderstorm, all of it blended into an exhilarating mash that was peculiar to Reef City itself. Veteran spacers claimed they could recognize ports by their odors as easily as with their eyes.

He counted to ten under his breath, then followed Frego down the alley. Immediately the temperature dropped as the hulking buildings cut off the bright morning sunlight. Thirty paces in, the stocky man was a dim figure waiting beside a nondescript painted steel door.

"Come on, kid," Frego called softly. "I don't like standing here." As Garry joined him, he glanced up. Garry followed his gaze and saw two spy eyes focused on them.

Frego nodded once, then touched the memory pad next to the door. Evidently he was known to whoever manned the spy eyes, because after a short wait the door slid silently open. Garry followed him down a dimly lit passage to another door, this one heavily armored.

"Notice how quiet it is?" Frego asked. "Six inches of armor plate all around us. The gas jets are in the ceiling."

Garry felt his lighthearted mood evaporating rapidly. He could well imagine that some guests of this dark corridor never left it breathing.

"Don't worry," Frego muttered, "I do a lot of business here." Again his fingers brushed the doorpad in a quick, intricate code. This second door opened much more slowly, revealing the oldest Human Garry had ever seen.

Garry wasn't very big, but this specimen barely came to his shoulders. One half of the man's face was covered with skin like translucent parchment—beneath it Garry could see heavy veins pulsing with thick slowness. Over the cheekbone spread a dark bruise—the eye that regarded them was a filmed and milky yellow, like spoiled cream. The top of the man's head and the rest of his face was an intricate steel mask from which glowed a single red orb. The rest of the man's body was a web of metal struts encaging wasted flesh. The cyber prosthesis was very strong, Garry knew. And appallingly expensive. Whoever this creature was, he had money.

"Well, Frego, what brings spying scum like you to my humble abode?" the ancient said, cackling. His electronic voice was harsh and full of static. His red eye blazed at Garry. "Branching out, mmm? Come to sell me a boy, maybe?"

Frego snorted. "No, Candy, not this time. You know more about that business than I do. As usual, all I want is your skill. If you've got any left, that is. You look worse than you used to—but then, you always do."

The man's head emitted a strange, haw-hawing bark that puzzled Garry until he realized Candy was laughing. "Don't worry about old Candy, scutball. He was here before you came, and he'll dance on your grave after you've gone." Again the awful barking noise.

"Right," Frego said. "So can we come in, or shall we continue this delightful conversation and forget about business?"

"Not so quick!" Candy buzzed. "Who's your sweet young friend?"

"He's a friend, you rotting old lech. And not for you, either. He's the business I'm talking about."

"Ah. Well, that's different then, isn't it? Come in, come in." Candy moved backward with eerie smoothness, his exoskeleton emitting a slight humming sound. As Garry passed he felt fingers glide down his arm, a touch as feathery as spiders. "So young," Candy whispered, and Garry shuddered.

The second corridor debouched onto a large, low-ceilinged room filled with odd bluish indirect light. Garry wondered for a moment what planet the old monster might have originally called home. Around the walls of the room was scattered the largest collection of data processing equipment he'd ever seen in one place, from antique IBM minimains to the most modern products of Interstellar Data Module. He even thought he recognized the distinctive shape of a meatmatrix tank, but that was impossible; the big meats were outlawed throughout the H'hogoth Confederacy. In the center of the room was an articulated surgical chair with massive, padded head clamps. He moved the chair around and fiddled with its controls. When he was finished, he glided over to Frego. "So? What is this business you've brought me?"

"First, I want him"—Frego jerked a horny thumb at Garry—"scanned and mapped."

"Both? That's expensive."

"What's the matter? My credit suddenly no good?"

Candy speared him with an evil glance. "Maybe I should trust you, huh? Well, we'll see." Garry heard him muttering at one of the machines. After a time he returned. "Okay," he said grudgingly, "anything else?"

"I'll tell you later. Do him first."

"You're the spy with the money," Candy said. "Come on, kid. Into the chair with you."

Garry glanced at Frego. "Go on," Frego said. "It won't hurt."

That wasn't what Garry was really worried about, but he nodded and moved toward the chair. Then he paused. "Frego, what's a scan and map?"

"Candy here is gonna scan you for any kind of cyber bugs and whatnot, and also do a gene map and a retinal analysis."

"How come?"

" 'Cause I said so. Okay?"

Garry shrugged and sat down. He realized that Frego had no intention of discussing any more than he had to in front of Candy, and that made a lot of sense. What you don't know, you can't tell. Or sell. Candy looked like he would sell *anything*.

He settled back in the chair. Candy lifted the head clamps into place. Then he said, "I'm gonna put you under, kid. So don't jump or anything, okay?"

A moment later he felt the sudden sharp chill of a contact hypospray on his neck. Then, nothing.

He awoke feeling stiff and sore, and decided he must have been under for quite a while. When he moved his head a quick knife of pain lanced through his skull, and he let out a short groan.

"Hey, you back with us?" Frego said. He walked over and stood looking down. "You feel okay?"

"A little stiff."

"That figures. The gene and retinal stuff take a while."

"Can I sit up now?"

"Sure." Frego reached down and did something to the chair. A moment later Garry found himself in a sitting position.

"Better?"

"Yeah," Garry said. "So what'd you find out?"

"You're clean, for one thing. A couple of odd bits about your brain structure, though even that was within normal limits. But no bugs or anything like that."

"I could have told you," Garry said.

"Uh-huh, you could. But now I know. Anyway, we'll be able to do what I wanted."

"Which is?"

"Did you think we were gonna smuggle you onto a outbound ship through a cargo hatch or something?" He shook his head. "Not hardly. What you get, my friend, is a new identity. Then we can go where we want without setting off anybody's alarm system."

Garry found the subject interesting. "How are you gonna do that? Change my identity, I mean. I thought it was impossible."

Candy chuckled. The result was a weird, crackling sound. "All the snoopies would like you to think so, my young friend. They tell you that retinalysis and gene maps are impossible to fool. But there will always be people who'd rather not be who they are, so there will always be people like me, who help them do it." Candy breathed metallically for a moment, then continued.

"I can change your retinal pattern with computer-guided laser surgery, and as for gene mapping—that's a little tougher, but it can be done too. They always use blood for their samples. That can be fixed as well. If you've got the money."

Garry shook his head, trying to wipe away a moment of dizziness. He looked at Frego. "Do we?"

"What's that?"

"Have the money?"

Frego laughed suddenly. "Yeah, kid, we got the money. Let's say somebody does, and we can use it." He and Candy seemed to share some inside joke as their eyes met.

"Okay, I guess. When do we do whatever it is?"

"Huh?"

"You know, make the change. Whatever he does." He pointed at Candy.

This time the deformed man's laugh was a rising buzz saw. "Oh that. It's already done. I've made a new man out of you, kid." And the horrible laughter pealed up the register one more time, finally tailing off into an electronic wheeze.

"Oh. So what's next?"

Frego came over next to him. "Not much. As soon as Candy finishes putting together your ID chip, we'll be out of here."

And, indeed, less than ten minutes later, they were back on the streets of Reef City.

"When we get back, I'll sleep-stuff you on your new identity, okay? I don't think there'll be any problems, but you never know. And we'll both feel better if you can answer any questions that might come up."

Garry nodded, his eyes on the bright storefronts they passed. "I guess so," he said.

"By the way, I'm your uncle now. You can call me Uncle Frego."

"You aren't going to change your own name?"

"Frego isn't my own name," he replied.

Frego had slowed to an amble, his twisted hands in his pockets, his eyes squinting against the sun. Garry matched his pace, listening to the myriad sounds of the Reef—whispers, calls, shouts in a dozen languages and dialects, horns honking and hovercycles pop-popping their way through the crowded streets, distant sirens, music from darkened club doorways—a general cacophony that was suddenly split by the jaw-grinding howl of a freighter shuttle taking off from Port.

The big ships never touched down, Garry knew. Designed and built in space, they would crumple like cities made of tin foil on a planet. Yet their shields and force fields protected them in the unimaginably greater gravity well of a black hole, as they entered these gates between universes. It made a strange contrast, but not the first Garry had discovered in his life.

"That Candy guy was pretty weird," he said.

"Weirder than you'll ever know," Frego agreed. "Crazy as hell, but he does good work. And he keeps his mouth shut, as long as he gets paid. I always pay him, so we ought to be okay."

The strange, ancient little monster hadn't struck Garry as being extremely trustworthy. "You sure about that?"

"Why not? In his business, Candy gets a reputation for loose lips, somebody comes along and sews his mouth shut. You understand?"

Garry swallowed. "Makes sense."

They were nearing Frego's apartment. Across the square at the end of the block, people lined up for entrance to the workers' gate of the Port.

"When are we going to leave?" Garry asked.

"When I find out where we're going," Frego replied. "It could be anytime. Or we might wait a week. I doubt if they'll risk hanging around much longer. Everybody on H'hogoth must be looking for them by now."

"How many people are looking for me right now?" Garry asked quietly.

"A lot, probably. Not as many as for the cube, but some of Thomas's people would no doubt like to get rid of any witnesses to what happened at the Golden Ball. Which is you, my young friend."

"I wish my dad was here," Garry said at last.

They stopped in front of Frego's building while he fumbled for his entry chip. A worried look flickered across his scarred features. "So do I, kid."

Garry walked aimlessly around Frego's apartment, pausing every once in a while to stare down over the square in front of the Port entry. The area was almost deserted now, only a bored pair of guards lounging in the shack behind the fence. It was a gray afternoon, two days after his trip to Candy's house of horrors, and now the sky was full of clouds. Sometimes he felt his mind suffered the same affliction, as his thoughts grew fuzzy and swollen and bumped against each other.

Still no word about Garth, other than that his condition remained the same. Frego had tried in various ways to crack the veil of secrecy surrounding Garry's father, but had come up luckless each time. Garry himself, outfitted with his new ID and a fresh set of blue contact lenses, had returned to the computer shop for another try at Hal. He'd been gratified to meet the same clerk, who waited on him again with no recognition, but less pleased to find that his home comm-line, his only way of reaching Hal, was no longer in service. He tried to use the implant, but as he feared, he was too far away from Hal's pickups.

What did it mean? Was the line gone, or was Hal destroyed? He feared the second, because Hal was a witness too, his testimony filled with the sort of detail only the dispassionate speed of metal and crystal could provide.

"Mrowp."

"What? Get off my foot, Matherbel."

The ginger-colored tabby ignored him, continuing to butt her blunt face against his ankle. He laughed a little, bent down, and picked up the obese animal, who responded to his touch by going as limp as a bag full of Jell-O. He carried her to the sofa and sat her down beside him. Her agate eyes regarded him calmly as she circled her sharp white teeth with a single swirl of pink tongue.

"What would you do, Mather?" he asked.

She didn't reply.

Frego had been gone when Garry woke up, evidently rushed, because the bathroom was a mess. Or maybe he just expects me to keep house for him, Garry thought. I've been doing enough of that lately, God knows.

Frego made it plain that Garry was not to leave the apartment, and Garry more or less agreed—what was he supposed to do? He didn't know friend from enemy, could think of no way to break the chain of guardians visible and not visible which surrounded his father, and knew of no other place to turn.

Moreover, after his conversation with the Garth analogue hidden in Hal's memory, he understood that great forces were balanced precariously in his situation. He could well imagine the frantic desperation with which the Human Confederacy would seek any clue to a realtime stardrive. And anything of interest to the Confederacy was of interest to the Potential Worlds, for their own convoluted reasons. Finally, if only in response to their deep-seated racial paranoia, the H'hogotha would be just as eager to come into possession of the cube.

It was a staggering problem. He'd never realized how much the environment he'd grown up in had taught him to distrust the authorities—nothing overt, just the simple understanding that cops weren't for the likes of Garth or Garry or the business of the Golden Ball. But now he felt cut off, almost helpless. He chafed under Frego's rule, even as he told himself it was all he had, and things would work out.

"Dammit!" he spat suddenly, and slapped the cushion next to Matherbel, who landed three feet away from the sofa, hissing and flexing her fur.

He threw himself toward the window, his narrow frame a coiled piece of steel screaming for action. Something, anything to do. His whole world had come apart in a single night, and now he didn't even know where to find glue, let alone the shattered pieces.

Something silent and malignant bloomed against the lowered sky. He froze, his hawk nose against the glass, until the sound finally rolled to him, shivered the cold hard surface, grumbled in his ears, shook the floor beneath him.

"Jeezus!" His breath painted the word on the window. "What the hell—"

His bones knew it before he did, as his body began to vibrate with the rhythm of the distant explosion. Now the fireball boiled into the sky, crowned with a greasy flame, stained and smudged with debris.

"Ohmygawd. The hospital. It's the *hospital*!"

He leaned against the pane, shaking and frozen at the same time, and felt something unnameable and entirely real stretch itself inside him, becoming thinner and thinner, and at last, irrevocably, snap.

Matherbel hissed once in the silence.

"Dad," Garry whispered. "Oh Dad."

All things are coincidence, he thought as he watched the tall man walk slowly across the square toward the entryport. The man was dressed in nondescript workman's clothing: boots, a drab brown jumpsuit, a shabby leather belt. Garry ignored the everyday garb and watched the man's gait instead. Like dice clicking in a bony hand the slow, gliding shuffle etched itself on him like stones, and he knew—for Garry never forgot things. Once, younger, he'd thought it a curse. Now it was a joy of vengeance.

He stood on a roof and looked down. Frego stood behind him, his face a map of lines like knife cuts just beyond blood.

"It's him, isn't it?" he said.

Garry nodded. "That's him. That's Hyarl Thomas."

Chapter Six

"What were you able to find out?" Garry was amazed at the sound of his own voice. Frego didn't seem to notice, but to Garry the change was obvious; something young had been leached out of his words, leaving them cold, old as rust, deadly. Always it seemed the fireball bloomed behind his eyelids in some secret subliminal place. Garth, the fireball said. Father.

"Not much." Frego shook his head. The dim light of the room rolled off the shiny skin of his skull. He sighed heavily. "Not much hope, either. Two hundred dead so far, Garry. They're still finding . . . pieces. The explosion was centered beneath the intensive-care wing. Some of that isn't even dug out yet."

Garry nodded. His head felt like a puppet's wooden globe, controlled by invisible strings leading to some distant place. "He's dead," he said.

"We don't know for sure yet. . . ."

"Do you really believe that?"

Frego was silent for a moment. Then he shook his head. "No. I don't."

"That's it, then. I didn't want a funeral anyway. Do you think my dad wanted a funeral, Frego?"

"Garry, don't talk like that."

"Why not?" Garry said harshly. "He's dead, that's all. It had to happen sometime, didn't it? Sooner, maybe, in his . . . line of business."

"Garry, your father had his reasons for taking the risks he did. It's not for you to judge him."

"So that's it, then? I have no right? Fine. Next case."

Frego stared at him with the look of a man who'd picked a rose and seen it turn into something chill, toothed, and slimy in his fingers. "Do you think Garth would be proud of you right now? He's dead, and all you can feel is self-pity. Is that it?"

"What should I feel? What would bring him back?" Garry knew he *was* in shock, and was grateful for the cottony distance it gave him. He felt apart from the explosion, the death, some kind of observer. And glad of it—now things had to be done. Garth had lived his life a certain way, made commitments, believed in things. It seemed natural to Garry that those commitments must be kept, those beliefs must be honored. If in so doing revenge might be found, then so much the better. And there was no room for seventeen-year-old innocence, childish grief, useless tears in that. "I have to avenge him, Frego," he said slowly, as if it were a new thought.

Frego nodded. His scarred, lumpy features observed Garry intently. Finally he said, "It's not work for a kid, Garry."

Garry couldn't help it. There was something vicious, whiplike in his reply. "Oh, no. Of course not. Not for a kid. Keep secrets from the little kid, okay. So when his dad gets blown up, his home destroyed, everything he knows vanished, then he's got nothing left. That's good for the kid, right? Keep him safe and warm and ignorant. Worked out pretty well, wouldn't you say? Frego?"

The older man nodded slowly. "I'm glad you have things figured out so well. Blame me. Blame your father. That's a very mature thing to do, Garry. Right now I'm sure your dad would be proud of you." Then his voice went hard. "If you don't want to be treated like a kid, then stop acting like one!"

It was like a dash of cold water. Garry sat back. He opened his mouth and then closed it. Opened it again. "Oh, Frego, oh my God. I'm so scared."

Frego leaned forward and wrapped the boy with his massive arms. He said nothing. He waited. Garry tensed against him and then, at last, the tears came. Still, in the cracked emerald agony of the boy's eyes, he sensed some of the strength of the father, of the man to whom he'd given undivided allegiance decades before. Maybe that hint of strength would be enough, he decided.

He felt the boy shake against his chest and knew that life wasn't fair. Garry was still, in many ways, a little boy. Yet children had led armies, fought revolutions, overturned palaces. And he also knew that in other parts of man's empire, often wilder, more unsafe parts, children Garry's age were men who plowed virgin ground, raised families, gave wise counsel.

It would be harder on Garry than on him. Garry still had a few illusions left. But he owed it to Garth Hamersmidt, and Frego always paid his debts.

"Okay," Frego said at last, stroking the back of the boy's head. "We'll do it. We'll get those scuts that killed your father."

And only disliked himself a little for what the promise meant.

"Okay, remember," Frego said, "your first name is still Garry. I left it that way so it's harder for either of us to make a slip. But your last name is—"

"Hardwick. I know."

"Where were you born?"

"Kenilworth." His voice took on a singsong tone. "A poor frontier world, where I was delivered in a log cabin. Which explains why nobody took my footprints at birth."

Frego nodded. His voice was dry. "At least the sleep hypno took."

"I could have remembered all this stuff without it."

"Maybe. But why take chances? This way, you'll still parrot it back, even under light chemical trance. Here's one of those things I can teach you, Garry. In this business, never take a chance you don't have to. But if chance is all there is, then jump on it with both feet."

They were halfway down the long line waiting to board the shuttle to the *Star of Orion,* a medium-class liner bound for Petersburg, an established Potential World.

"I'll remember that too, Frego. I'm sorry, I'm not trying to be stubborn. I've always been able to remember things." He paused. "And good old Garry Hardwick is an orphan. At least that's right."

Frego didn't reply to this. "Got your chip ready?"

Garry showed the thin plastic card in his hand. "Uh-huh."

Frego inhaled slowly. "If anybody's looking, they'll be looking here." He glanced forward at the small group of uniformed Sector patrolmen who, along with a pair of uniformed H'hogotha, were checking travelers through the security gate leading to the loading area.

Finally they approached the checkpoint. "Look good, now," Frego whispered.

Garry nodded.

The boarding procedure was designed to be fast and efficient. Garry stepped through the steel arch that scanned him for weapons and explosives, then presented his ID chip to a uniformed man who fed the bit of crystal into a terminal that was on-line to the H'hogothan data pool. At the same time, another man motioned him to take a seat and, when he did, swiftly lowered a device that resembled an aluminum half egg over his head. Garry stared into the darkness until two tiny blue stars exploded silently before him. The egg rose.

He hadn't even noticed the tiny prick in the ball of his thumb, where a blood sample for gene mapping had been taken.

Thirty seconds later, the first guard handed his chip back to him. "One thing," the guard said, looking at his face. "It says your eyes are green."

Garry smiled, reached up, and touched his face. "Oh. Sorry." He held one finger forward, showing a glistening plastic disk. "Contacts."

"Right on. Green they are." The guard smiled and motioned him forward.

After the short shuttle jump, and a similar inspection in the orbiting boarding station adjoining the *Star of Orion*, Frego and Garry spent a few minutes unpacking in their small stateroom.

"I hate that security," Frego said. "It makes things hard as hell for an honest spy."

Garry unfolded his favorite shirt, a silky thing that shifted colors as the temperature and humidity changed, and carefully hung it up. "We live in paranoid times," he said. "The lizards are paranoid by nature—their brain structure demands it—and the rest of us are paranoid because of the lizards. The drive dictates so much of the way the H'hogoth Confederacy is structured, you know."

"You're got all that schooling," Frego said. "That's good. Don't forget what you already know, Garry. But don't be afraid to learn something new, either."

Garry shrugged. "It's obvious, if you just look at all the details. The only way the worlds communicate with each other on a day-to-day basis is via ship. Despite the roundabout routes—through the wormholes, back in time, forward in time—the ships arrive at their destinations essentially in realtime. So anybody who controls access to the ships controls the worlds. For the first time in man's recorded history, borders mean something. If you can control what goes on the ships and comes off them, you control the same things for your planet. Which is, of course, why boarding and disembarking the interstellar ships is so rigidly monitored. The mice can't slip between the walls anymore."

"We did," Frego reminded him. "So did Hyarl Thomas."

"No wall is perfect," Garry said. "And, for that matter, neither of us may be exceptions. You—and I, I suppose—represent a planetary force. Terra and the Confederacy. As does Hyarl Thomas represent—who? The Potential Worlds? Himself? Maybe all our preparations were for nothing, and those guards at the gate knew exactly who we were. Perhaps our passage is allowed by others, of whom we know nothing—not their reasons, or their plans, or their goals. Could be we are puppets, Frego."

The older man stared at him. "Puppets don't bleed, Garry. Keep that in mind."

Garry smiled suddenly and the odd patina of knowledge dropped away. He was a kid again, and Frego was almost able to forget what was coming, and the terrible lessons Garry had yet to learn.

"I'm a weird kid, right?" Garry said.

"You sure are," Frego replied.

They both laughed.

The jump to Petersburg would take about three weeks of shiptime. After the hectic routines of getting under way were done with, and the *Orion* was safely in the groove for the black hole that was her entrance to the wormhole, Garry found himself settling into the peace of shipboard routine. There was an almost psychic quality to the relaxation he felt, as if in leaving the physical borders of H'hogoth he had somehow erected mental borders between himself and the horror of Garth's death. Yet now, for the first time in his life, unanswered questions began to haunt him.

"Frego," he said after dinner one night as they sprawled

in two chairs in the ship's lounge, thick mugs of Terran beer in hand, "did you know my mother?"

In the diffuse, pseudo-evening illumination, Frego's face resembled that of a brass satyr, red and cheerful, the scars softened by shadow. Around them the quiet murmur of conversations in several languages made a sound like electric surf. Lizards warbled and men croaked and beneath it all the drive made a sound like an eternal bell. The odors of the ship were concentrated, despite the best efforts of the maintenance systems—sweat and perfume and the cinnamon taste of reptile. Garry felt almost sleepy as the beer took hold, but he noted Frego's long pause in replying. The older man tasted his beer, set it down, stared at the foam on the top of the mug. Finally he nodded.

"Yes, I knew her."

"What was she like?"

Again the strange pause, of which perhaps only Garry might have sensed the strangeness. He'd always known he observed more than others, so that things often seemed perfectly clear to him, yet unexplainable to anybody else. Now this faculty, heightened by the events of the preceding several days, functioned with a poignancy he'd never before experienced. Frego's pauses now resonated with hidden meaning. His mother had died shortly after his birth—so Garth had told him. He'd told him little else, however, and Garry had never pried. Even as a child, he'd recognized the barrier of pain that surrounded his father's memories of his mother. Pain, and . . . something else. Something involving him, he now sensed.

"Your mother was a wonderful woman, Garry. She was pretty—no, beautiful—and smart. Smart like you. She seemed to know things. . . ." His voice trailed off into a fog of remembering, and Garry realized Frego had loved his mother. He had no memories of his own to cherish, and for a moment he envied Frego desperately. As far as he knew, he had no family left. He was alone. Yet something deep within him said the opposite. He felt that somewhere, somehow, there were those who might understand him, cherish him, be to him something both smaller and much larger than "family." As he watched Frego's face, a living memorial to a woman he'd never known, this feeling of loss and possibility almost overwhelmed him—and with it, unnoticed before, a sense of purpose growing like an iron weed. When this was done— when Hyarl Thomas was bloody dust and the cube, whatever it was, was safely returned to Terra, then he might go looking. That might be his purpose, he decided. To find those beings he felt within himself who were his true family.

"Garry? You still with me?"

"Huh? Oh, sorry. Just thinking."

"Mmm. So was I. Your mother, Garry . . . she loved you very much. I remember when you were born. . . ."

So I am Human, he thought to himself. For a moment there, I wondered. But something was still wrong.

"She was so happy," Frego continued. "Garth once told me that they thought they couldn't have children. Some kind of incompatibility. So when you came along . . . well, it was everything they'd hoped for."

Garry grinned. "You make it sound kinda unplanned."

"I don't know. She was pregnant when they first arrived on H'hogoth. I was just a runner for the local Search, and Garth came in to take over. He was the boss and, for some reason, he took a liking to me. Promoted me a couple of times, kept me close. He always told me you were very important to him, Garry. You know, come to think on it, right from the very beginning it was always understood that was part of my job. To keep an eye on you. He gave me the recognition code when you were only two months old."

Garry laughed. "So that makes you what? My unofficial godfather, maybe?"

A mothlike wash of hurt twitched its wings in Frego's riveted gaze. "Maybe I always felt that way," he said.

"I'm sorry, Frego. And it's true. I suppose it always has been. At least you're here now, when I need you."

Frego brightened. "You better believe it, kiddo."

On that note they finished their beer in silence, while Garry examined a few more enigmatic facets of the puzzle that was himself.

As he lay on his bunk that night, serenaded by Frego's rattling snores from the bunk above, Garry thought about Petersburg, their immediate destination. Frego's sources had pinpointed the Potential World as Hyarl Thomas's goal. Except for the one flashing glimpse of Thomas strolling unconcernedly into the Port, there had been no word of him on H'hogoth. The only outbound ship reasonably available to him had been one headed for Petersburg, although his name hadn't shown up on the passenger manifesto. Moreover, hasty messages to Terran Searchers on Petersburg had turned up no trace of him there, either. Which, Garry thought, wasn't altogether surprising. Thomas would have reached ground before Frego's messages even arrived, and Thomas had not struck Garry as the kind of man who'd wait around for the chase to catch up to him.

It might be a dead end, he decided, but it was the only end available. He had no intention of deviating from his immediate goal—the recovery of the cube and destruction of Thomas and whatever he stood for.

He sighed and rolled over on his stomach. So much had happened, and now, more and more, he found himself contending with the strange things happening inside his own skull.

Polymath.

He considered the word, and its meanings. Terran dictionaries defined it as, simply, a person who had a wide range of knowledge. He knew there was more to it than that. The word related to another, older term: polyhistor. The root of that word was "knowing," hence, "much knowing," while polymath itself could be inverted to "much to learn." He felt keenly the imperatives of both meanings, for he understood that while he knew much already, there was yet an immense amount to know. Now, as his mind drifted idly over the seventeen years of his life, fueled by the new eye that seemed to have opened in his brain, he began to wonder.

Why had he, from the very start, sought to know things simply for the joy of knowing? He'd discovered early on that he never forgot anything, whether visual, verbal, or written. And Garth had fed that hunger from the beginning, with books, computers, conversation—anything that Garry wanted. He had clear memories of even his earliest childhood—including something pink and warm and moist that he hadn't wanted to leave.

He shied away from that recall, even as the anomaly presented itself—if he could remember his own birth, why not then his own mother? What had Frego said? "She died after you were born."

But how long after? Weeks, months? Seconds?

He shook his head silently. The implications were frightening; but Garth had never hinted such a thing, talked little of it at all. And never showed Garry anything but love.

There was a mystery here, he realized suddenly, but he wasn't sure how to solve it. Or whether he even wanted a solution.

He turned his thoughts to Hyarl Thomas in relief. That was something simple and straightforward. A few weeks to Petersburg and then—what? Suddenly he realized he had little plan beyond letting Frego take the lead, himself dependent on the older man's skills and the resources of the mysterious Terran organization called "The Search."

Now, staring into the dark, he knew it wouldn't be enough.

Finally came the day when the ship's lounge seemed especially crowded. They'd come in just after lunch, or they wouldn't have gotten their usual table. Now, approaching dinner time, all the seats were full, and men and lizards stood in small groups, talking and drinking quietly. Frego stared at his beer morosely.

"Something the matter?" Garry asked.

"Does it show?" Frego lifted his beer and finished it with one deep swallow, then looked around for another. There were extra waiters on duty, and one immediately brought him another.

He tasted it, then set it down. "Yeah. I've done twenty, maybe thirty jumps, you know. But I never get used to it. Nothing goes faster than light. Except in a black hole and out. *Into* a black hole, Garry. Doesn't that bother you a little bit?"

Garry shrugged. "I don't know. I guess not. Either the shield holds, or it doesn't. If it doesn't, we'll never know. And we don't go faster than light, either. Not once we're in the wormhole universe. We trade off distance for time, so that both are conserved in our 'real' universe. You know that."

"That's what I mean, Garry," Frego said. "You know all about the technical end and you're not bothered by the reality. But the reality can kill you."

Garry grinned. "We're safer now than if we were jay-walking in the Reef, you know."

"I know the statistics. But some ships don't come through."

"That doesn't mean the hole got them. Something could have happened afterward, on the timeband drive back to the present."

"Yeah. Think about that. Something goes wrong with your drive, and you're thousands of years in the past. Nobody around to help. Not that it matters. Stray longer than the parameters of your flight plan allow and the ship blows up anyway."

Garry realized Frego didn't really understand the principles of the wormholes, nor did he want to. But he wasn't like a lot of the others on the ship, suffering from a phobia induced by a situation a writer named Arthur C. Clarke had once pointed out: that any sufficiently advanced technology would appear as magic to the uninitiated. Garry had given much thought to what his father's analogue had revealed, and now felt he had a better grasp of what was involved. By controlling the drive, the H'hogotha dominated almost every aspect of human culture, simply through their ability to determine what went where. He suspected the lizards had no compunction about blacklisting certain cargoes, if they felt those cargoes represented a threat of any kind.

Their force was so final. If a ship deviated in any way from its flight, it simply disappeared. Perhaps if it deviated in other ways it suffered a similar fate. Sometimes Garry wondered if that was all the Kurs'ggtha artifacts were—debris from disasters of the present, translated into the distant past. Yet the artifacts were strange—nothing about them resembled Human or H'hogothan work.

He raised his beer. "We either will, or we won't. And nothing to do about it except—"

"Yeah," Frego said. "Except order another beer."

"Right," Garry replied.

So they did, and as the beer arrived the great liner eased silently past the Schwartzkild radius of their own target. They slid into the holes beneath the universe and, after a time, out into the light of younger stars.

They ordered another beer and drank it, and after a

further time the ship *Orion* took up an uneventful orbit about Petersburg.

It was all unwieldy and roundabout and perfectly ordinary, and Garry wouldn't recall what had touched him then until much later. But he would remember.

After all, he never forgot anything.

Chapter Seven

The most noticeable thing about Petersburg was its aroma. As Garry disembarked into the main reception terminal he stopped.

"Wow!"

"Stinks, doesn't it?" Frego grinned.

Garry thought he'd gotten used to close-quarters fragrances during the three-week trip from H'hogoth, but this was something else again. A wall of odor surrounded him, invaded his nasal passages, and battered his brain.

"What is it?"

Frego pulled him out of the hurrying streams of travelers into a small bar. "What is it? Twelve or fourteen different races, as many of their pets, plus every kind of stench you can imagine a planet to generate. Don't worry. You'll get used to it." He paused, then grinned again. "I did. Eventually."

The tiny lounge was deserted. A blank-faced metal cybartender presided over rows of fake bottles. The temperature was comfortably cool but the air seemed thick and muggy.

"Let's get a beer," Frego said. "We aren't in a hurry right now."

Garry nodded. "Sounds good," he said.

Frego carried two frosty mugs of dark brew to the table Garry had selected in the far corner of the bar next to a window wall overlooking the front of the port.

"Here you go, kid," Frego said. He slid into a chair opposite Garry and raised his mug. "To luck," he said. "The good kind."

Garry lifted his mug in return but didn't say anything. His attention was on the throngs surging in and out of the main gate of the port. Beyond the low metal wall that

marked the edge of the port area stretched a broad
boulevard lined with strange, twisted trees, and beyond
those a mass of wooden buildings.

"Wood?" Garry said in disbelief. "My God, that's
barely out of the Stone Age. Haven't they heard of steel
and stresscrete?"

Frego chuckled. "Sure they have. But there are disad-
vantages. You'll see."

Garry started to question Frego further, but a tall,
obese stranger interrupted him. The man did not appear
threatening, but he walked right up to their table, so
close that his massive thighs touched the edge of the top.
Frego looked up.

The stranger glowered back at them but said nothing.
Suddenly Garry had a very disconcerting feeling. For
some unknown reason he felt he should identify himself
to this stranger and welcome him to their group. But
before he could open his mouth Frego touched his shoulder lightly and shook his head. Then Frego turned back
to the stranger.

"I'm sorry," he said. "We are visitors here, not native.
I'm sure you must realize." He cocked his head and
waited for a reply.

When he'd finished, the stranger burst into a radiant
smile. "Oh, no, good sirs. It is my fault. I detected no
specific pheromones, but thought perhaps you wished to
remain alone. That should have tipped me off right there,
though. Allow me to introduce myself. Fandor Archel, at
your service."

Garry wrinkled his nose at the sharp odor of cloves
that accompanied this announcement, but all the same
felt a strong urge to reveal his own name. Again Frego
shook his head slightly.

"Well, Mr. Archel, thank you very much, but we wish
to maintain our privacy. I'm sure you understand we
mean no offense, but we are not native. Please forgive
us."

Archel's expression turned glum and stiff. "I see. Well,
forgive me for intruding." And with that the big man
turned and marched stiffly from the cocktail lounge. Garry's nostrils wrinkled. The odor he now smelled resembled nothing so much as a dung heap.

"Whew." He inhaled sharply. "What was that all about?"

Frego shrugged. "That guy was a Petersburg native. You in the mood for a little local history?"

Garry sipped his beer. "Sure."

Frego leaned back in his chair and wrapped his fingers behind his thick neck. His belly protruded right to the table's edge and Garry grinned. Then he remembered the way Frego had moved and quit grinning.

"Petersburg is one of the earliest colonies. You can probably guess from its name that the Russians were the first to hit dirt here. But it wasn't plain old communists. Even then the Marxists had all kinds of schisms. The group that emigrated here was a real funny bunch. They thought orthodox communism was too liberal. That it didn't go far enough. Their philosophers were believers in the idea of man as a herd animal, of a *real* communist system."

To Garry, this conversation was straight out of his history lessons. Communism had fractured so many different ways that its few remnants were as strange and archaic as what was left of the Catholic Church—that is to say, almost the stuff of fairy tales. Yet he understood that each of these institutions had once been vast forces on Old Terra, and even to this day their offspring, perhaps altered beyond recognition, remained potent social structures in one way or another.

Frego grinned. "Of course, like a lot of the Potential Worlds, they took things further than anybody would have dreamed. The original colonists here wanted to live close to each other. Very close. And like all new colonies, some things were quite efficient and some weren't. Their sanitation systems weren't the best, for instance. In short, they had to get used to the smell of each other. Which led one of their genius types to an ideologically perfect solution."

Garry drained his beer. "Body odor was good Marxism?"

"Something like that. Actually, they had a very powerful pack of software dealing with genetic surgery. This genius type remembered that some insects, even some mammals, used odor to communicate with each other. Pheromones. So they did some work and pretty soon the children were born with heightened olfactory organs. They increased the area of the 'smell patch' in the back of the nose. A few other things. And they modified the sweat glands to produce specific odors on call. The result, after a few hundred years, is Petersburg today. We made that guy mad, you know."

"Who? That fat one?"

"Uh-huh. Did you feel anything when he left?"

Garry scratched the side of his nose. A big laser bus landed outside, its firecracker roar shaking the glass wall. "Something smelled real bad."

"Yeah. If you were a native, it would have been like getting punched in the nose. These folks need each other, need the closeness more than we can imagine. The atmosphere here is very moist, good for retaining the molecules that stimulate smell. They prefer to surround themselves with that—which is why you see all those low wooden buildings. First, wood is a cheap construction material here. Second, they like to live three and four to a room, and they like to be aware of the people on the other side of the wall. Concrete and steel tend to make them feel walled away. And third—well, with any luck, you won't need to find out about the third reason. Anyway, separate a Petersburger from his fellows and he feels lost. That was why that guy just naturally joined us, even though the rest of the bar is empty."

The cybartender whined slightly. Garry glanced up. "You think that thing is wired?"

"Sure. But not for us, Garry. Don't worry, though. Somebody will be along in a minute."

Garry's eyes widened. "You mean we're expected?"

This time Frego's ugly features split into a sunny smile. "Why? You didn't think we were gonna do it all by ourselves?"

They ordered another round of beers. Something seemed to be wrong with the cybartender. As it prepared the mugs it creaked and moaned. One of the mugs filled with foam and the cybartender had to pour another one.

"Where are we staying?" Garry said at last. He was staring through the window at the wooden houses. It was a strange sight. He had grown up on a world of ancient stone and modern steel. The houses looked flimsy to him. He didn't much like Petersburg, he decided. The chill, muggy air. The clouds. The endless changing smells. No, stinks was more like it. Petersburg *stank*. It was all so unfamiliar and it made him feel queasy. And irritable. He hadn't asked for this.

The alcohol began to fill him with self-pity as he stared at the crowded wooden houses with their red and brown and green shingled roofs. Each house had many dark windows like empty eyes. That meant many rooms. He imagined the rooms filled with sweating, exhaling bodies. He shivered.

"Frego, what—"

"Shh."

The Golden Girl came into the tiny lounge and looked around.

"She's been waiting outside," Frego said. "To make sure. Garry, you may never forget what you see, but you have to learn to see everything. She's been there for ten minutes. Didn't you notice?"

"No."

"Well, then." Frego sounded satisfied. As if he'd just delivered a lesson.

Garry stared at the Golden Girl and tried to imprint her on his memory. She was shorter than he was and very slender, almost anorexic by his standards. Her skin was really golden, not the *café au lait* color most people think of when they use the word. She had bright red hair. Her eyes were very wide, almost round, and flecked with silver sparks on a gray background. She moved like a dancer made out of rubber, without joints. Her mouth was small. She wore no makeup, so her other features faded away and all you remembered were the eyes and the hair and the skin. She was one of the most alien creatures Garry had ever seen.

"What weird planet is she from?" Garry whispered.

"Terra. Old Terra," Frego replied.

Garry blinked.

The Golden Girl ordered a fizzy pink cocktail from the cybartender. It came with a bright blue umbrella stuck on the rim. She took the drink to a table on the other side of the room and sat down. She didn't look at them. As she drank the drink she doodled on her cocktail napkin with a small pen. After a while she finished. When she sucked the last of the drink through her straw, it made a razzing, bubbly noise. Then she got up and left the bar.

Frego waited a few more minutes. "Let's go," he said, and drained his mug.

Garry didn't understand, but that was all right. He had

to trust Frego on this. If Frego didn't know what he was doing, it was all useless anyway.

They walked past the table where the Golden Girl had been seated. Frego bumped the table and knocked over the glass. Ice cubes splattered everywhere. The cybartender whined again.

"Sorry," Frego mumbled as he swabbed at the mess with the cocktail napkin. He looked at the cybartender. "My fault. Sorry." They walked out of the bar. Garry looked back. The cocktail napkin was missing from the table.

They picked up their luggage from the incoming carousel and went to the front of the terminal. When they stepped outside, a thick, moist wind slapped them in the face. Garry began to sweat immediately. His armpits felt slick and greasy as he moved. The breeze smelled of a hundred nameless things.

"The People's Marriott," Frego instructed the computer that operated the groundcab. The low-slung car took off with a lurching, rusty heave.

Garry touched Frego's knee. Then he made a motion with his hand, as if drinking something from an invisible glass.

"Later," Frego said.

Garry nodded. The cocktail napkin was in Frego's pocket. He wondered what was written on it.

The People's Marriott was a low, rambling wooden affair sprawled across the top of a low rise facing a long, L-shaped lake. The hotel was at the bend of the L. Rambling wooden stairways led down to a wide white-sand beach. The waters of the lake were slow and leaden beneath the clouds. Wisps of fog rose from the water and curled above the sand.

"Nice room," Frego said.

Garry finished hanging his clothes in the closet that ran along one wall of their room. Two beds were on the opposite wall. The third wall was filled with sliding glass doors that led out onto a patio made of wooden blocks sunk into gravel. Beyond the patio was a view of the lake. Far out, almost hidden by the fog, a light blinked twice, like a tiny star.

"Does it have an air conditioner?" Garry asked.

Frego nodded slowly. "Sure. This is a business and

tourist hotel. But Garry, you should try to get used to this world. Man is on hundreds of different planets. Some of them don't have Marriotts. Then you have no choice. Better to learn to adapt when you have a choice. Then when you don't, you don't have a problem."

"You sound like a schoolteacher."

"Isn't that what I am? Garry, hasn't it sunk in yet? They killed your father. They would probably have killed you, if you hadn't been very lucky."

"I had a little to do with that."

"Yeah. A little. That bit in the bar, with the gamblers. But what if I'd been working for Hyarl Thomas when I stuck that knife in your throat? Your luck would have been out then."

Garry shrugged uncomfortably.

"Maybe if I can teach you enough, you won't have to depend on luck. We aren't playing games anymore. Hyarl Thomas isn't playing games. Or maybe he is, but his games have real blood in them. They blew up the hospital and killed two hundred people to get your dad. Isn't that real enough for you?"

Garry went to the window and stared out at the lake. The far-off light blinked once again. He wrapped his arms across his chest and grasped his shoulders. It looked very cold out there. "I keep trying not to make it real, Frego. Two hundred people. How can I think about that?"

Frego came up behind him and touched one of his hands. The fingers felt cold. "You have to, Garry. It may be a nightmare but it's not a dream. If you let it be a dream, it will kill you. It will kill me first, but then it will get you. Make it real, Garry. Then you can fight it."

Garry nodded. Finally he turned away from the window. He'd taken out his contacts and his eyes were as green as moss. "What was on the cocktail napkin?"

Frego dropped his hand. He fumbled in his pocket and brought out a sodden wad of paper. "Here," he said. "Read for yourself."

"It's just a number."

"Uh-huh," Frego said. "Did you think she would leave us her address?"

Garry stared at him. "I don't understand."

"I sent word ahead that we were coming. The Terran Search only has a skeleton group here, a few people.

This is a Potential World. Not one of the dangerous ones, perhaps, but sympathies here don't lie with Old Earth. So people are careful. This is how we make contact. The Search here has the story. They've had a chance to do a number on Hyarl Thomas. I thought there might only be a message. But it seems they want a meet."

"All this from a number? Is it a code?"

Frego shrugged. "It will be a cutout. That's a security code for a shielded infobox. Check the local services. Somebody will have the code listed."

Garry nodded. After a moment he went to the data terminal that dropped from the fourth wall, between the door and a six-drawer fake mahogany dresser with a mirror over it. He entered his room number for billing and started at the top of the local mailbox service directory. On the third try the code activated a message. He read the words that appeared on the screen.

"Hand only," Gary said. "What does that mean?"

Frego looked irritated. "There's such a thing as too much security. Somebody wants to check us out. It means we have to pick up the message at the office itself."

Garry wiped the screen. "Is that dangerous?"

"I don't know."

"I'll come with you."

"No, you won't," Frego said.

Frego put on a heavy jacket and left a short time later. Garry glanced at his watch. He'd adjusted it to local time, but his stomach told him the time was off a bit. Here it was late in the afternoon. Shiptime was standard and different. They'd landed just after breakfast. Now he wanted lunch.

Frego hadn't said anything about staying in the room. Garry locked the door carefully behind him. Frego wasn't saying much about anything. The secrecy irritated Garry. All he got from Frego were lectures. It was becoming tiresome.

He went down the hallway and turned right. Another hall led to the main lobby. He remembered seeing a restaurant there. There was a human hostess standing there, a young girl. She had straight blond hair and soft blue eyes.

"Can I get something to eat?" he asked her.

She smiled at him. He suddenly smelled the odor of

violets. It was a nice smell. Then he realized he'd developed an erection.

She smiled more widely. "Welcome to Petersburg," the girl said. Garry put his hands in his pockets and made fists. His cheeks felt hot.

"Right in there. Take any table," the girl said.

He nodded and edged past her. He decided he hated Petersburg. But he looked over his shoulder and saw her watching him. Pheromones or not, she was attractive. It might be interesting after all.

"It's an address and a phone number and a time," Garry said. He thought about what Frego had been teaching him. "Isn't that awfully exposed?"

Frego shook his head.

"Look at the address. Finial and Leninprospekt. A street corner. It will be a comm-booth. We go there and call the number at the time listed. Somebody will be on the other end. These people don't trust us."

"How do you know that?"

"Because they want us naked. We have to go to a place in the open where they can see us."

Garry rubbed his chin. "Is it a trap, then?"

"I don't know. Only one way to find out."

"This time I am coming with you."

"Yes," Frego said. "Now you are."

Evening had brought heavier fog. The air was filled with the smells of water and fish and salt. The lake was a salt lake. His footsteps were muffled as he walked up to the comm booth at the corner of Finial and Leninprospekt. The sidewalks were wide here. A street lamp glowed above the booth. Buildings taller than usual surrounded the square. The streets came together on a broad plaza. The area was deserted and open. Garry felt very exposed. Anybody could be watching.

He fed his chip into the unit and entered the number. There was a long pause and then two clicks. Then a voice said, "Three-sixty-one Betancourt Place. Go there now." That was all. The unit hummed at him.

He looked around. The streetlights hung like faded, fuzzy suns in the shifting fog. It had gotten cooler. He punched up a local map and found the address. It wasn't far away. He memorized the map and his own location.

After he left the comm-booth he walked a few meters out into the plaza and stopped. When he was sure he had his bearings, he continued across the open space. The plaza was paved with wooden blocks, like his patio. The fog swirled around him. For a moment he was disoriented. He shook his head and saw the dim glow of a lamp ahead.

Was it footsteps he heard behind him, hidden in the night?

Don't let it be a dream, he told himself.

Number 361 Betancourt was in a run-down neighborhood. Garbage was piled on the street. The sidewalks were muddy, only partly covered with rotted wooden planks. He tried to step carefully but slipped here and there and had to pull his feet from the muck with moist, sucking sounds.

The building itself was nondescript. It was only one story high. The wood had once been painted but the paint had peeled away, exposing a grain that looked like streaks of blood. He took a deep breath and wished he hadn't. The stench here was overpowering. The neighborhood seemed quiet and watchful. He heard no human sounds, but somewhere nearby water dripped.

He climbed the wooden stairs to the porch of 361. There were four windows. All were dark. He imagined eyes behind them, watching him. The damp cut through his jacket and made him shiver. He felt shaky with tension.

"Come on," he whispered. He knocked on the door. It was unlocked, not even tight to the jamb, because it opened beneath his knuckles. A line of wan, yellow light illuminated the porch.

"Hello?" he called.

No answer.

He swallowed and pushed the door wide enough to step inside. He closed the door behind him. The hallway beyond was filthy. Old bits of newspaper, rags, a shredded doll. Something brown and shapeless he didn't want to look at too closely.

There was a door to his right. The sound of soft music came from behind it. He went to the door. "Hello?" he said again. "Anybody home?"

He waited. Then he pushed the door open.

A small discplayer sat on the floor. It played cheery

music. There were two moldy chairs, rump-sprung, one with a rusted spring poking from its side. A scarred wooden table teetered between the chairs.

The Golden Girl sat in one chair. Her small mouth was open in what might have been a smile. Beneath her chin was another kind of smile. It was very wide. It went from one ear to the other. Inside the lips of that smile was something black and wet.

As he watched, a small insect buzzed and landed and walked on the smile.

The door behind him slammed open. Rough arms grabbed him.

Garry screamed.

Chapter Eight

"No, no, no." Someone whispered the word in his ear over and over. Garry was trying to scream but nothing came out. Something was over his mouth. When he tried to move, the arms around him squeezed tighter and held him motionless.

"No, no," Frego's voice said again.

Finally he closed his eyes so he didn't have to look at the black wet smile and the bug crawling on the white lips of it. After a while Frego loosened his arms and took his palm away from Garry's face. As soon as he did Garry felt a great painful knot rise in his gut and fill his throat with sour grease. He bent over and vomited on the floor.

Now Frego held his shoulders but his grip was gentle. Frego held him until the last of the dry heaves went away. Shakily Garry wiped his forehead. It was cold and wet.

"You okay now?" Frego said.

Garry turned and looked at him. "She . . . they . . ."

"Yes," Frego said. "She's dead. They killed her. I told you it wasn't a game."

"But—"

Frego's voice changed, went harder. He spat out the words. "And we don't know who they are, Garry. So we have to get out of here." He stepped around the boy and went to the Golden Girl's corpse. Now Garry looked closer and saw marks on her arms, on her face. They looked like tiny angry burns, but pale, leached of blood. There was a dark shiny puddle on the floor beneath the chair. Her lap was full of blood. He felt nauseated again but there was nothing left in his stomach.

"Look at this," Frego said.

"What?"

"Here. On the table."

Garry moved closer. In the bleached yellow light of the room he saw what she had done. The fingers of her right hand were coated with blood. There were red-black trails on the tabletop next to her.

A scrawled word glittered on the wooden top.

"Arius," Garry said softly.

Frego nodded. "We have to leave, Garry."

"But what about her?"

Frego shook his head. "It's too late to do anything. We've got her message." His face was grim.

"We can't just leave her."

Frego took his arm and pulled him toward the door. "What do you want to do? Take her with us?"

Moisture welled in Garry's eyes. He shook his head.

"She's dead," Frego said. His voice was harsh. "She left her message. Now we have to stay alive if we want to do anything about it. You understand me?"

Garry nodded mutely.

"All right." Then Frego's voice softened. "I know. It's rough. We'll talk about it later."

Garry paused in the doorway and forced himself to look back. I have to learn, he told himself. I have to learn it's not a game.

He could still hear music playing softly as they left the house.

Frego made Garry walk six blocks through the fog back to the plaza at the intersection of Finial and Leninprospekt. He held on to Garry's arm the whole way. Twice he had to hold Garry upright when the boy stumbled. He was walking blind. Frego waited until they were in front of the comm-unit where they had called the house.

"I'll get a cab now," Frego said. "We had to get out of that neighborhood. It might have been a setup for us. It probably was."

Garry thought his voice was coming from far away. He had seen the explosion that had killed his father and a couple hundred others, but he'd never seen death face-to-face, as it were. There was a sick empty feeling in his stomach. His chest hurt from the dry heaves and his throat was sore. His mind didn't seem to be functioning right. Frego's words didn't make any sense.

"What . . . setup?" Numb, Garry shook his head. He didn't know what Frego was talking about.

Frego glanced at him sharply. "Stand there," he said. "Don't move."

Frego punched up a cab number and gave their location. Then he went back to Garry. There was a worried glint in his eyes. He drummed the fingers of his right hand nervously on his thigh and looked around. The fog had lifted a few meters and hung over the plaza like dirty laundry. Beneath, the street lamps illumined the barren expanse of wood paving. They were alone in the dark.

"Damn," Frego said at last. "It's all screwed up now."

Garry touched his shoulder. "I want to go home," he said. "Please take me home."

The expression on Frego's battered features might have been pity. "It's too late for that," he said.

Garry was lying on his back on the bed when someone knocked at the door and he jerked around. His face was white and blank. His eyes stared wildly. Frego had been watching him while he stared at the ceiling and shivered.

"I'll get it," Frego said.

Garry licked his lips. "Who is it?"

"Room service. I ordered some stuff."

Frego opened the door and pointed at the top of the dresser. The uniformed bellman carried in his silver tray and set it down. The tray held a bottle, two glasses, and a bucket of ice.

"Something for you," Frego said, and plugged his chip into the bellman's reader. The young man smiled at the figure.

"Thank you, sir," he said.

After he had gone Garry pushed himself higher against the headboard. He was propped on two pillows and he had hardly moved since they returned to the hotel room. He had not spoken at all except for a grunt or two.

"What's that?"

"It is Glenfiddich Scotch," Frego said. "The real thing. From Terra."

"Scotch?" Garry said.

Frego pulled the cork from the bottle and poured each

glass half full. He added ice cubes. Then he carried one glass to Garry. "Here. Drink."

"I'm not thirsty."

"Drink it, Garry. It will help. I promise."

Garry took the glass. He held it up to the light and stared at the amber liquid. After a very long time he nodded and put the glass to his lips. Sputtered. Shook his head. "Wah. That's—"

Frego grinned slightly. "It's very good Scotch, Garry. Very smooth. Drink some more. Just sip it, though. It will get better."

Garry ran his tongue over his teeth. The small warm bomb exploded in his gut then and he sighed. "Ah." He tasted the drink again and leaned back against the pillows. A little bit of the hard wet glare went out of his eyes. And then without any warning at all he began to cry.

Later, they were very drunk. Garry had seemed encased in a thin film of ice, but the ice had melted in the heat of the Scotch. Frego had let him cry until he had trailed off. This time he had made no move to touch or hold the boy, simply allowed him time. Then he made him another drink. Now the bottle had only an inch or so of liquid in it and Garry had begun to slur his words.

"The blood looked black," Garry said.

Frego nodded. "It was the light. Sometimes it does that."

Garry stood in front of the sliding glass doors and held his drink. He was staring out into the night across the lake. His breath made small round foggy circles on the pane. "Frego. Who was she? Why did they do that to her?"

Frego had his shoes off. He was sprawled in the one chair on the far side of the dresser, next to the closet door. He stared at his sock feet and wiggled his toes. "Who was she? I don't know. Somebody in the local Search organization. Maybe not even somebody important. Just a runner, a messenger."

"What were those little marks on her hands and face?"

"Burns. They burned her. Torture."

"But why?"

Frego tasted his Scotch. The lamp on the dresser emitted a dim, dusty glow. In the light he looked a hundred years old. His face sagged around deep lines like half-healed wounds. "They didn't have much time. They wanted her to tell whatever it is they wanted to hear. Drugs will do that, but it takes time. Torture is fast but not reliable. It takes time too, because you have to ask the same questions again and again. But drugs and torture together are very fast. If you know what you're doing." He rattled the ice in his glass. "I think they knew what they were doing. Only one mistake."

Garry's face was a pale, featureless oval. "What mistake?"

"They didn't make sure she was dead. I hope it was a mistake."

"I don't understand."

"The only other possibility is that she was dead. She didn't write that word with her own fingers and her own blood. If that's true, then it's a trap all around." He shook his head. "I don't know."

"Word. What did it mean? Arius?"

Frego sighed and poured himself some more Scotch. He seemed to be getting more sober, not less. "Well, lad, that's another story entirely."

As the night wound down into the empty hours before dawn Frego said, "Could you do it, Garry?"

"Do what?" Garry's voice was hard to make out, a thick, furry mumble. He was almost asleep.

"Kill somebody. Like that. Torture, murder." Frego's eyes were bright and glittering.

Garry was silent. After a moment Frego understood that his steady breathing meant he was asleep. He sighed and stood up and turned off the light.

"You may have to," he said softly. "Because it really isn't a game." Then he went to bed.

When Garry awoke much later in the day, he felt as if he might die. His head throbbed. His skin itched. His breath felt like moldy fire in his mouth.

Hangover, he thought. He wasn't comforted. He'd never gotten drunk like that before, kept on drinking until oblivion. Now he realized if he hadn't been drinking and felt like this, he would go to a hospital. If a normal person was this bad off, he would assume he was terminally ill.

But as sick and awful as he felt, he felt better. The terrible vision of the Golden Girl and her black, fly-ridden smile no longer appeared whenever he closed his eyes. Now she had become a part of his memory. The picture was filed and not on permanent exhibition. He wondered if Frego had realized that would happen. Probably. Frego seemed to understand a great deal more than he'd given him credit for originally.

Or was it just that he was seeing more? At the beginning of this he'd decided it would be simple. He'd never met anyone who was his intellectual match. Perhaps Hal, but Hal was a computer. Even his father, he'd discovered, was not as smart, as quick as he was. He'd filed that bit of information and it had made no difference in the way he'd felt about Garth. The way he'd loved him.

Maybe my brains came from my mother, he thought muzzily. But I never doubted I would track Hyarl Thomas down and kill him and retrieve the cube. It might be difficult, but any game was difficult. He always won games, though.

A quick fractured picture of the Golden Girl flicked up from his memory and he shuddered. It wasn't a game. Frego was right. It was something else Frego knew and Garry had to learn. Now Garry understood. It wasn't a game.

He opened his eyes.

The dim light admitted through the drapes over the sliding glass doors seemed abnormally bright. Every detail of the room was etched with a painful silver gloss. He blinked and even that small movement hurt.

"Oh, my God," he said.

"Awake, are we?" a cheerful voice replied.

"Just shoot me," Garry said.

Frego was repulsively cheerful. He slapped Garry on the back as the boy got up, and Garry winced. Inside the bathroom Garry stared at his face in the mirror. His green eyes had gone dull. The white around the green had a yellowish cast, and even his skin seemed flat. He used a depilatory carefully and took a long, hot shower. He put in his blue contacts and even their color was not quite right. Afterward he felt a little better, but not much. What about those books he'd read, when the hero had a terrible hangover but a shower and a cup of coffee fixed him right up? He shrugged. His head throbbed. That was probably another myth. He wasn't a hero. This wasn't a game.

He was suddenly very afraid.

"How about some breakfast? A couple of nice poached eggs, good and runny. Some fat sausage links?"

Garry stared at him. "You are an evil man, Frego."

"I know." Frego grinned. He held a fist out and opened it. On his palm were two orange capsules. "Here. Take these."

"Will they kill me?"

"No. Sorry."

"Oh, well."

Garry rinsed out one of the glasses from the night before. The smell of stale Scotch made him gag. He rinsed several times to make sure all the Scotch was gone. Then he took the capsules. Less than a minute later, like a delayed but welcome sunrise, his head began to clear. He felt a moment of dizziness and held onto the sink until it passed. It was amazing how good he felt. It was the best he'd ever felt in his life.

No, it's not, he realized. It's normal. I feel normal. But compared to just a minute ago . . .

He went back to the main room.

"Okay now?"

"Great, Frego. What's in that stuff? It's wonderful."

Frego moved his shoulders. "It was invented a long time ago. Back in the late twentieth century. It interferes with alcohol molecules attaching to receptors in the brain. Instant sobriety. They discovered it in a nation called the United States."

Garry nodded. He'd read about the United States.

"They banned it, of course."

"What?" Garry thought about the inexpressible relief he felt. "Why? Is it dangerous?"

"No. Not at all. Their logic was that a hangover cure would only encourage drinking. They were officially a very moral people. They felt that humans could be morally perfected by laws." Frego nodded to himself. "They were fools."

Garry thought about it. Outside, the sky had become dull pewter. He was certain there was a sun somewhere over the clouds, but he hadn't seen it yet. Beneath the clouds the lake moved slowly, like a bowl of mercury.

"Why would they ban something like that?" Garry said. He recalled from his studies that the United States at that time had done many strange things, but proscribing something as useful as this was beyond him. He wanted to understand.

Frego paused, as if searching for the right words. Finally he said, "Their social philosophy blamed the victim. If you had a hangover, it was because you got drunk and you didn't deserve the cure. If you were poor, it was because you didn't work hard enough and therefore it was your fault. Even if the system wouldn't allow you access to education and housing and security and skills. It was still your fault and you didn't deserve help. If you were crazy, it was somehow your fault and they turned you out on the streets because it was too expensive to feed and house you. And on and on."

Garry shook his head. "That's not fair. It's not even logical."

Frego laughed. "But it's life, Garry. Come on. Are you hungry now?"

Garry managed a smile. "You mean it's not my fault I got drunk? I get to have breakfast?"

"Who cares whose fault it is? You still have to eat."

He was surprised at how hungry he was. The waitress had stared at him when he ordered. "That's breakfast," she'd said.

"Is it a problem?" Frego asked. "I know it's afternoon."

Garry glanced at his nailtale. He'd reprogrammed it by pressing on the nail soon after he'd arrived. The tiny telltale blinked the time: two in the afternoon. This world had a twenty-five-hour day.

The waitress was mollified by Frego admitting they were eating the wrong meal for the time of day. She smiled. "No. The chef will make an exception, I'm sure."

And what if he doesn't? Garry wondered. Do we starve? Do we spend our tourist dollars elsewhere?

She brought the food quickly and smiled again as she served. Garry smelled the faint odor of violets and felt a stirring in his crotch. Oh no, he thought. Not again.

"Friendly folk, aren't they?" Frego said. "I think she likes me."

"Down, boy," Garry said, and forked up something

that tasted like potatoes. "Sometimes food is better than anything."

"You're learning," Frego said with approval.

"I want to talk now," Frego said. He was chewing a slice of ham. "If you have anything to say, say it with your mouth full."

"What? Why?"

Frego's voice took on what Garry had begun to call his teaching tone. "Because," he said patiently, "it's impossible to read lips if you chew and talk at the same time. Even a computer can't sort it out. Our room might be bugged. But I doubt if the tables here are. They might use a laser to read our lips, but there's too much noise for a long-distance mike. This is the safest place."

Garry nodded. It was all so confusing. So many rules in this game that wasn't a game.

"You remember the word," Frego said.

"Arius." A quick flash of ragged black scrawls on rotten wood. He chewed. "What does it mean?"

"It's a place. A planet. I'm not surprised you haven't heard of it. A Potential World, but very secretive. And very powerful in a strange sort of way."

Garry tasted his eggs. "What do we do now?"

Frego said, "If the woman's killers left the message, it's a trap. But if they didn't, then it was her message. Hyarl Thomas has something to do with Arius. Or he's going there. Either way, we have to go. Because there's nothing left for us here. Do you understand?"

Garry shook his head.

"I followed you to the meet to see if anybody was following you. I was careful, I think. Careful enough. There was nobody. Whoever it was went before us, but not much. Just enough to . . . interrogate the woman. But they must know about us now. Whatever she knew. The Search here has been compromised. That's obvious."

"By who, though?" The question had been nagging at him and he hadn't even realized it.

"Who knows? The local government, Hyarl Thomas. The lizards. Maybe even Arius. But this is a dead end. The word is the only information we have. So we go on. We have no choice."

Garry didn't like the sound of it. It was weak and flimsy. But what else to do? Frego said go on.

"All right," he said at last.

"We have somebody on Arius," Frego said.

"Who?"

"You'll see."

They packed quickly. Outside, the bellies of the clouds had turned a burnished brass color. The lake was like a bowl of fire. The streets were crowded right up to the spaceport.

Garry struggled with his bag against the crowd. His head was turbulent with smells. The thought clicked in his head and he wondered why it hadn't come to him before.

"What if they try to kill us?" he said. "In the port. Out here."

Frego's eyes were hooded. "Remember what I said earlier? About a third reason the natives use wood so much?"

"Uh-huh."

Frego reached into his bag and came up with a small, dull gray object. They were standing directly across from the spaceport entrance, where the surging throngs were thickest. Then he fumbled in his pocket and came up with two tiny clear pluglike contrivances. "Here," he said. "Filters. Put them in your nose and don't take them out."

Garry took one filter and put it in his nose. Immediately he smelled nothing. The air still came through, almost unimpeded. But no odors.

"Don't breathe through your mouth," Frego said.

Garry nodded. A wave of cool, damp air slapped him on the cheeks and reddened them. His jacket felt sodden. The air was full of sounds. Now that he wasn't distracted by all the smells, he could hear them. The chatter of the crowd. Footsteps. Horns. Dull roaring noises from the spaceport. A distant speaker announcing an arrival. The flat, firecracker sputter of a lasercab.

He realized he had been becoming used to the smells, now that they were gone. Just as Frego said.

"Stay with me," Frego said. "Whatever happens, stick with me."

Garry moved closer. He took a deep breath and then closed his mouth. Don't do that again, he told himself.

Breathe through the nose. He wondered what Frego was going to do.

Amazingly, far out over the lake the clouds parted. A single golden shaft illumined the water like a spotlight. For one moment Petersburg was beautiful.

Frego shook his hand and something extremely thin and evanescent appeared from one end of the dull gray object.

Monomole switchblade, Garry thought.

Then it began.

Chapter Nine

Right next to them was a very fat man with a bald head. He wore a business suit and carried a PortaAI. He was sweating. Garry saw and remembered all this because time had slowed down for him. He was like a camera, clicking and clicking.

Individual snapshots. Frego turned. A monomole switchblade is merely a hardened ceramic handle containing a length of single-molecule wire. The wire can be extruded from the handle to its full length and stiffened by a static charge. Then it is a sword, and it is sharp enough to chop down a concrete building. Or it can be any smaller length. Garry saw that Frego had it set short, almost like a pocketknife.

Frego slashed the fat man across the upper part of his arm. Fabric parted. First the suit. Then the shirt underneath. Then the flesh beneath that. Bright red blood spurted. It soaked the man's suit immediately. So much blood.

Frego bent down and slashed the man's leg across the thigh. Blood dripped down and covered his shoe. The fat man opened his mouth in a round O. He screamed, a thin, high-pitched sound. And something else came out of his mouth. It was like a small gray cloud.

The crowd around them panicked.

It was insane. Now everybody was screaming. Even through his skin Garry felt it. The blind urge to run, to fight. The crowd surged this way and that, trying to get away. Panic spread. Garry wondered what it was like to feel the full force of those pheromones.

Panic turned into stampede. Into riot. The voice of the crowd was a dull roar. He felt himself pushed and pulled.

It was hard to keep his feet. Frego grabbed him and jerked him into the street, toward the spaceport gate.

Cars smashed into each other. Frego and Garry fought their way through as fingers clawed at them. The fat man had disappeared into the maelstrom. They reached the gate. Even some of the guards there had gone berserk. They waved their shocksticks like bats and ran out into the mob. Others—some were off-worlders, Garry saw—remained calm. One of them pushed nose filters into the face of another. These men used their sticks to keep the crowd away from the gates. Frego and Garry burst into this circle of relative calm. One guard, red-faced and shouting, surged toward them.

Frego waved their gate passes and yelled at him. The guard lowered his stick and waved them through. A moment after they were safely inside, the gates slammed shut behind them. Garry looked back. As far as he could see, the crowd danced madly. People slammed into the wooden walls and clawed their way up. The flimsy buildings shivered. Two collapsed as he watched.

He saw something else. A man who seemed unaffected by the general rage clawed at the gate. He looked directly at Frego and Garry. He was shouting something. The guards shoved him away with their sticks and he disappeared into the crowd.

"Wooden buildings bend and give. But concrete crushes. And glass shatters into razors," Frego panted. "That's the third reason. Come on."

They made their way into the filtered safety of the spaceport terminal.

Inside, people moved with an air of barely suppressed tension. Men in uniform jerked past at a trot, their faces set. Even through the thick panes of glass, the stresscrete walls, the cry of the crowd was audible like the sound of surf pounding on rock. The noise was a backdrop to everything, low and ominous.

They were boarded through their gate quickly. The attendants seemed nervous and jerky. They heard the noise too. They knew what it meant.

Frego was silent until the laser launcher flung the shuttle into the sky and weight pressed silently on their chests. "Did you see him?" he said at last.

"The man at the gate? Yes."

"I think we were very lucky," Frego said.

"What did he want?" Garry asked. He knew, but he had to ask anyway.

Frego glanced at him. "He wanted to kill us."

Garry closed his eyes. He wondered if he would ever get through this. Somehow vengeance seemed very far away. From H'hogoth to Petersburg to Arius. It was like a rhyme. He couldn't get it out of his head. It no longer felt like a chase. It felt like a hunt and he was the quarry.

Oh Father, he thought suddenly. What were you? What am I?

The sound of the shuttle was thunder in his ears.

"Why Arius?" Frego said. He was thinking out loud. Their stateroom was small. It contained two bunks, one up, one down. A table folded from the opposite wall. There were two chairs bolted there. A data terminal was hidden behind the fold-down table. The air was clean and neutral and cool. It had a filtered taste to it.

Garry lay on the lower bunk and stared at the bottom of the upper. Frego sat at the table, next to the dirty plates and dishes from lunch. Before, they'd eaten in the ship's mess, but now Frego used room service. It cost more, but Frego said they should stay in their cabin as much as possible.

"I don't know," Garry said. "I don't know anything about Arius. I tried to call it up on the terminal, but the ship's library only lists the name and coordinates. Nothing else. Not even when it was colonized."

"It could be a trap," Frego mused. He had been preoccupied since they'd boarded. That was all right with Garry. He felt so tired. All he wanted to do was sleep. It had gotten beyond him. He kept seeing the Golden Girl's face. Or the maddened face of the man at the gate. People wanted to kill him. He'd understood it before as an intellectual exercise. As a puzzle. But now he felt it a different way. Somebody wanted to cut his throat. Leave his corpse drained and bleeding into its lap. For the flies.

It nauseated him to think about it. It paralyzed his thoughts. He didn't know if he could go on, but he didn't know how to stop. There was no place to hide. It could be anybody. Old Terra. Hyarl Thomas. The lizards. Somebody else.

Only Frego, and the older man was as hunted as he was. Yet he seemed more cheerful, as if all this didn't bother him much. Perhaps he was used to it. He was a spy, after all.

"Do you think it's a trap?" Garry said. His voice sounded far away.

"It could be," Frego said. "But I told you before. There's a good chance it isn't. Except why Arius?"

It was the third time he'd asked the question. That was irritating. Did he expect Garry to answer? How could he? Garry was the amateur in a professional world. He wasn't a spy. He wouldn't coldly slash an innocent by-stander into ribbons to make his escape.

Would he?

So many questions.

"Because Arius is where Hyarl Thomas went," Garry said. He didn't know if that was right. But it was an answer.

Frego glanced at him sharply. "Okay. That's a start. Take it further."

"I can't. Hyarl Thomas went to Arius, or is going to Arius. The Golden Girl knew. She was killed but she left a message."

"What happened to that fine young brain, Garry?" Frego's voice was mocking. "I thought you could do whatever you wanted. Figure anything out."

Garry rolled over onto his side. Anger flamed in little red spots on his cheeks. "Then I was wrong, wasn't I, Frego? I'm just a kid. I really don't know anything, do I? Okay? Is that what you want to hear?"

But Frego didn't get angry. If anything, he seemed satisfied. "No, Garry. You're a man now. Whether you want to be or not."

Garry flopped to his previous position, but his cheeks remained red. Frego nodded to himself and stared at the dirty plates.

It was so hard to stay awake. Garry continued to stare at the bunk above and tried to keep his eyes open. He could hear Frego breathing not three feet away, but he didn't look at him. He was so tired. What had happened on Petersburg had leached something out of him, and he wasn't sure what it was. He remembered what he'd been like before all this had begun. Was it possible he'd been so carefree, so confident?

He almost wanted to laugh. What had he vowed?

Hyarl Thomas would pay. He'd actually hoped the man would find him. Now he couldn't imagine why. If Thomas did find him, he would end up like the Golden Girl.

I am a coward, he thought suddenly. The thought surprised him. He'd never felt anything like it before. Coward. The word carried such a freight of self-loathing. Thomas killed my father and I'm afraid he will kill me.

There it was.

And I don't want to die.

He tried to shove the thought away, but the word kept repeating itself. And beyond the word that named him shuffled vast forces and powers. It was too much. The lizards. The Potential Worlds. Old Terra and the Search. Arius, whatever it was.

Too much. His eyelids felt heavy. He just didn't want to think anymore.

Coward.

His eyes closed.

The ship entered the wormhole while he slept. Frego watched him. Occasionally he took his handkerchief and wiped Garry's damp forehead. Frego's muddy green eyes were sad as he listened to the boy whimper in his sleep.

Bad dreams.

Of course.

The ship slid into the wormhole as slick as an animal and went far back in time. Arius was a great distance away and they had to go very far back.

The dream took him slowly, like a mother lifting a baby:

Light.

He was spiraling around a great yellow star. Then, without warning, a green planet loomed beneath. A snapshot. Then clouds surrounded him as he fell like an angel.

He had the sense of flying. Not as if he had wings, but as if all he had to do was move his arms slightly and kick his legs. It was like swimming through the air. He arced down and figures became visible below. There was a mountain tipped with snow. Below the snow line rocks glittered hard and black, and below them were trees. They reminded him of pines, but he understood that wasn't exactly right.

The buildings were small, blocky affairs that looked

like they were carved from sugar cubes. He moved his arms and swooped closer. Now he began to make out their real size. Tiny figures moved on walkways and plazas among the buildings. It took him a moment before he understood. People. The buildings were huge.

Somehow he knew it was a dream. It was silent. He could see the trees below bending before a wind, but he heard no sound. The air parted before him. Now he flew above a long white walkway and a great structure bulked before him. Two immensely tall doors were open and he flew through them, over the heads of people hurrying with that blank-faced intensity that is meant to signify dedication.

The people were humans. It was a human dream.

He flew down long hallways. He turned and turned again and somehow knew which were the right turnings. Eventually he came into a large open space roofed with glass. The space was occupied with a single glowing cloud. The cloud contained all colors, and none. One moment it was blue. Then red. Then a featureless silver.

The cloud called to him. He knew it was a gift. For the first time in many days he felt safe. He knew he'd been wounded in some way but didn't understand how. Yet the cloud would know.

The cloud knew everything.

Smiling, with the warmth of it on his face, he spread his arms wide and flew into the cloud.

"Garry Wake up!"

"Leave me alone. I'm tired."

Frego shook him. "I said wake up. We're here."

"What?"

"We're here. Arius. We dock with the orbiting terminal shortly."

He opened his eyes. Dimly he remembered something. Huge and shining and warm. He tried to grasp the thought but it slipped away. There. Gone.

The dream drained into the thin light of the cabin. Frego's face was close. His river-colored eyes were wide. "Come *on*, Garry."

"All right," he said. He knew he sounded cranky and irritable but he didn't care. "All right, leave me alone. I'm awake."

Frego stared at him. "Not very cheerful, are we?"

"Go to hell."

"Garry."

Garry shook his head. It felt so heavy. Now even the
dream was gone and nothing warmed him. He felt cold
inside. "I'm sorry, Frego," he said. "I'm sorry."

Frego touched his shoulder and started to speak.
Thought better of it. "Well. Let's get ready."

"Sure," Garry said. "Whatever you say."

The orbiting terminal was large and seemed even larger
because there were so few people on it. Only two other
passengers had disembarked with them. But everything
here was modern, clean and harsh and brightly lit. They
were checked through by robots. The robots made no
comment about Garry's blue contact lenses. That worried
Frego.

They checked a data screen, which informed them of a
small hotel. They could stay in the hotel while they made
arrangements for the shuttle service downplanet.

For they would have to make arrangements. Merely
arriving at the terminal did not guarantee admission to
the mystery planet below.

"What now?" Garry said. He was carrying his own
bag. It felt heavy. He wondered what the gravity was on
this satellite.

"Check in to the hotel," Frego said. "Then I'll have to
make arrangements."

"What if they won't let us in?"

Frego shrugged.

"What if somebody tries to kill us? What if it's a trap?
I've never heard of a setup like this. No direct shuttle
downplanet. It could be a trap."

"No. I've never been here, but I've been told. It's
always been like this. Arius is different. Very security
conscious. Almost paranoid. You explained once. About
how the mice can't slip through the walls. Well, here they
can't."

Garry remembered his little lecture. It seemed that
someone else had given it. Had he been that pompous,
that sure of himself?

He felt ashamed. And more tired and empty than ever.
When it came right down to it, he didn't care anymore.
Eventually somebody would come and kill him. Then it
would be over.

Maybe it would happen on this satellite.

"I remember," he said.

"Come on, Garry. We'll go to the hotel. Then I have some things for you to do."

"Okay," Garry said. He followed Frego's broad back and tried not to think about anything.

They had no problems checking in. The hotel desk was down a broad corridor leading from the main entryport. Everything here was on a large scale. Garry couldn't figure it out. The terminal was obviously designed to handle large groups, but it appeared nearly deserted. On the way to the hotel they passed only one person, a uniformed employee who didn't look at them. The uniform was made of a spotless gold material that shimmered. Garry thought of the Golden Girl and looked away.

Frego took care of the desk and came back with a pair of black doorchips. "Come on," he said.

The room was as spacious as everything else. It was really a suite. Two king-size beds occupied a large sleeping alcove that could be screened off from the rest of the area. There was a soft leather sofa and two matching chairs arranged around a low glass coffee table. A complete data terminal with a desk was across from the grouping, as well as two dressers, one with a mirror. There was even a small bar with a quick fridge, and a dining area with a table and three chairs.

"Look here," Frego said. He touched the master control panel just inside the door. One wall was nearly blank. The drapes on it swept slowly back and Garry looked straight out into space. Below, Arius loomed in enigmatic grandeur.

Clouds covered most of the planet. Only a little greenish brown showed, and the hard bright sparkle of water.

Despite himself Garry was impressed. "Wow," he said.

"Nice room," Frego said. He seemed pleased with himself, like an amateur magician who had pulled off a difficult trick.

Garry stared at the planet a moment longer and wondered what awaited him down there. If he got that far. Suddenly the tiredness hit him like a hammer. He dragged his suitcase to a stand at the foot of one bed. He yawned.

"Gotta take a nap," he said.

"You just woke up."

"I'm tired." He tried to keep the whine out of his voice, but knew he hadn't quite succeeded. Frego clicked his tongue against his teeth.

"Well," he said. "If you have to."

Frego was disappointed in him. Too bad. He still had to sleep. To get away from the cold. And maybe find the warmth again.

Frego regarded the sleeping boy from his spot in one of the chairs. He'd been afraid of this. He'd seen it happen before. When he'd let Garry go to the meeting house alone, he'd had a plan in mind. He didn't really think they would be followed, but tradecraft dictated he do it a certain way. Somebody had to go, and somebody had to check the backtrail. Garry didn't have the skills for the second job, and so it was his by default. But he wanted Garry to do something, to come in contact with reality. To Garry it had been a game. He'd hoped the loneliness of the walk, the meeting with the Petersburg agent, perhaps even a dash of fear, would bring the truth home to the boy. That it wasn't a game. That it was deadly and treacherous and real.

Scare the boy a little, just enough. But he hadn't expected the Golden Girl and her black slit throat.

He thought he knew what was wrong with Garry, but he wasn't sure how to fix it. Even he was a bit shaken. He'd been wrong once. He could be again.

And Hyarl Thomas was a devil.

Why Arius?"

"How do you feel?"

"I dunno. Tired, I guess."

"That's okay. You've had a rough time." Frego slapped Garry's shoulder. "But we've got to go on. We have no choice. You understand that, don't you?"

Garry thought about how there was no way to stop. No place to go back to. Even nameless relatives on Old Terra weren't an answer. Whatever he was mixed up in might be able to reach even there. Maybe even had come there. The Kurs'ggtha artifact was so powerful, so valuable it destroyed every certainty. There was no certainty.

There was only Hyarl Thomas and whatever he represented.

"I understand," he said.

"You look pale. You hungry?"

"Yeah."

"You haven't been eating much lately. We'll go out for lunch. How's that?" Frego was treading as gently as he could. Garry was very fragile and he didn't want to break him. But he was afraid events wouldn't give him time.

"That's good," Garry said. His face was waxen. He mouthed the words slowly, with no emphasis.

"Look, Garry. I want you to do a computer search. I don't know much about Arius. We need to know more. I checked already, there's a complete file on Arius. Can you do that? Generate me a synopsis?"

Garry glanced at the fancy data terminal. It was AI-driven and voice responsive. Verbal icons for search vectors. He hadn't worked with a machine like that in a long time. Slow and dim, a spark began to grow.

"Yeah," he said at last. "I can do that."

"Good," Frego said.

They had a choice of three restaurants. The one they picked was done in soft earth tones. The tables were covered with white tablecloths and the waiter was human. The restaurant might have seated a hundred people, but they were the only two guests. There was an eerie anticipation to the place, as if the restaurant waited. Polished and glistening and fully staffed. Frego wondered what it waited for.

Did it wait for them? He shook his head. That was paranoia.

"What?" Garry looked up from his plate. Some kind of meatburger on a thick bun.

"Huh?"

"Why did you shake your head?"

"This place. I mean this whole satellite. Empty. Why?"

Garry chewed. He'd spent almost two hours at the data terminal. The machine was very fast, but it took him that long to ask the right questions. Not all of his questions were answered, but a pattern began to show. Arius winked its enigmatic eye at him and he was beginning to understand.

There was something awesome on the planet below. He only saw glimmers now. He didn't even understand how he sensed it, but that was all right. This was something he was good at. Something Frego couldn't do.

A measure of hope had returned to him. A small measure, but still hope.

"Why?" he asked. He finished chewing and put down his fork.

"Because you were right. This whole planet is a trap. I don't know what for, but I know what it is. And something else." Garry's eyes flashed blue.

"What?" Frego was staring at him with an odd expression on his face.

"Hyarl Thomas is bait. I wonder if he knows it."

Chapter Ten

Frego watched Garry carefully. He took a long time about it. His eyes were clear and blank, as if he were savoring each word. "That's an extraordinary thing to say," he said at last. His voice was gentle and controlled.

Garry finished his meatburger and wiped his lips with a napkin. It was a dainty motion, somehow theatrical. He smiled.

"Why is that?"

"Did you realize that Hyarl Thomas might be on this satellite with us? The timing is a little strained, but we don't know when he left Petersburg. If he did. But it should be obvious that there aren't daily shuttle flights downplanet. He might have been held up. Just like we are."

"I don't think there was any holdup for Hyarl Thomas. If he came here, he was passed right through."

Frego paused again. He watched Garry as if the youth had just pulled a small furry animal from beneath his dinner plate. "Garry, how did you arrive at this conclusion?"

Garry leaned back in his chair. His face was thin and intent. Someone laughed far away and there was a clatter of metal. It sounded like pots and pans being clashed together. Two thin, vertical lines grew above Garry's nose. "I did a synopsis. Do you want to read it?"

"Later. Why is Hyarl Thomas bait? What does he have to do with Arius?"

Garry slowly licked his lips. He looked very young and a little frightened. But he also looked secretly proud. "There was a large file on Arius. You were right about that. History. Social structures. I think much of it was lies. But when you analyze data, lies can tell as much as truth. If you can figure out the lies and why they were told."

Frego nodded. "Yes." His voice was dreamy. "I understand lies. Tell me about the lies of Arius, Garry."

"It was one of the earliest colonized planets. I think that's true. It correlates with much other information. But did you know how early, Frego?"

Frego shook his head. He listened carefully but didn't say anything. He could be a good listener when he wanted to.

"Arius was one of the first. Maybe even the first. It was colonized before the lizards intervened. Before we knew there were lizards. It may have been the flight that alerted them to our presence."

Frego absorbed the words slowly, like a sponge in syrup. His face looked ugly in the dim light of the restaurant. His scars burned white against his flesh. "Go on," he said.

"After the end of the Matrix Wars. When Luna and Old Terra were finally united and the meatmatrices banned." Garry reached for his water glass and sipped. His eyes had gone remote and blank. He seemed to be consulting a hidden source, something written inside his skull. "The history says the colony ship originated on Luna."

"It was a turbulent time," Frego said. "What does it have to do with us now?"

"It's impossible that it could have been that way. The ship couldn't have come from Luna. Independent histories agree on this. Luna was never a colonizer world. Only Old Terra. And some of the early colonies themselves. Not Luna. Not ever."

Frego pulled at his ear. "History can lie."

"Luna was exhausted after the Matrix Wars. Even if it had wanted to, it didn't have the Resources. Premier Nakamura ruled both worlds, him and the Spirit Corporate. The first ships came from Terra. From the Russians and the Japanese. Not from Luna."

"Then who colonized Arius?"

"I don't know," Garry said. "I don't even know why. But there is one thing. Arius is not what it appears to be. And if that is the case, then why is Hyarl Thomas here? He must not be what he appears to be, either. He appears to be a trap. Therefore he must be bait."

Frego moved his fingers on the tablecloth. His fingernails made soft scratching sounds. "Do you have any facts?"

"Some. In the synopsis. A lot of it is hints and my own intuition. Can you trust my intuition?"

Frego stared at his fingers. "I can. But I don't understand what it means."

"There is a pattern," Garry said. "We have to go downplanet to find it. I think that's what is expected. Hyarl Thomas won't stop us. He isn't here."

"How do you know that?"

"It isn't the job of bait to frighten the quarry."

The permissions to go downplanet came through that evening. They were instructed to board first thing in the morning.

Frego slept deeply. It was a trick he'd learned long before. The possibilities he saw frightened him. There might be trouble. But he was an old fighter and still alive. He ate a heavy meal and went to bed early. Who could know how long he might have to go without food or sleep?

Garry said it was a trap, but he didn't say who the trap was for. Frego read the synopsis and destroyed it. It didn't tell him much. He was put off by long rows of statistics. The numbers meant something to Garry but less to Frego. Yet he agreed with Garry for reasons that had little to do with the synopsis.

He felt treachery. It was a familiar feeling and it filled him with chilly anger. So he ate and slept because there was nothing else to do.

Thus he didn't see Garry sitting up late, his eyes bright, staring out the broad window at the shimmering planet below.

Something was beginning to happen. It was hidden in the numbers and the movements of the strange dance he was only beginning to learn. The heat of the dance beat on the cold ball inside him and began to melt it.

The planet that was a trap dressed itself in gauds and glitter. But he could sense the teeth underneath.

He was so afraid.

There was no customs gate. They boarded the shuttle after a quick breakfast. The shuttle was huge. There was space for two hundred people, but they were the only travelers. Yet the shuttle itself was but a gnat on the side of the enormous satellite terminal. All through their visit

the feeling of emptiness, of waiting persisted. They rode
the shuttle down a pillar of laser-driven fire and landed
on a barren concrete plain next to a vast ground terminal. Their luggage plopped efficiently out of a tunnel at
their feet. Nobody checked them. Nobody said anything
as they walked down echoing stainless-steel corridors.
Finally they were outside. Neither had spoken. The silence was overwhelming.

"Now what?" Garry said.

Overhead the sky was a blue dome. A warm breeze
slapped him gently on the face and brought the smell of
trees just beginning to turn green. Something large and
winged—a hawk?—flapped over their heads with the sound
of laundry on a line. Beyond the immense perimeter of
the spaceport was a ring of mountains. The mountains
were young and jagged and covered with something like
pines. There was a deep perfume in the air. The sun
burned out of the bowl of the sky and made them squint,
made their eyes water.

A sharp hissing sound jerked them around. They turned
and watched a low silver hovercraft float toward them.
The vehicle ghosted to a halt and one of the doors raised
up like an aluminum wing.

"A hotel," Frego said. He tossed his bag inside and
gestured Garry to enter. Garry glanced at the port one
last time. There was a feeling to the great empty buildings. They were very modern, very up-to-date, but he
sensed age and antiquity. The buildings were like monuments. Cleaned and polished and dead.

He wondered what they waited for. Was it him?

He climbed into the cab and the wing folded around
them.

As the cab lifted off the ground he saw a flash of light
in the pines of the far mountains. It was like a tiny star,
but he knew it had nothing to do with them.

The hovercab took them out of the spaceport onto a
twelve-lane superhighway suspended on concrete pylons
above the low forest beneath. Once on the highway it
accelerated and pressed Garry and Frego back into the
soft leather seats. Each stared out his own window, lost
in thought. Garry watched the trees grow taller as the
highway dipped and wove around humped dark rocky
outcroppings, above tumbling streams far below. The
highway ribboned up toward a towering peak. Something

about it was vaguely familiar, but the faint tug of memory stretched and broke. He sighed.

Now they were in a high canyon. Steep walls rose on
either side. Wind roared dully through the window glass.
In all this wilderness he'd seen no sign of habitation
beyond the white road.

Yet the computer search had insisted that at least a
billion citizens lived and worked and played on Arius.
What did it mean?

Where did they live?

Up ahead the walls of rock dropped suddenly down
and became smooth concrete. A gigantic opening appeared, far too large for the road itself. A tunnel of some
kind.

There were no doors. The car didn't even slow. It
flashed past the concrete jamb, then the opening was a
receding shining hole behind them. But in the moment of
passage Garry's young eyes had seen something. What
had Frego said? Observe, observe!

The edges of doors pulled back. Steel doors twenty
feet thick. There is only one purpose for an open door,
Garry reflected. An open door can only close.

"This isn't a hotel," Frego said. He leaned forward
and banged on the control console of the cab. "I said a
hotel, you stupid machine."

Garry touched him on the shoulder. "It's all right," he
said.

"How do you know? What are you talking about? This
cab took us to the wrong place. What's the matter with
you?" Frego seemed almost frantic. Garry wondered if
the strain was breaking him down. He could understand.
He was afraid all the time now. The fear was like a dark
liquid filling him up. He was immersed in fear to the
point that it had almost become normal. It was normal to
be terrified.

"Frego. We don't have a choice."

Frego sat back. His breathing was hard. "You're right.
But you don't know everything. I contacted somebody.
Someone who—"

"Our contact. The Terran Search."

Frego stared at him. "Yes."

The winged door sighed up. Garry tilted his head.
"Out there," he said.

And the bizarre creature bowed his head into the cab and said, "Welcome to Arius. I've been expecting you."

"Where are the billion people? Why, all around you," Chasm said.

He said his name was Chasm. His full name was Chasm, Incorporated-A, but they could call him Chasm. Everybody did.

Garry stared at the strange little man and tried to impress every single detail into his memory. He never forgot anything, but sometimes he didn't see enough. He was trying to remedy that fault.

Chasm was about five feet seven inches tall. He was neither thin nor fat, nor was he well built. His body was, in fact, entirely average. But his head was memorable.

It was too large for his frame and completely bald. It bulged in the back, as if chunks of cauliflower had been stuffed beneath the skin. Most astonishing was the ridge of flesh about three-quarters of an inch thick and an inch high, which began at the peak of his forehead and traveled all the way back and down to the nape of his neck like a crest.

Chasm's skin was completely black. His teeth were shiny gold. His flesh was covered with an intricate tattooing of threadlike glowing neon. The patterns flickered bright and dim according to the volume of his voice. When Chasm spoke, it was like listening to an organ recital. Garry wondered how that flat, unremarkable chest could generate such slow, vibrant tones.

His hands were big and smooth, with long, flat fingers. He had tiny feet. He wore tight black pants and a flowing red shirt that reminded Garry of ancient pictures he'd seen of some forgotten Terran tribe; Gypsies, they were called. From other studies he had wondered if the Gypsies had actually existed, just as he wondered now if Chasm were real.

"But you don't see them, do you?" Chasm said. "That's the beauty of it. Arius is a planet of mystery. But I will make all plain to you."

He's preaching to us, Garry thought. Why is he doing that?

They had been shown to a grand room by a shining housebot. The ceiling of the room was twenty feet tall and gilded with curlicued wood. Paintings that Garry was certain had to be copies hung from velvet walls, each illuminated by a single brass lamp. Doors on either side of the room led to smaller but equally lavish bedrooms. Each bedroom had its own bath. The pile of the antique Oriental carpets came up over his bare toes.

Frego was still agitated. "Garry, be careful. Don't say too much." He put his fingers to his lips and glanced around the main room. Garry understood. The room was probably bugged. Of course it was. But what difference did it make? They were on Arius. He remembered what Frego had said about pain and drugs. Either one would work, but together they were faster. He suspected there was plenty of both available here, if needed.

But he nodded to show he understood and said, "I'm gonna unpack. Is this place something, or what?"

Frego's eyes bulged slightly. Garry moved his mouth as if chewing gum sloppily. Just a kid, he tried to project. Just a dumb, stupid, kid. After a moment Frego nodded and grinned.

Chasm said, "Arius has standard, you might call them notions, that are different than other places." He stood as he talked, bouncing on the balls of his feet, his big flat hands fluttering gracefully. He was always in motion. His face moved and stretched. His wide lips tasted each word. His eyes glittered and slanted up toward his forehead. Even their color changed from blue to green to gray to silver. Those eyes couldn't be natural.

Chasm couldn't be natural.

They were in a room more grand than their own. Everything was polished; mahogany, brass, pewter, crystal. From some invisible place came the sound of strings, so real a quartet might be hidden just around a corner.

Each man held a thick crystal tumbler. Chasm's drink was clear and syrupy and he gasped slightly each time he sipped. Frego and Garry's drinks were Scotch. Some kind of single malt, Frego said, but he couldn't identify it. They had eaten in another splendid chamber, served by silent robots. Chasm had been voluble all through the meal without saying anything. Then they came here.

Garry tasted his drink. It warmed him and dissolved a bit of the fear. Alcohol was strange. He knew he should be more frightened but the smoky Scotch helped. It masked him from himself.

"Chasm, tell me about the population of Arius. You're the first native I've seen."

"Yes, yes, yes." The little man warbled the words. He shivered with the sound of his own voice. It seemed like a performance. "Well, I am part of the population. I certainly am. In fact, I'm three parts of the populace. What do you think of that?"

Garry closed his eyes. His forehead felt tired and itchy. Was there something in the drink? "I don't understand," he said.

This weird creature talked like a nursery rhyme.

Chasm pointed to the fleshy crest on the top of his skull. "I'm an Artificial Intelligence. My crest. It's full of silicon. Memory chips and hardware. And I'm a corporation. A rather large one actually." He caressed the cauliflower lumps on the back of his head. "And I'm me. A human."

He spoke the last almost belligerently, as if he dared anyone to contradict him.

Frego glanced up from his Scotch but didn't say anything.

"And each of those things is a full-fledged citizen of this planet. Of Arius." His slanted eyes changed color so quickly they seemed to spin.

"Uh, Chasm," Garry said. "Is everybody here like that?"

"What do you mean? As good-looking?" Chasm had a huge hooked nose. He tilted it up in the air.

Garry laughed. The little man was too ludicrous for belief.

He'd expected the fear to catch up with him here. Waited for the ominous. Instead he got a schizophrenic clown. Was schizophrenic even the right word? "No. Multiple . . . is personalities the right word?"

Chasm danced closer. His hand fluttered as he shaped the words. "Perhaps. My AI has a personality. A definite one. And the corporate part of me—well, my competitors say Chasm, Inc. has a definite sort of feeling to it. And then I, myself. Would you say I have a personality?"

"Oh yes." Garry swallowed some Scotch and let the warm bullet override his urge to giggle. It was like playing with a toy. Chasm in a great room, push a button, make him sing.

The little man's voice dropped, went softer. "I know you think I'm ridiculous. But I'm not. I have rules. You can't imagine. My society is not like yours. Perhaps you would seem stupid to me if you had to be on my world. Perhaps you do seem stupid to me. Especially if you laugh at what you don't understand."

The glorious room was suddenly chill and dusty. Garry stared into Chasm'a face and felt like a fool.

"We mean no harm," Frego said then.

Garry sighed. The first bit of humor, of warmth he'd felt in weeks turned out wrong. Became treacherous. Had he made an enemy of this man, even as he accepted his hospitality? Insulted him in his own home. "I'm sorry," Garry said. "Frego keeps telling me I'm stupid. And he's right. So are you. I was thinking—doing exactly what you said. Please accept my apologies."

Chasm brightened. His eyes lit up. An array of fractured patterns chased themselves over his skull. "That's good, young man. I know what I seem like. I go off-planet not much, only as necessary. But I accept your apology." The little man bowed gracefully.

"Chasm, I have questions," Frego said. He seemed calmer now, Garry thought. Perhaps the food, the rich surrounding. Or the Scotch was helping. It made Garry nervous when Frego appeared to lose control. Frego was all he had. He didn't want to think about not having Frego around.

"Certainly," Chasm said. "Ask them."

"Are you conversant with what has happened?"

"I have read reports forwarded to me from H'hogoth and Petersburg," Chasm said slowly. "Would you like to add anything to them?"

Frego shook his head.

"Good." Chasm set his drink on a priceless mahogany table. He ignored the ring of condensed moisture that appeared around the bottom of the glass. "Hyarl Thomas is an interesting problem."

Garry's fingers felt cold around his tumbler. Just the ice, he told himself.

"Thomas has been a factor in many plans, many operations," Chasm continued. He rolled syllables as a musician would run his hand up a keyboard. "It appears he has decided to become a factor again."

Frego gnawed at the knuckle of his right hand. "I know Thomas," he said. "The question is, what is he doing *now*? You have access to the best data pools in Potential space. Have you turned up anything?"

"I have interrogated the Aryan files, yes," Chasm said. His voice was cool and noncommittal.

"And?"

"It appears that Thomas may be here. On the planet. Now."

There was a long silence. Then Frego exploded. "Dammit, that's impossible!" His voice had dropped to a husky rasp. The words were sudden, harsh. Garry looked at him in surprise.

"I assure you our data files tag for probability. We show a positive factor of ninety-six percent."

Frego had half risen from his chair. His big fists clenched, unclenched. He regained control and sank back. "That's not what I meant. How could you allow it? Hyarl Thomas downplanet? Madness!"

Chasm shook his head. His eyes had gone a deep, clear green. "We did not allow it."

Frego stopped dead. He stared at Chasm. After a long time he spread his thick hands wide. "But Chasm," he said softly. "How can that be?"

Chasm seemed not to hear the question. His eyes faded to silver, to gray. He shrugged. He walked slowly back to the table and picked up his drink. He tasted it and set it down again. He glanced at Garry.

"How can that be?" Frego said.

"Hyarl Thomas is an interesting subject," Chasm ventured.

"How can that be, Chasm?" Frego's voice was insistent. He sounded as if he could ask the question forever. Until he got an answer.

The odd little man whirled. His eyes were the color of blood. His words played out from the deepest part of the organ.

"I—*we*—don't know!"

Frego crumpled slowly into the back of his chair. Suddenly he looked old and gray and sick. "Then we are well and truly screwed."

"Yes," Chasm said.

Chapter Eleven

It was the day after their first meeting with Chasm. They walked outside on the rim of the mountain and looked out into morning. The warm smell of pine surrounded them. Brown needles crunched beneath their feet. A few lumpy clouds shambled across the horizon; gauzy shadows flowed across the blue plain far below like lazy travelers.

"Frego, what you said last night. It doesn't make any sense. Why were you so surprised that Hyarl Thomas might be here on Arius? I thought you were certain he'd come here."

Frego's features had relaxed. He seemed at peace with himself. Fatalistic, as if something important and beyond his reach had been decided.

He brushed against the thick bole of a tall pine and ran his fingers over the shaggy bark. "I thought he would come here. But I didn't think he'd get downplanet. Now I don't know what to think. I had read things a certain way and they haven't turned out."

Garry sensed secrets encased in secrets. Frego had become a secret. A faint curl of fear turned in his belly.

"Frego. Tell me your secret. Tell me what you haven't told me." His voice was quiet. There was a dreamlike quality to the morning, to their walk. To this conversation. The secrets would come alive and kill him. There was nobody to trust. He glanced at Frego. Had there ever been?

"Chasm works with the Search. For his own reasons. I don't know what they are," Frego said.

"Go on."

"This planet is more than a planet, Garry. New Chi-

cago is the nominal head of the Potential Planets. But I
think the Potential heart is here."

Heart. The Potential heart. Garry tasted the words.
There was a kind of poetry to them. "Say what you
mean, Frego."

"The government here has never been opposed to the
Search. Tolerant, actually. People like Chasm couldn't
work for us without official support. The government
rules Arius totally. When it appeared Thomas might come
here, it seemed a good thing. Perhaps Arius would help
us. Or if they didn't we would know. We wouldn't be
allowed downplanet. But Thomas may be here. Without
the government's permission. That's inconceivable, Garry.
It would mean Thomas was more powerful than Arius. I
thought that was impossible."

Garry picked up some dusty brown needles and rubbed
them between his fingertips. "Maybe Chasm lied. Maybe
the government lied to Chasm."

Frego sighed. It was a long, whistling, mournful sound.
"We would never know, Garry. But if Chasm lied, then
we should be dead."

The cold that waited inside him widened. "Yes," Garry
said. "I was afraid of that."

He couldn't take his eyes off Chasm. The strange little
man fascinated him. His constant movement, his organ
voice kept him mesmerized. Now Chasm pointed at an
elaborate dish one of the housebots presented for lunch.

"Krigel fish from New Chicago. Very rare," Chasm
said.

Frego ate his food with mechanical concentration. He
chewed and swallowed without raising his eyes.

"Is it hard? What does it feel like?" Garry said.

Sparkling eyes. Red, moist lips. "What?"

"All the stuff inside your head. The AI. The corporation. How do you keep track?"

Chasm fussed at the housebot a moment, then clicked
his teeth and served Garry with his own hands. "It's not
bad. Less complicated than you'd think." He took his
own place across from Garry at the spotless table and
ignored Frego, who sat at the end of the table. "The
corporation sells the products of the AI. The AI is cross-
wired with my own brain. It gives it a unique perspective.
I specialize in predicting the outcome of social patterns.

My corporation markets data all over the Confederacy. Even the H'hogotha buy from me."

Garry tasted his fish. It seemed full of garlic and charcoal and a hint of chocolate. The combination wasn't as awful as he'd suspected. He swallowed and gazed at Chasm's crest. "You must have an awful lot of storage there. You really do keep everything in your skull."

The little man grinned, revealing his double row of perfect gold. The effect was startling, like lighting a lamp in a dark room. "The AI has its own personality, you know." His voice dropped an octave. Sly half notes crept into the harmonies.

"Doesn't that get uncomfortable?"

Chasm shrugged. "It depends on who has the upper hand." He tasted his own dish. "Too much salt," he announced. "By the way, I've located Hyarl Thomas." He shook his head. "You just can't find good help anymore. I pay a fortune for chef software and—"

Garry stared at him. "You what?"

"Good chef software," Chasm said, "and I still can't get a decent plate of—"

"No, you said something about Hyarl Thomas."

Frego put down his fork and swallowed. "Chasm." His voice was choked. A faint flush put his scars into white relief.

"Now don't you start on me. I didn't ask you to come chasing in here with that maniac one step in front of you."

Frego sighed. "You agreed, a long time ago. I don't know why, but you agreed to work for us, for the Search. We've helped you. Helped your corporation. It was a part of the bargain. Don't bullshit me, Chasm. It's time now. Now you get to pay, so quit fucking with me. Do you understand?"

Chasm's eyes flashed through a spectrum of colors. Some Garry had never seen before. "We had a deal, yes." His voice was slow and cold.

Frego was patient. "No, we still have a deal. And if we don't, then there will be another deal. It will involve you but you won't be in it." He spoke as if explaining something very simple to a child. When he finished, he looked at Chasm and nodded.

"I'm safe here," Chasm said at last.

"Nobody's safe anywhere," Frego replied. He waited.

Chasm tossed his napkin onto the table and made a petulant sound. "You are so serious, Frego. But I suppose you have to be. Very well. You want to know about Hyari Thomas. Finish your lunch and I'll tell you. Better yet, I'll show you."

Frego nodded one more time. "That's good," he said.

After lunch Chasm took them to another part of his home. This room was white and antiseptic looking. He ushered them inside and dimmed the lights with a word. There were several chairs arranged in the center of the room facing one wall, theater-style. On that wall a small electronic unit of some kind protruded from the smooth surface about three feet above the floor. Something about the shape of the unit made Garry think of computers, although it resembled no hardware he'd ever heard of.

"Take a seat, gentlemen," Chasm said. He bowed slightly. Garry was amused again by the exaggerated courtliness of the elfin man.

Chasm waited until they were settled in their chairs. Garry moved in his and found that it swiveled a full three hundred and sixty degrees easily. Then he realized that a slight pressure on either arm caused the movement, and held himself still.

"Good," Chasm said. He went to the unit on the wall and pulled a dark knob from it, as if tugging a cork from a wine bottle. The knob came loose and trailed a thread of fire.

Garry squinted. "What is that?"

"Superconducting monomolecular cable," Chasm said. "Much more efficient than fiber optics. Much higher capacity."

Garry rubbed the side of his nose. 'I never heard of stuff like that."

Chasm flashed his golden grin. "Perhaps in some areas we are more technologically advanced than the rest of the Confederacy. It doesn't matter. Like the stone ax and the plasma beam."

"How's that?" Frego said.

"Either one can kill you. Either one gets the job done."

Frego looked at the floor.

Chasm lowered his head and exposed the back of his neck. A black socket appeared at the base of his crest.

He fitted the plug into the socket. "Quicker this way," he said.

Garry was interested. "What kind of interface is that?"

"Direct. The AI does the filtering. Human memory storage is holographic in nature."

"Wait a minute. You're going to project your own memory?"

Chasm turned and faced the wall. They couldn't see his face in the dim light. The monomole cable fanned out behind him like an exotic bridal train. The individual wires shimmered like moist insect wings. "It's not a problem with the proper interpretation software. Memory is memory."

Garry nodded slowly. His eyes were half-closed. He picked his words slowly, carefully. "Nobody has that kind of ware. I've heard of something but it was long ago. Old Terran. The bioelectronic brains. What did they call them? Meatmatrices. But they're banned. They don't exist anymore."

Chasm pivoted slowly until his eyes were visible. They had become a rusty red, like dried blood. "I have a brain. I have two, in fact." He made it sound like an explanation, although Garry knew it was a puzzle. Another part of a puzzle.

"Here," Chasm said, and the entire room flashed into light.

The room disappeared and they were surrounded by a wide expanse of grass at the mouth of the small canyon. From the canyon a stream moved quickly and smoothly, like molten clear glass. The canyon widened as it climbed away from the meadow, and far above it disappeared entirely on the flank of a massive peak.

The mountain seemed familiar to Garry. He didn't understand the familiarity, and for a moment his forehead wrinkled. Then he decided it must be a similarity with the mountains he'd seen on his way here.

At the far edge of the meadow, beyond the stream, was a low gray stone building. It had an orange tile roof. There was an air of genteel decay about the structure, a sense of abandonment.

But then the door opened and a man stepped out into the light.

Garry sucked in his breath. Even Frego stirred slightly.

"Yes," Chasm said. "Hyarl Thomas."

The man walked out into the meadow and paused. He shaded his eyes with his right hand and peered up the canyon. He looked like a man expecting a visitor who was late.

Garry watched the long liquid stride of the man and saw once again the same feline grace that had flowed across the floor of a pawnshop light-years distant.

This is the man who killed my father, he thought. He tried to summon the flame of the rage he'd felt then, but the familiar warmth wouldn't come. Only a chill. Only fear.

He watched Hyarl Thomas shake his head and turn and walk back to the gray building. For a moment he paused in the doorway and Garry thought he saw Thomas's eyes. It seemed they looked right at him, as if the man were aware of Garry's observation.

He shivered. I don't want him to see me, he told himself.

He felt something else in that moment too, a kind of yearning. A need he barely acknowledged. They were bound, the two of them, by ties of blood and death.

Now the flame stirred just a bit. For an instant its heat burned away the chill.

Sometime, Garry thought. But not yet.

"That's all," Chasm said. And the room became a room again.

Garry let his breath out. He hadn't even realized he'd been holding it. He looked up and saw Frego staring at him curiously.

"I'm okay," he said.

"I didn't ask," Frego replied.

"My government is concerned," Chasm said. "That place, that building. It has significance."

Garry sniffed. The air of the room was cool and without odor. He thought about the research he'd done on the history of Arius. The hidden things, the lies. The history of Arius was a secret. "What significance?" he said.

Chasm unplugged the monomole cable from his crest and fed it back into the wall. His eyes were blank and empty. No color at all. "When Arius was colonized, that was the first installation. The home of our forefathers you might say."

Garry thought about it. "That? That small building? For a whole colony?"

"It is an iceberg. The tip of it. Most of the installation was underground."

"Why underground?"

Chasm shrugged. "Ancient history. The original colonists had their reasons."

Like an iceberg, Garry thought. An iceberg is a great secret mostly hidden. Only the sharp point protrudes into the light. He felt the secrets gather around him like a cloud of buzzing insects and squeezed his cold fingers into fists. "Why don't you tell me the truth?" he asked.

"It is the truth," Chasm replied.

Garry couldn't think of anything else to say. His mind was filled with Hyarl Thomas, with his slow, gliding assassin's stride. The sureness and confidence of it.

"How did he get here?" Frego asked. "And if you— your government didn't allow it, how did you find him?"

"Satellite imaging. ELINT. Electronic intelligence. He was discovered through routine analysis. Much after the fact, of course. The building has been watched since, but he hasn't been seen again. There are questions at the highest level."

Frego nodded. He patted his belly, which was like a hard beach ball. "I'll bet. Have you any answers for the questions?"

Chasm glanced at Garry. "Perhaps," he said.

Anger animated Frego's voice. "Of course you do. And the answers involve us, don't they? Did you know that he was coming here? Maybe you set it up in the first place. It would be easy if Thomas worked for you. Did you know two hundred people died on H'hogoth? Including this boy's father? What are you doing, Chasm?"

The little man moved toward them but he was dull. He was tired. For the first time, Garry wondered how old he was.

A faint pattern of silver lines chased themselves across his black face. "We don't know about Thomas," Chasm said. "He is a mystery to us."

And Garry knew it was the truth.

"We have to talk," Frego said when they returned to their apartment. Garry sat in a spindly wooden chair that was all polished curlicues. It was like sitting in a picture, a work of art. It made him feel young and clumsy.

"Is it safe?"

"You mean is the room wired? Probably. But this whole planet is wired. We have to talk anyway. We have to decide what to do."

Garry nodded. He felt slightly sick. He was a puppet dancing on hidden strings, but he didn't know the puppet master. Was it Chasm? Was it Frego? Hyarl Thomas?

Was it his dead father twitching the strings from beyond the grave? He felt so tired. This is what it's like to be old, he thought. So sad.

"What do we do?" he asked.

Frego raised his eyebrows. He didn't like the change in Garry. The ugly death of the Golden Girl had altered him in a bad way. Now on some days he would be okay, like a kid. Then his face would go pale and white and his eyes empty. He wondered if Garry was going mad.

He wished that it didn't matter. He'd never done a job like this. But Garry was the wild card. He didn't understand that, but it was true. Garry was important. More important than an old, crafty agent named Frego.

"Remember what we set out to do," Frego said. He tried to keep his voice brisk and precise, without emotion. "Remember how it started. The artifact. And Hyarl Thomas. Forget all the rest; it's smoke. We came for the cube. Thomas has it and we want it. If Thomas is here, then the artifact must be here also. Look at it that way and it becomes simple."

Garry nodded. "Yes. We have to go get the cube. We have to go to that building. The Aryan shrine. Do you trust Chasm, Frego?"

Frego was startled. "Trust? No, I don't trust anybody."

"Not even me?"

"Well, of course I trust you, Garry."

Another lie, Garry thought. But it was all lies and secrets. He thought of Alexander and his sword. Cut through the Gordian knot with a single stroke. His muscles felt heavy and congested. They craved action.

His brain was tired but his body eager. Very well. He wondered if he would live through it, and was surprised to discover he wanted to survive very much. He'd never even considered survival before. It is a given when you are seventeen. Like breathing and eating and laughing. You are immortal at seventeen.

He felt a loosening in his chest. He'd discovered his own mortality and the universe, of which he was the center, had forever changed.

"We have to go to that place," he said. His right hand twitched and he stared at it and thought of the Golden Girl and Hyarl Thomas, of death's sure stride. "Frego," he said.

"Yes, what?"

"I don't want to grow up. I thought I did, but I don't."

Frego came and put his thick, twisted fingers on Garry's thin shoulder. "Nobody does," he said. "But you don't get a choice. Or if you do, that's even worse."

Morning.

They were outside, standing at the edge of a small concrete plaza at the mouth of yet another tunnel. The mountain was honeycombed by tunnels. Garry tried to guess how many people lived in the mountain. But that was wrong. Corporations lived here too. Artificial Intelligences. Citizens of Arius lived in computers, gathered in data banks. The flesh was only part of the story.

There was a low ring of the slightly alien pines around the plaza. It was early. The sun was barely over the horizon and the dew had not burned off. The slanting rays of the sun caught the tiny droplets and turned them into a net of jewels. But the air was brisk and refreshing on his cheek and for a moment he could forget the fog and dreams that clouded his mind. For a moment everything was clear and simple and new.

He stretched. He wore a thin, supple leather jumpsuit that fit his wiry frame tightly. It was almost like a second skin. At his hip a new holster held the familiar weight of his short-barreled .44. An odd thing that weapons traveled so easily through the entryports of the planets. People were weighed and measured, but their weapons were ignored. He remembered an ancient slogan from Old Terra: "Guns don't kill people. People kill people." Perhaps it was true.

It was a nasty weapon. Chasm had procured explosive slugs from somewhere. They would tear flesh into shreds, leave great gaping holes. The slugs moved at such high velocity that a hit in the arm was enough to ensure death.

Systemic shock would do it. He tried to imagine putting a slug into Hyarl Thomas's chest.

"Garry, you ready?"

Frego's voice was tight and high with tension, but Garry felt relaxed. He felt helpless, at the mercy of events. Nothing was left to him but action, yet that was a release. To do something, to seek a resolution. He had thought too much, touched too many secrets. Now it was time for something direct and simple.

His body felt loose. There was a space in the pit of his stomach. The smell of new leather filled his nose. He touched the wooden grip of his revolver. "Yes," he said. The sun burst over the tops of the trees and illumined the plaza. "I'm ready," he said.

The expedition was small. Two helicopters with odd, screwlike vanes and jets beneath the main pods. Inside, their army, a dozen shining metal constructs. Some resembled spiders with tiny heads and single eyes. Articulated laser platforms. And others, multilegged steel things with three or four arms. Mechanical shock troops. All were carefully programmed, but Frego could override their software with his own instructions through a mike bead embedded in his lower lip.

"Quick in and quick out," Frego had said. "Thomas can't have an army in there. Or if he does we lose anyway."

Garry had gotten out of bed early and taken a long shower. He shaved carefully, rubbing depilatory on all the scattered bits of whisker. He put on a cologne that smelled of cedar and musk. It seemed like a ritual and it was, although he couldn't know of all the young men who'd dressed themselves for battle and joked about it. Better to die young and good-looking. He glanced in the mirror.

Yeah. Looking good.

A flight of bright redbirds exploded overhead. They made throaty hacking noises as they flew, like dry rough sticks scraped together. Garry climbed into the co-pilot's seat of the lead copter. Frego slid in behind him and punched him lightly on the back.

Garry nodded. Suddenly he felt very alive, very connected. The morning sparkled and the cool air filled his lungs. Colors were bright and immediate.

He felt young and empty.

For one instant fear was gone and he was filled with—

The cyborged pilot threw the copter into the air and the feeling disappeared. Garry heard the harsh whine of the second copter rise behind them. They breasted the ring of pines and mountains arched up in black-green splendor.

Look out, he thought wildly. Here I come!

Chasm, Inc. watched the small flight disappear over the trees. His black face jittered with the movements of hundreds of thin blue threads. His eyes were bright and green.

He licked his lips and tugged at his right ear. He paused with his head cocked as if listening to something. After a moment he nodded to himself.

He made no motion, nor did he say anything, but a large, armored gunship rolled ponderously out of the tunnel. It came to a halt in the middle of the plaza and squatted there like a vast, predatory bug.

Chasm stared up at the empty blue sky. His eyes flashed red for one instant, like the shutter of a camera clicking. Then he climbed into the copter.

The armored door rolled shut. The gunship lumbered slowly into the sky.

A single redbird landed on the plaza and began pecking at the concrete. In a while more joined the first.

On Arius they were called the wings of red desire, and they knew no secrets at all.

Chapter Twelve

When it finally began, it happened quickly. They had come over the mountain and landed their two helicopters on the broad upland where the narrow, deep canyon broadened out onto a high rock plain. Every sensor and every sense they possessed had been aimed down the canyon toward the small building invisible in the morning mists. There had been no alarm. The landing was uneventful.

They made a hasty camp and settled in to wait. Frego said it was better to approach the building after dark on foot. It would be even better to drop from the sky, but if anybody was watching, there was no way to disguise the arrival of two gunships loaded with robot troops and heavy weapons. They would start down after sunset with the helicopters in reserve.

Garry slept part of the day, comforted by the feel of massive stone beneath him. Before he closed his eyes he watched clouds hurtle by. He felt small on the great mountain beneath the high clouds. Small and almost safe. He tried not to think about sunset, about the night.

Frego checked his weapons again and again. It wasn't nerves. It was just the endless cautionary habits of a veteran fighting man. The battery pack on the laser must be charged. The gun must be loaded and clean. The edge of the blade sharp. Such things could save a life. Better to check, and check again.

Garry closed his eyes. The last thing he saw was the high blue sky and a single dark V like an exclamation.

It might have been a hawk.

His breath smoked silver in front of him. The wind came from downcanyon, funneled by the black walls, harsh and frigid. It slapped his cheeks and stung his eyes. The night was alive with the faint chink and jingle of their steel troops. They clambered over the rocks with jerky motions, catching and releasing claw holds with machine certainty. One of the laser spiders was out ahead, scouting the point. Frego carried a tiny analyzer. He watched the figures scroll down the screen. The faint light washed his face a ghostly blue.

"Nothing," he said softly. "There's nothing down there. They don't have any sentinels out." His voice was puzzled. Surely Thomas would guard himself. Perhaps he wasn't there. "It might be a wild-goose chase," he said aloud, without realizing he'd spoken.

Garry's fingers were numb. The wind pushed fog ahead of it, but he could sense the low ceiling above the rim of the canyon. There were no stars, only the wind and the moving fog and the black rock. Not far ahead the canyon ended like a deep knife slash in the side of the mountain. Beyond the stony mouth lay their objective.

"It's like an iceberg," Garry replied. "Mostly underground. Maybe the entrance isn't guarded."

Frego brought the party to a halt. His black leather combat gear was nearly invisible. Garry caught a flash of scar, where the blackout grease had covered imperfectly. "Could be."

He seemed to talk with himself, though he spoke in Garry's direction. "How would I do it?" He considered for a long time. "I'd leave the entrance open. I'd make a trap."

Garry stared down the canyon. The wind howled and hair rose up on the back of his neck. The wind sounded alive and in pain. "Maybe he's not expecting anybody. Maybe he's just hiding."

Frego consulted his tiny screen. His eyes were black holes in his face, blank and empty. "Maybe," he said.

But he sent another laser spider ahead. "Can't be too careful," he said.

They began with fire. The two laser spiders emitted a humming noise and bright green lances began to criss-cross the gray stone walls of the building. The smell of molten rock began to fill the air. Then Frego made a signal and one of the troopers clambered forward and aimed its railgun.

The portable railgun was a terrible weapon. A ball of metal was accelerated down a tube ringed with superconducting electromagnets. The metal ball achieved an unimaginable velocity. It hit one corner of the building like an avalanche and blew out five feet of stone. The roof above the corner sagged and smoke began to billow up and mix with the fog.

"Go!" Frego said, and scuttled forward. Garry sucked in moist, cold air and followed. His heart was beating very fast. Events became images. Click, click.

Something white and broken and shiny gaped through the ruined corner. He imagined shattered teeth in a ruined mouth.

One of the laser spiders burned the door off its hinges. It fell backward into darkness.

Now the rest of the troops opened fire and lines of brilliant-colored light illumined the darkness. Their weapons made strange hooting sounds or screamed like children. Garry narrowed his eyes and followed Frego's broad back.

When they rolled and tumbled inside the building and Frego slammed him down just beyond the door, it was almost an anticlimax.

Empty.

Nobody home.

The interior was ruined. The railgun had fired two more times and the entire back wall was gone. A wall of some kind of machinery had buckled out of the corner opening. They were the teeth he'd seen. A chair was on its side, legless. Another piece of furniture, no longer recognizable, smoldered next to it.

The silence was oppressive. Nothing moved. Then Frego rose to a crouch. "Stay down," he said. He scuttled forward into the smoke from the wrecked furniture.

Garry lay frozen. His revolver was in his hand, but he hadn't pulled the trigger. The metal was cold to the touch and heavy. It took all his strength to lift it and aim toward the center of the building. If there was something, it would come from there. He was sure of it.

So he almost blew Frego's head off before he realized who it was.

"Jesus! Be careful with that thing."

"I'm sorry. What's going on."

"There's an elevator back there. A big one. The railgun took out the wall around it, but the mechanism looks okay. That's all this place is, just a cover over a big elevator. Chasm should have known." Frego shook his head. He didn't want to think about Chasm and what he should have known. It just reminded him of what he didn't know. It made him think about treachery.

But Garry understood. Chasm should have known, but he didn't tell them. What else had he kept silent about?

"So?" Garry said. He knew the answer, but he wanted Frego to tell him.

"We go down," Frego said. "What else is there?"

Garry stood slowly. Fire ran down his back. His shin hurt from where he'd slammed into the edge of the doorway and not noticed. His muscles felt twisted and full of acid.

"All right," he said. He thought about riding a steel platform into the dark earth. Down to where Hyarl Thomas waited.

Down in the dark, in the secret places.

Down beneath the tip of the iceberg.

"Let's go," he said.

"This is stupid," Frego said. They had crammed themselves, one of the laser spiders, and three troopers onto the elevator platform. Despite what Frego had said about damage, something was broken in the machinery, perhaps something that controlled the magnetic rails that lifted the platform. As they descended, the floor tilted slightly and long groaning sounds wailed beneath them. Or maybe the mechanism was simply old and worn out.

"We don't even know where we're going. There could be a hundred levels down here. He could be anywhere."

Garry nodded. Every once in a while his teeth would begin to chatter and he could clamp his lips shut until it passed. Frego noticed this but ignored it. There was nothing to do anyway. What could Frego say? Don't be scared, this isn't real?

Of course it was real.

"Start at the bottom. If this thing goes down that far."

"It's a perfect trap," Frego said. "If somebody—if Chasm—wanted us out of the way, this is how to do it. Send us down into a hole in the ground. We're ducks here."

"You want to go back up?"

Frego sighed. "Yeah, I want to go back up. I want to go back to H'hogotha and hang out in spaceport dives and cheat the tourists." He grinned. "But I can't."

No, Garry thought, once a thing is broken, you can't ever put it back together again. My life is broken.

There was the smell of smoke and rancid oil. Hot metal. The elevator screamed with agony and lurched to a halt. They looked down. They were halfway below the top of a dark opening.

Frego got down on his hands and knees and peered out. He couldn't see anything. He looked back over his shoulder at Garry.

"I guess we get off here."

Garry felt the weight of the revolver in his nerveless fingers. He raised the weapon slightly. "You think they got stairs in this place?"

Frego edged forward. He held a laser rifle in one hand and pushed it ahead of him. Warm air pushed against his face from the opening. It smelled dry and musty.

"That's what we have to find out, isn't it?"

"Among other things," Garry replied.

They strapped small bead lamps to their foreheads. In a way it made them targets. The center of the lamp was the skull and behind it the brain. But the lights were bright and designed to shift, to confuse a would-be assailant. And they needed their hands free.

There was a panel beside the gaping elevator entrance. The doors had jammed open. Frego looked carefully and saw streaks of corrosion. It was an old breakdown. The panel listed many floors, at least sixty. They hadn't come that far down.

"What do you think? Down, or up?"

Garry shook his head. The light danced and strobed. "Up," he said at last. "The elevator would have stopped for them here too. But we found it at the top. So they didn't come down this far."

"Not on the elevator," Frego said.

Garry turned and flashed his beacon out into the darkness. There was a gray patina of dust on everything. The vast room was deserted. Columns grew like perfect tree trunks in the gloom. But there was nothing but emptiness and open space.

"There are other elevators," Garry said.

"No, only this one."

"Others," Garry repeated. "Look at this place. Look how big. Sixty levels deep. And only one elevator? There are others. In other places. This was only one of the entrances."

"He looked like he was waiting for someone."

"Who?"

"Thomas," Frego said. "He came out of the little building and looked up the canyon. Like he was expecting something. But what?"

"Maybe it was us," Garry said.

They found a stairwell after crossing a deserted space the size of two football fields. They moved slowly, from pillar to pillar, with two of the troops and the laser spider out front. It had been a tight fit, getting them out of the elevator. The door to the stairway was thick steel. It shrieked once when they pried it open. Amazingly there was dim light in the stairwell. Ancient chemical glowstrips still burned, acting out their phosgene destiny. The light was low, barely enough to see by. They edged through the door. The laser spider went first, its jewellike snout pointing up like an expectant eye.

Nothing.

The spider barely made it through. It would move up the stairs slowly, wedging itself along, inching through the turns. It wouldn't be able to maneuver very well, but it would block anybody who tried to come down the stairs.

Even trade-off, Garry thought. They began to go up.

It was sweaty, muscle-deadening work. The tension wouldn't allow them to relax, and the unnatural watchfulness as they rose kept them bent at an exhausting angle. Garry's neck began to ache. His back had already gone numb.

They stopped at each floor. Some of the doors wouldn't open at all. Others had to be pried, and popped open with the sounds of a tomb being violated. These would be the worst. They knew the noise would alert anybody on the level. But nothing was there.

Three floors below the top—the levels were marked in faded black paint at the side of each door—Frego held up his hand.

This door was open just a crack. Frego turned and

stared at Garry. His voice was low, his face intent. "Garry. The elevator was at the top."

Garry nodded. "Yes."

"Don't you see?"

"What?"

"He took it down, he took it up. He is *above* us."

Garry thought about it and knew he was right. Thomas might not even have been in the building. He might have watched the attack from beyond the meadow, hidden in the rocks. Perhaps laughing at their stupidity. Their vulnerability.

Above them. The trap was above.

They had to go through Thomas to survive.

Or else he was gone and they were in an empty hole in the ground.

"What difference does it make?" Garry said at last.

Frego shifted the laser rifle a bit and looked at the door. His face had thinned out, become harsh and stark in the bitter chemical light. His scars glowed.

"Yeah. You're right." He stepped back. "I'll send the spider first." He spoke softly to the mech and moved out of its way. It chink-clinked delicately around him, moving slowly up to the door. "Put one of the troops in the back," Frego said.

Carefully the spider opened the door with a pincer claw. The door opened silently, as if it had been freshly greased. It was pitch dark beyond. Silence breathed out of the darkness. The spider twitched its way through the opening and paused, its murderous head seeking a target. Moved forward. Paused again.

Frego took a deep breath and aimed the snout of his rifle into the outer room and stepped forward. Dropped to a crouch.

After a moment he said, "Come on."

Garry bent over and scuttled through like a crab. He held his revolver in both hands and extended it forward.

He felt a troop push gently against his back as he waited.

Their lights revealed dusty shapes, great boxy instruments long abandoned. Dust coated the floor. It was thick and gray and the footprints that disturbed it showed up very well in the glare of their lights.

Footprints.

The dark exploded.

Something jagged and hard slammed Garry brutally to the floor. It was the troop behind him lumbering forward, its machine gun already chattering. Right behind, another troop lurched out into the room. It carried a railgun and swept the area forward, looking for something to kill.

Garry edged back against the wall beside the door. He still held his revolver, but he'd forgotten about it. He was petrified with terror. Something struck the spider and it shuddered heavily. Garry saw that one of its steel legs was gone. The stump jittered wildly and the big machine sagged, off balance. The laser cannon in the center of it erupted with a short siren sound and a pile of dusty machinery flared suddenly red.

Frego was a dark shadow limned momentarily against the strobe flashes of the battle.

"Stay back," he called. Garry watched him crawl forward on his knees and elbows, the laser rifle cradled in his arms. "Back in the stairwell," Frego shouted.

But the words galvanized him. Frego was advancing so that Garry could retreat. Frego was sacrificing himself for Garry. He had no idea what was out there, but he went forward. It was suicidal.

Garry watched him. He was frozen by fear. Hyarl Thomas was out there waiting to kill him. It had been inevitable from the very first, when Thomas had destroyed the pawnshop on H'hogotha.

Frego stood up into a half crouch and triggered his laser rifle. Sparks flared in the darkness. Then a spear of light transfixed the short, ugly man and he threw his arms up. Garry saw light all around him, like the corona of a sun in eclipse. Now Frego was falling backward, his rifle thrown by reflex away from him. Tiny curls of smoke rose from his black combat leathers.

"No." He didn't know where it came from, but the icy ball in Garry's belly dissolved. It rose in hot waves and warmed him finally. "Noooo!"

His arms and legs moved of their own accord. All he could see was Frego's huddled form and the flashing, spinning webs of fire. He stumbled forward and grabbed Frego's arm and began to drag him toward the doorway. Toward safety.

Incredibly the man was still alive. His face was burned black and bubbling and his eyes were dull, but he moved his lips as Garry tugged him across the dusty floor. "Go Leave me. Get away."

Garry shook his head. He kept on pulling. His strength seemed superhuman. He dragged Frego with one hand and aimed his revolver with the other. He saw nothing, though the laser bolts continued. Now the spider was down and one of the troops. The second let off a bolt from its railgun and blew a hole as big as a man through two of the huge, enigmatic machines. Then another sizzling streak sawed it in half.

Plasma, Garry thought absently. How can there be a portable plasma weapon?

Finally he made it through the door. Frego smelled like bacon frying. Garry felt moisture on his cheeks and paid no attention. He pushed the third troop back and slammed the heavy door shut.

The sudden silence was like a benediction. Whatever was on the other side would wait. There was still a chance.

"Garry . . . get the hell out here. I can't . . . I can't."

"Shhh," Garry whispered. Frego's eyes were closed now, puffy slits of swollen flesh. The troop jittered nervously. All its weapons were out as it tried to cover both directions of the stairwell and the door itself.

"A minute," Garry said. "Maybe a minute. I'm going back up and get the rest of the troops. We can get you out of here."

But the pain had claimed Frego. Pain and shock had dumped him into coma and he made no reply.

"Just a minute," Garry said. "A minute."

He glanced down the stairwell. He arranged Frego on his back against the wall. It wasn't much, but it might keep him out of the line of fire.

"Kill anything that comes through that door," he told the third troop. Its eyes, now masked for infrared, blinked redly at him.

"I'll be back," he said to Frego. "Just a minute. You hold on."

Then he turned and ran up the stairs.

At the top of the third flight he came into a small room. The room was completely empty. A single narrow slit window admitted a faint hint of starlight. After the blinding explosions of the short ambush it was barely enough to see by.

Garry scrabbled his way around the walls of the room until he felt the outlines of a door. There was no knob. He gritted his teeth and slammed his shoulder into the door.

Pain crashed into his shoulder blade and collarbone. He thought he felt something crack. He threw himself against the door again. This time he felt the metal give. And the agony almost made him pass out.

He bit his lip and tasted salt and copper. He closed his eyes and surged forward one more time. The door flipped open easily and he fell on his face.

"Ah . . . goddamn!" The cool night air washed across his face. After a moment he was able to take a breath. He pushed himself up. Overhead the stars were a glittering bowl. The sudden feel of vast open space disoriented him. He spun around. He was in a small defile at the base of the canyon. Finally he located the wreckage of the gray stone building. He shook his head and gulped air until the wave of dizziness receded. Then he began to run toward the building. The rest of the troops were there. They could rescue Frego.

He felt as if he'd run a marathon when he came up to the ruined walls, though it was only a couple hundred yards.

His lamp made bright, bizarre shadows in the destruction. He stopped.

"Oh no. Oh . . . my—no!"

Slumped all around in terrible regularity like the remnants of some hideous dance were the metal corpses of the rest of his troopers.

The trap had closed.

He stood in the night and waited. There was nothing else to do. Strings of anguish jerked up and down his limbs. His fingers twitched. He was empty inside. Nothing left. Even the fear seemed to have gone, leaving only desolation. And the waiting.

He felt as if he'd been waiting all his life.

Hyarl Thomas came then, as he knew he would.

A fleeting, liquid shadow against the destruction. He came out of the flames where the crumbled walls of gray stone still smoldered.

Garry raised his revolver and then lowered it. Too soon. He couldn't trust his own reflexes.

Hyarl Thomas walked across the grass that was black in the starlight until he stood only a few feet away. Garry could see his face, but it was empty, devoid of expression.

"First the father and now the cub," Thomas said. He raised his right hand. Something bright flickered there.

Garry tried to lift the revolver but Thomas was much too fast. He stepped forward like a dancer and waved his hand across Garry's face.

Garry didn't even feel the pain. Just a faint, itching line across his throat and a sudden gush of liquid down his chest.

"I've hunted you a million years," Thomas said. His voice was without expression. But it was final. The voice of Hyarl Thomas was an ending.

The night began to spin. Garry thought about the Golden Girl. He stared at Hyarl Thomas. Only a minute, he thought.

He raised his revolver and pulled the trigger and saw a black rose bloom on the older man's chest. Now there was an expression on Thomas's face.

It was surprise.

Garry felt no fear as the spinning earth took him. No fear at all. The last thing he saw was darkness coming down, blotting out the stars.

Chapter Thirteen

So this is death, Garry thought.

He floated over a vast blue plain. Above was a dome of darkness. Directly ahead, overhanging an invisible horizon, was a dim sun, wrinkled and orange with age.

He felt a sense of movement, of great speed, although as far as he could tell, he wasn't moving at all. Perhaps this place was in motion, carrying him along.

Nothing happened for a long time.

A part of his mind nibbled at the question. He was familiar with the postdeath experience. It was common enough in the worlds of man, although the lizards reported no such occurrence. Patients who died on operating tables. Victims of accidents, of drownings. Those whose hearts stopped, for whatever reason. Brought back by medical technologies, they reported visions. Tunnels from darkness into light. Meetings with old relatives, friends. The return to the body. They returned, for the most part, forever changed.

Am I changed? he wondered.

This didn't fit the pattern. But I am really dead, he thought. He remembered everything perfectly. He remembered the razor strike of Hyarl Thomas's knife, the painless feel of his own throat open and spilling blood down his chest. Remembered killing Thomas in his own final moments, before the darkness pressed down and carried him here.

Death isn't so bad.

There was sadness, of course. Who would bury his body? It didn't seem important, but the thought of his corpse rotting on that mountain bothered him. And Frego. Was Frego dead too?

Perhaps they would meet again. Frego, even Garth, his

father. The thought cheered him. That would be nice. They could sit down and talk about it.

Now that they were all dead, none of it mattered anymore.

Would Thomas be here too? He hoped not. Although he was no longer afraid of the man. Death had taken away the fear.

Too late. There would be no second chance.

The jumbled memories dimmed. None of it was significant. Even death was past, a gateway. What was this place?

He saw a figure.

The little man walked up to him and smiled. It was a crooked, lopsided grin, soaked in cynicism. The man wore odd clothing. Tight denim jeans, boots, a black leather jacket of ancient cut. He had a big nose set in a small, foxy face. His eyes could have been any color.

Garry felt a sudden kinship. "Have you come to show me the way?"

But the little man only grinned again. He turned and flipped one hand toward the horizon, toward the wasted sun, like a master of ceremonies introducing a new act. A line of light began to grow at right angles to the horizon. The light had a shape. It might have been a sword.

When Garry looked back, the little man was gone. He was the little man who wasn't there.

The feeling of movement began to increase.

The light was blinding and he closed his eyes. Painful afterimages burned on the inside of his eyelids, then subsided. After a time he heard voices.

". . . awake yet?"

This is wrong, Garry thought. Death was peaceful, calm. This hurts.

More voices, unintelligible.

"Vital signs approaching normal." This voice was brisk. He identified the tone. Clipped, professional. A doctor's voice.

Were there doctors in hell?

He found that idea funny and felt his lips twitch.

"Garry?"

Chasm. He could never forget that organ voice. Had Chasm died then too? But how could that be?

"Garry, can you hear me?"

"Yes . . ."

"Oh, good." The voice dropped into lower registers, rich harmonics full of worry and sympathy. But why? Garry wondered. Everything's okay. I'm dead. Nothing can hurt me now.

"You made it," Chasm breathed. "Can you open your eyes?" A pause. "The lights, of course. Somebody dim the lights."

The bright glow faded from the back of his eyelids.

Suddenly he felt tired. This was too real, too mundane. Now he felt the hard bed beneath, and when he tried to move his head, something restrained him.

"Don't try to move," Chasm said. "It was touch and go."

Garry opened his eyes. In the faint light Chasm's dark face glittered like a Christmas tree. "We were so worried," Chasm said.

"I'm alive," Garry told him.

"Of course."

Something momentous slipped away from him. He began to cry.

"I died."

"Yes, for a while. Your heart stopped beating. I told you, it was touch and go."

"Tell me what happened," Garry said.

They were in the small room where Garry lay recuperating, surrounded by shining machines that sparkled in the shadowy light. Garry lay flat on his back. Wires and tubes extended from his body to the machines. In the clear plastic tubes liquids pulsed and bubbled. Connected, he thought. I am connected to the world again.

He was seventeen. He felt a hundred years old. They killed my father, they killed Frego. They killed the Golden Girl.

They killed me.

But I have come back.

"I followed you, of course," Chasm said.

Garry stared at him.

"Yes. I told you before, my government has an interest in Hyarl Thomas. That he was in that particular place."

"It was empty. Deserted, abandoned. There was nothing there. Nobody for a long time."

Chasm shook his head slightly. Light flickered across his face. "You don't understand us. Here on Arius it is different. That's all right. We have made it so. There are secrets here and we keep them."

Garry blinked. It was amazing how strong he felt. How unafraid. Death had freed him.

"Secrets in that place?"

"Perhaps."

He felt hard and powerful. Chasm had diminished in his eyes. He spoke harshly, brutally. "Then Hyarl Thomas broke your secrets. He was there. He violated your hidden place, before I killed him."

Chasm's head rose. His eyes cycled through a spectrum. "You killed him? Who?"

He felt as if he were explaining to a child. Patience. "I killed Thomas. After he killed me."

Chasm spread his hands. "Then where is his body?" he said.

Three days later he was able to get up and walk around. He stared at himself in the mirror in his bathroom. He touched the faint red line, like a necklace, that ran from one side of his neck to the other. There was no pain. The machines had done their work well. He had been very lucky, Chasm said.

"We set down just after your troopers were destroyed. There was a firefight. We were afraid we would be too late. I had waited, hidden above your original camp. We watched and monitored, and when the fighting ended, we came down. And found you."

"Found me."

Chasm nodded. "Yes. You had a terrible wound. We got you into the copter and put the medics to work. They were able to . . ."

Garry nodded. "Save me."

"Yes."

"And you found nothing else?"

"There was no other force. No bodies. We investigated the installation and found the wreckage of the rest of your team. The troops, the laser spiders. But we didn't find Frego, either. Are you sure it happened as you remember? You were in awful shape."

"It happened that way."

"How can you be sure?"

Garry smiled. "I never forget anything. Ever."

He combed his dark hair. It had grown longer than he liked. On a shelf beneath the mirror was a case with blue contact lenses inside. He opened the case and frowned. No more reason to hide. Frego was gone. Thomas was gone. The artifact was gone. Only he remained.

He emptied the case over the toilet and watched the thin blue disks sink to the bottom. He still felt weak, but he knew it would pass. He would recover and go on with his life.

What life?

He stared at himself in the mirror. His already thin face was wasted and gaunt, his eyes wide green pools above cheekbones like scalpels. There were new lines at the corners of his eyes, and two deep vertical slices over the bridge of his nose.

I look old, he thought with surprise.

Seventeen. Three more years of college. And then what?

It all seemed so distant, so far away.

He brushed his teeth. And when he finished, when he looked at those alien eyes in the mirror—eyes that had seen death—he thought he finally understood.

At least he could be grateful for one thing. He wasn't afraid anymore. That would make it easier, what he had to do.

He sighed and bent down and fished the contact lenses out of the toilet and rinsed them off and put them away.

Garth, Frego, the Golden Girl.

The artifact.

Hyarl Thomas.

It wasn't over yet.

Chasm, Incorporated-A sat in his interface room and listened to the sounds of the universe. The neon tattoos on his face rippled to the beat of his pulse. His eyes had cycled down to a dull pewter. They were empty as cups that would never be filled.

Twinkling threads connected him to silent machines. He sat in a chair that molded itself to his body, accepted his every move. A chair like a hand, caressing, supporting.

It was all a game, of course. The equipment was so

primitive. So unnecessary. But appearances had to be maintained. The lies had to seem real.

It was a world of secrets. Arius was a secret. He was a secret. The secrets coiled within themselves like Chinese boxes, each secret larger than the last, yet somehow encased in it. How could the large fit into the small?

On Arius many strange things were possible.

His flat, long fingers twitched on the arm of his chair, were still.

It had been a mistake. He saw that now.

Perhaps I'm getting old, he thought. So many years since the beginning. So much time.

Thomas was worse than he had feared. His power was appalling. Thomas had his secrets too, and revealed himself only a little bit. A flash here, a hint there.

He was the wild card. He was what they hadn't planned for.

Chasm himself, and himself, and himself sat in his chair and thought about Garry Hamersmidt. Thought about the terrible wild card named Hyarl Thomas. And waited.

Heaven was worth a wait. Even on Arius.

Especially on Arius.

"'You look better," Chasm said.

Garry spooned up something that looked like hot grain cereal, but had a distinctly fruity taste and consistency. "Thanks."

"How are you feeling?"

They sat alone at a huge ironwood table; Chasm at one end watched Garry eat breakfast at the other. The spoon paused between the bowl and Garry's mouth. He seemed to consider the question carefully. "Okay. A little tired. Not as weak as I was."

Chasm's voice soared into a high, cheerful register. "The latest medical reports say there is no permanent damage. There won't even be a scar."

Garry swallowed. "Good."

"A young man like you, it would be an awful thing to be disfigured. The young women."

Garry carefully placed his spoon by his bowl. He dabbed at his lips with a white linen napkin. "Cut the shit, Chasm."

"What?"

"You're treating me like a kid. Think about it. Then quit doing it."

Chasm tilted his head. His eyes ran through a tentative series of blue: turquoise, indigo, lapis, azure, aquamarine.

"Garry. You are seventeen. Legally you are still a child on most planets. On your own planet."

"What is that, Chasm? Is it H'hogoth? But my father is dead. Old Terra? I don't know anybody there. Maybe it's here now. Maybe Arius. Am I a kid on Arius, Chasm? I died here, after all. You could say I just got born again. Would that make me a kid?"

The sarcasm was so savage Chasm had to look away from the steady green eyes. Those eyes frightened him a bit. They were too old, too knowing for the young features. They were the eyes of a secret. But what secret did Garry hold?

That was the question.

"Yes," he said at last.

"Yes, what?" Garry replied.

"Arius is your planet now. If you wish it. I am a wealthy man. I feel responsible, although I'm not. But I feel it. So this is your planet. This house is your home. If you so desire."

For a moment Garry's face, so much like a stone, softened. He blinked. "That's . . . that's very kind of you, Chasm. Very . . . thoughtful." He shook his head. His voice turned cold. "But it's a lie, of course. Not your words. Not what you say. But what they mean, that's a lie, isn't it?"

Chasm stared at the boy. This was awful. The cynicism, the chill blank knowingness that suffused every word nauseated him. He felt sick at his stomach but he let none of that show. He couldn't. Because Garry spoke only the truth and they both knew it.

"Your home . . ." Chasm tried again.

"Never mind. I accept."

"You do?"

Garry stood up. His face was pale and tight. "Yes. I have to stay somewhere, don't I?" He turned and started slowly for the door, then paused. Without turning his body, he turned his head and stared at Chasm. "And you *are* responsible."

Chasm didn't move for a long time after Garry left the

room. When he finally did move, he placed his right
hand over his left, to still the shaking.

The woman did not knock when she came into Garry's
rooms. He looked up into eyes as green as his own, but
shadowed and cracked, like flawed emeralds.

"Who are you?"

It had been another week. He had wandered the halls
and galleries of Chasm's great house in the mountain and
seen wonders that left him cold. Eventually even Chasm
had begun to avoid him. He didn't care. What he had to
do would turn upon events yet to happen. He would be
thrust forward by events. As he had been through all of
this.

"Glory. You can call me Glory." She had a chopped
rag of dark hair on top of a fine-boned face. She moved
like a dancer, all knife blades and icy certainty. He
realized that she dominated the room, and he didn't care.
If she was an event, she would make herself known.

"Why should I call you anything?"

She wore a skintight black top and black leather pants.
Her fingers were long and white. They were the only
calm thing about her. She prowled to a chair across from
where he sat and leaned against its carved wooden arm.
"Frankly, Garry, I don't give a damn," she said.

The corners of his mouth twitched. "You like old
movies?"

"I am an old movie, bud. How about you?"

Suddenly he realized he could like her. It wasn't a
sexual thing—although those leather pants caused a stirring he thought he'd forgotten—but her air. She carried
her own ambience and infused the room with it. Something about her reminded him faintly of Frego. A certain
deadly competence.

And no bullshit. Absolutely no bullshit at all.

He hitched himself up on the sofa. "Is there any reason at all I should trust you?"

Her green eyes flickered. She raised one pale hand and
stared at it. Blood-red nails. "I don't recall," she said,
"asking for your trust."

He grinned suddenly. "Good. We'll get along."

She lowered her hand. "I didn't ask about that, either."

"What are you to Chasm?" he asked later.

She smoked incessantly, lighting one cigarette off the smoldering butt of the last. It was not a habit he appreciated, but he suspected his preferences were of little concern to her. Now she ground out one cigarette on the rim of a priceless vase and fired up another. She exhaled a long blue cloud of smoke.

"What do you think?"

"I don't know. Lover. Friend. Employee, perhaps?"

Her laugh was a surprise. It was low and hoarse, throaty. Immensely sexy. He felt the stirring again and remembered a girl on Petersburg. He shifted and crossed his legs.

"Some of those," she said. "Does it matter?"

He realized he was enjoying this. Enjoying her. It had been a long time since he'd felt loose and open. Since the thrust and parry of a simple conversation had given him any joy. There were depths to her, but he had no desire to probe them. The shallow surface was enough.

He shrugged. "It depends."

"On what?"

"What you want, and whether you want it from me."

She smiled. Her lips were wide and thin and lazy, and her smile was the most enchanting thing he'd ever seen. "If I want it, Garry," she said at last, "I'll take it."

"Just like that?"

"Yeah," she said. "Just like that."

They went to lunch together. Chasm was absent. They sat in the huge dining room. Normally Chasm sat at one end of the table and Garry at the other, so far apart they almost had to shout. But when the housebot seated them so, she laughed again and walked around the table and sat down next to Garry. "Over here, tin man," she said. "Haul the plates over here."

"Chasm," she said later, "can be a pompous ass."

They ate odd things and chatted about not much. Garry enjoyed the meal. Even the strange food tasted good.

"Why am I responding to you this way?" Garry asked.

"Because I'm the first person to treat you like a Human since you managed to get your throat sliced. Chasm caters to you because he doesn't know any better."

"And you do?"

"Sure."

A beat of anger throbbed in his forehead. "Did you ever get *your* throat sliced?"

She reached up and tugged down the neck of her shirt. He stared at the dull red line that ran from her right ear straight down to her knobby Adam's apple.

"You could get that fixed," he said finally.

"I like my memories straight," she replied.

Late that afternoon they stood on a high balcony carved out of a cliff on a part of the mountain he'd never seen before. The cliff dropped a thousand feet straight down to a pool the color of cornflowers. Sunlight slanted golden from behind the mountain and turned the lichen-covered rocks around the pool to brass. A brisk wind slapped their cheeks and reddened their noses.

"You get winter here," he said.

"Yeah. There's a strong axial tilt. Some say Arius reminds them of Old Terra."

He tilted his head back and felt stiff muscles pop in his neck. "How about you? What does Arius remind you of?"

"Home," she said slowly. "Arius reminds me of home."

He was astonished at the hook her words sank into him. Suddenly he recalled H'hogoth. The dark ancient humped mounds of Great Goth, the towers of the Confederate Enclave, the never-ending rude pageantry of Reef City. Home.

"What do you want?" he said.

She stared at him. "I want to help you."

It broke then, and he shook his head. "Go away."

"Why? Something I said?"

His voice had thickened. He didn't understand why he felt so sad. "Maybe you want me to trust you. You want to help me and I should trust you. Isn't that the second line of the lyric?"

"Testy, aren't we? You a bit young to be so cynical?"

He didn't reply.

"No," she said finally. "Not too young, I guess. So that's one good thing."

He didn't want to, but he spoke. To hear the words, to keep it from ending. "What's a good thing?"

"That you aren't an innocent. A naïf. It would make it so much harder."

"To help me?" His words were bitter.

faces, the connections. The central computers are elsewhere. I can't take you there."

"I know. But I want to see the room. I want to understand."

She lit another in her interminable chain of cigarettes and tossed her head. The shaggy black mop above her green eyes moved and settled in a different mop. "Understand?"

"Yes," he said. Explanations were a kind of trust. He wasn't ready for that yet.

She took him to the mouth of a tunnel where a small cartlike vehicle waited. The tunnel pierced directly into the heart of Chasm's mountain. She drove with abandon, laughing. The wind whipped their hair into their eyes and Garry forgot the darkness that waited inside him, and for a moment felt warm.

The interface room was small. There was a single thronelike chair covered with soft red leather. Monitors lined the walls like blank eyes. Interface connectors dangled from outlets beneath the monitors and from the top of the chair. There were two touchpads, although the installation could be voice-activated as well.

"Go ahead," she said. "Sit in the chair."

He did, and felt the buttery leather melt around his body. He was conscious of the vast weight of rock that surrounded him. He liked the feeling. It made him feel safe.

"You don't have a socket," she said.

"No." He'd never needed one. The carbon interface cyber socket was for professional programmers, those who needed a direct interface with the heart of their machines. He'd always made do with voice. Hal understood him quite well. He'd only used touchpads for information that required more technical entry.

"Do you have one?"

She brushed a chunk of hair away from her right ear. He saw the bright metal ring around the black center of the socket. "Sure."

"You a real programmer?"

"I have been."

"Tell me again, what you do for Chasm?"

"I didn't say I did anything."

He stared at her. It was true. She had admitted nothing to him and he knew nothing about her. Except that she was with him in all his waking moments. He suspected she even kept watch by his bed, while he slept.

Anything was possible.

"Do I need a socket? Can't I interface some other way?"

Her eyes went blank. He wondered what she thought about. Then she said, "Sure. You can use a ring. It won't be as efficient, but you can get by."

A ring. A cyberneural induction circle that fit like a crown on his head. It was an old and fuzzy way of doing things, but she was right. It would work.

"Okay," he said.

She went to the back of the chair and opened a small metal door and took out the ring. She placed it on his head.

"I crown you . . ." she said, and grinned.

"Kneel," he replied, "and receive my blessing."

"Kings don't bless," she said.

"Haven't you ever heard of divine right?"

A darkness passed across her features. "Don't talk like that."

"Why?"

"Just . . . don't."

He filed it away. Another strange thing. Another secret.

He savored the room. In a moment he would activate the ring and enter the world of information, where machine symbols and pictures danced a wild pavane with pictures and symbols from his own mind. But he liked this place and wanted to impress it on his memory.

The air was cool. It moved slowly, pushed by hidden fans. It was filtered and tasteless. The machines made no sound. He could hear her breathing in the silence. The monitors were gray and empty, and the interface plugs dangled from their shining cables like the tentacles of wondrous jellyfish. High-tech men of war.

The ring around his skull was a primitive miracle. He had thought about it once when he was younger. Thought about the mysteries of the mind. Centures before, educated men had scoffed at the idea of the psi sciences, at the possibility that man could manipulate his environment with the power of mind. Yet that process was with them then, and had always been with them. For what was existence itself but the triumph of mind over matter?

Of process.

Thought formed and directed. Across the evanescent bridge from thought to form something jumped. Something unknown broke the barrier and caused electrical pulses to move. Caused pulses to create chemicals between the synaptic junctions. Caused energies to quicken the nerves and squeeze the muscles.

Every time a hand touched a flower it was a miracle.

The mind moved mountains, and nobody knew how it did.

Miracles, he thought again. He smiled and activated the ring. The last thing he saw was Glory watching him.

He didn't know what to call the expression on her face.

It happened instantly. One moment he was watching her eyes and the light through them like shattered gems, and the next his world was blue. The vision had nothing to do with his eyes. The induction ring was a bridge between the electrochemical fields of his own brain and the vastly larger, faster processes of Chazm's mainframe computer. He had become a terminal, a remote entry point for the computer.

Dimly he understood this was wrong. He'd had enough classes to know that for a hundred years the progress of information technology had been a geometric curve. At its peak, the rate of increase had been almost straight up. Then, for unclear reasons, the rate of advance reached a plateau. Now, for over two centuries, machines had gotten smaller, faster, more complicated. But the heart of the machine mind was still a chip, still a bit of sand.

Vague references were made to other machines, bioelectronic giants of unimaginable power. But something had happened, something lost in the misty surrenders of the Matrix Wars. Perhaps it was only rumors. Only the kind of legends man always invents to justify his own history.

The blue field hardened. He felt a sucking sensation, as if the azure nothingness demanded completion. Cybernetic *tabula rasa*.

He thought the thought.

Hyarl Thomas.

The machine leaped to his bidding.

The eyes held him. They were the deep clear blue of ice under pressure, the kind of ice buried beneath a million-year glacier. He stared at the face conjured by the computer and wondered how the holo had been obtained. His vantage point was only a few meters away from Thomas's face, which gazed back at him with a disconcerting sense of aliveness. As if Thomas had been captured by the machine whole and only now released, a demon to the inadvertent summoning.

But he felt no fear.

He looked into the windows of those eyes and wondered what darkness waited behind them, and he felt no fear. Only an anticipation, a certainty. Thomas had killed him and murdered fear as well. Now he could face him.

Now he had to face him.

The computer responded to his silent command—a spark, a current, a bouquet of neurochemicals—and panned back. Once again he saw the full man with the bent nose and wide smile. His high forehead was unlined and pale, but he saw fine wrinkles at the corners of his eyes. The short blond hair was like silky fur. His body was well formed and strong looking. The holo was of a naked man. Thomas's sex organs were very large.

Garry flicked forward. He knew what the man looked like. It was the first time he'd seen him not in the act of murder.

But he would remember.

Now a dark and cloudy scene appeared. It was a spaceport somewhere. The picture was crude, as if captured by a low-grade security system. Passengers were disembarking from a wide tunnel. The view was from inside the port, facing the tunnel. There were no windows. The place had a musty, almost fortified feeling.

A robot scuttled by. Pieces of luggage were balanced on its wide back. Travelers passed unseeing beneath the camera, their faces tired and intent, as they hurried elsewhere. Then Thomas glided out of the mouth of the tunnel, his slow, graceful shuffle unmistakable. His hair was different, darker and longer. Perhaps it was the poor quality of the camera or the bad lighting, but his eyes seemed darker, more opaque. He walked quickly beneath the camera and disappeared. The video ended.

When Garry requested data, block letters appeared over the frozen scene. "FIRST SIGHTING. CHICAGO NEW O'HARE GROUNDPORT. 2057."

As his vision faded to blue, Garry felt the rush of his own blood. The scene was over two centuries old. Thomas looked no different today than he did on Old Terra two hundred years before.

How old was he?

What was he?

And how did Chasm's computer know about it?

Now the screen of his mind devolved to an endless melange of images. Thomas in drab rooms. In gilt palaces. Under skies wet with rain, in winds that tugged and tore at his clothes. With people whose faces were empty. And faces full of terror. Stars overhead in patterns strange and wonderful. There were lizards and machines and incomprehensible movements.

He realized suddenly that Thomas had a vast and ancient history, and what he watched was only part of it. Instead of having too little information, he had too much. Thomas was obscured by his very obviousness. He was everywhere, had done everything.

No wonder everybody seemed to know him.

But the earliest sighting was two hundred years old. Why not earlier? Or later?

He withdrew from the flood of data. The pictures, the words overwhelmed him. Each picture was a question.

He had to find the answers.

Everything depended on it.

Everything.

He lifted the induction ring from his head with his own hands and let it fall. It took a moment for the blue haze to clear from his vision.

"Well?" Glory said. She leaned against a clear space on the wall, hipshot, her hands clasped behind her back. Her eyes were glittery and serene.

He blinked. "Did you know him too? Everybody else does."

"Thomas?"

He nodded.

"I've met him. I don't like him."

He thought it interesting. She was the first one to offer a personal opinion. But she hadn't answered the question. "Do you know him?" he said again.

"No. I don't think anybody does. He isn't the kind you get to know."

"How long?"

She thought about it. "Years ago. Many years."

"He looks the same. He's at least two hundred years old but he looks the same. That isn't possible."

"There are treatments, techniques."

"No. None that good. What is he, Glory?"

"I don't know."

"Does anybody?"

She didn't reply.

"What are you, Glory?"

She didn't answer that either.

He tried once again in his rooms. She had swept back a wide wall of burgundy curtains that shimmered like silk in the fading dusky light. The great windows looked out from the side of the mountain across lesser hills to a cobalt shimmer of horizon. A few early stars picked their way out of the sky like tiny signal lights.

"Glory, we have to get this straightened out."

"Fine by me. Shoot." Her face was in repose and for once no cigarette dangled from her wide lips.

He had to pick his way carefully now. Choose exactly the right words and say them exactly the right way. "I have tried to figure out the heart of the matter," he said at last.

She had been half leaning, half sitting on the over-stuffed arm of a huge chair. Now she shifted all the way down. She fumbled for a moment and came up with a cigarette. She lit it.

"What have you figured out?"

He took a small breath. His forehead felt damp and cool. "Hyarl Thomas is not the center. He is only part of it."

Her eyes flickered slightly. "And?"

"I put together the chronology. First a guy appears in our pawnshop with a mysterious cube. An artifact. Then Thomas steals it back. He has friends, all kinds, all species. My father is killed and Frego tells me Thomas did it. I find out my father works for a mysterious group called The Search. For Old Terra. And that group indicates Thomas has gone to Petersburg. We follow. A girl is . . . killed. Her message directs us here. We come here, meet Chasm—yet another member of The Search— and go to a deserted hole in the ground. Thomas ambushes us, kidnaps or kills Frego, almost kills me. And disappears. Then I search Chasm's computers and find a huge history file on Thomas. And you know him. And so does Chasm."

She exhaled a swirling cloud of silver smoke. "From which you deduce . . . what?"

"Only part of the heart is Thomas. The rest is me."

"You take a lot on yourself. You saw the files on him. Thomas is an old and powerful man. A kind of force. Why should he concern himself with a seventeen-year-old boy?"

For the first time he began to think he might pull it off. "I don't know. But I don't believe in coincidence. He could have killed me in the pawnshop. Or on Petersburg. Or here. Why did Chasm arrive so precisely at the right time? Why did Thomas use a knife instead of something more certain?"

She shrugged. "Because you are mistaken. The artifact is the center. Thomas stole it and killed your father to conceal himself. Frego followed because he is part of The Search and it was his job to follow. He took you because you insisted. And for the rest, you were simply along for the ride. But Thomas is gone, the artifact is gone, and Frego is gone. The ride is over. You're safe, simply because you aren't involved anymore."

"But I am."

She lit another cigarette and stubbed out the first. "How?"

"I'm the only one left. I'm the last Searcher."

She laughed so hard she coughed. "Oh, but no, Garry. Not at all. Here on Arius. Me. Chasm. Here is the heart of the Search. Right here. And always has been."

He closed his eyes. "Then who is Thomas, and why does he want the cube?"

She hummed. It was a low, rough sound, the human equivalent of purring. Her eyes were half-open, barely revealing half-moons of dark green beneath. She regarded him for a long time and she hummed.

"Very good," she said at last.

He felt a trill run up his spine. He had done it. He hadn't been sure he could carry it off, but somehow he had. Perhaps it was his age. Seventeen. Adults removed children from their world, denied them their intellect. Children were . . . children and had no thoughts worthy of respect. He knew he was older, but knew as well the secret magic of youth. When the powers were full and bursting, eager to test the world, and yet a secret from the world. He had his secrets, yes, but some of them were simply the secrets of the young, and he was grateful.

She had put him in a niche, and that was where he wanted to be. Now she could be used. Now he could use her.

"Very good," she said again. "I didn't give you credit."

"For what?"

"For seeing the key. For beginning to understand Hyarl Thomas. And our problem with him."

He felt like purring himself. Our problem. Now it was our problem.

"It was obvious, if you looked at it right," he said. He paused. Had he overplayed things? "If he came here, there had to be a reason. If the reason wasn't me, then it had to be Arius. Finally, if he wasn't working for Arius, then who? It had to be The Search. If it was lizards, where better than High H'hogoth? And then you told me Arius is The Search. That canceled all possibilities. The question then was easy. Who does he work for?"

She smiled faintly and he kept his face still and solemn.

"Nobody," she said. "He works for himself."

"Oh. I didn't think of that."

Her smile widened and he made himself look chagrined. "You can't think of everything, Garry. No matter how smart you are."

Not everything, he thought. But some things. "I suppose," he said.

The sounds of the room ghosted around them, the sighing of the air conditioners, the filters, the distant electronic whine of the guts of the mountain surrounding them like a glittering skin.

The air wavered over a single candle burning on an elegant little table next to the door. The flame wavered slightly. He glanced at the window and saw a purple-black bowl of stars.

"Are you hungry?" he said.

"Could eat a cow." She grinned.

He grinned back. "How about pizza instead?"

That night he lay in a bed that dwarfed him and felt the watery slickness of silk sheets on his skin. He had opened the drapes on the far window so he could see the night. It was late; electricity thrummed in his body and he couldn't sleep.

He thought about Glory. Their relationship had settled as a ship does at anchor, without questions. At least she asked no questions and that was all he wanted. Without questions there was no need for answers, for trust. He was free of responsibility, except for the terrible responsibility of his own past.

He had asked the question and she had not answered; rather, she had given a different answer, and that had trapped her. She had revealed herself in the way she tried to manipulate him.

He felt no guilt at what he would do.

Outside his window alien stars twinkled in patterns new in human history. So many stars, so many planets. And all the races undiscovered.

Perhaps the Kurs'ggtha had sailed those stars above the universe, and left the wormholes to darker things.

Hyarl Thomas had come here and that was still the key. He thought he knew the lock.

He put his hands behind his head and settled into his pillows. The stars went soft and blurry as sleep fogged his eyes. He felt an unaccustomed sensation: warmth.

His eyes closed. He savored his own secret.

Tomorrow it would begin.

The beginning of the end.

Chapter Fifteen

It was a glorious morning. From the mouth of the small canyon the stream roared softly, swollen by melting snows far above. Garry stood at the edge of the stream and shielded his eyes against the sun. The breeze, thick with pine and new grass, rubbed against his face like a cat. He was thinner than he had been, and his face was pinched and pale, but his green eyes were bright and clear. He looked like he'd survived a long illness and was now on the mend.

Glory stood next to him, her vibrant power making him seem even smaller and frailer than he was. With her shiny black hair, her quick, strong gestures, and her red leather combat suit, she was a series of sudden exclamation points against the soft, slow morning.

Farther down, the wreckage of the elevator building was a scatter of soft black charcoal and melted rusting steel.

"We started from about here," Garry said.

She nodded. She ran her calm white fingers through her chopped black hair. "I saw the videos," she said. "Everything. The ones your mechs made, and the ones Chasm made. It was a stupid attack. Straight into it, my God!"

Garry shrugged. "We had no choice. Anyway, what are you, a military expert?"

"I had a good teacher," she told him. She smiled. "You should have laid back, waited. Watched until you were sure. Your way was suicidal."

"It was Frego's way. But I told you we had no choice. Your spy satellites had picked up nothing but the one sighting. Our instruments showed nothing. We had to go in. It was the only way to find out."

"It was a trap."

"Yes," he said.

They began to follow the stream down to the scorched ruin on the meadow. He swiveled his head back and forth and tried to see everything. Perhaps some detail would stand out. Perhaps things would become clear in the crystal morning light.

"Why are you here? What are you looking for?"

"I don't know," he said.

"Stupid." Her voice was hoarse and rough. She lit a cigarette as she walked.

"I'll know when I find it."

"If you find it."

He nodded, but he didn't say anything.

They stepped around small boulders tossed aside by the force of the stream. The water smoked and bubbled right to the edge of its banks. He imagined it overflowing in spring flood, scouring out the meadow in a sudden rush. If he squinted, he could almost see traces of past floods on the patterns of grass below. Yes. The high-water mark was within a hundred feet or so of the wrecked building.

The colonists must not have known, he thought. If this was their first encampment, it was a hasty one. An anomaly struck him. "Where is the ship?" he said.

"What?"

"The ship. If they landed here first, there must have been a ship. Those first colony ships weren't very big. Most of the colony was gene plasm and equipment. Just a few crew members to set things up and get them going. The ships were designed to land. On most worlds they are monuments now. First contact, first landing, that sort of stuff."

She blinked. "I don't know. I never thought about it." She looked at the meadow. "Maybe they took it apart."

"No." He was patient. "The ships were incubators. Places to live and work while they grew the colony. By the time the ship wasn't necessary any longer, there would be no reason to move it. No way, in fact. The power drives would have been the first reactors for the colonists. But they had to be removed. Later on the ship wouldn't be necessary. It should be here. It's only been a couple of centuries. There ought to be something."

"Is this important?"

"Why did Hyarl Thomas come here?"

She thought about it. "To make a trap."

He thought about icebergs. "For who?" he said. "Who did he want to trap here?"

"I don't know."

"Glory."

"What?"

"What was here first? What came on that first ship? Was it him? Was Hyarl Thomas your first colonist?"

They had been coming from upwind. Now the breeze shifted and they smelled the sour stench of the ruins. Burned, wet wood and soggy insulation and scorched metal. The smell of new rust, bitter and metallic. He felt a sudden exhilaration, as if a page had been turned in a story and now the plot would take off after long words of introduction.

"I was dead, you see," he said.

She glanced at him.

"But I came back."

"Yes."

"There is a reason."

She threw her burning cigarette away. It hit a greasy puddle and sizzled out. "There doesn't have to be a reason."

"There was a reason," he repeated. He climbed over the remains of a shattered wall and crunched toward the elevator.

No fear. Only a certain kind of raw joy.

The elevator creaked down with the wail of dying metal. They jerked to a ragged halt on the third level. They stepped out into the dusty darkness of a vast room and aimed the bright lamps they carried.

"Over here, I think," Garry said. He was trying to remember the layout and where the stairwell entrance should be. Great blocky shapes barred their way.

"What is this stuff?" Garry said.

"Machines. This was the first colony. You said yourself they had to build. To grow."

"But down?" he said softly. "This was a virgin world. Why did they have to hide? To bury themselves."

She didn't answer.

After a while they found the first mech. It had penetrated several yards from the main battle before something had sawed it into junk. One mechanical arm lay alone, circuits naked and exposed, the snout of a heavy machine gun protruding from the end.

He kicked at the arm. It made a sharp clanking sound, hollow in the dusty stillness. He remembered the beams blazing out of the dark, remembered Frego's voice warning him back. They had never seen their attackers. They had fought blind, in the dark, alone. They had lost.

He felt strangely calm, as if this was all ancient history. But it wasn't. Frego was gone but he might still be alive. Probably was, if his injuries weren't too great. They wouldn't have taken him if he were dead.

He savored the feeling of stillness, of somehow being centered. It was a puzzle. Frego said it wasn't a game and it wasn't. People had died. Been brutally murdered. The blood was real.

But it was still a game. There were players who moved pawns, who worked traps and captured other pieces on the board. He had too much information and none of it connected. It was a game and it had rules, even if he didn't understand them.

It was real to the victims who bled and died, but it was a game to those who moved them. He had been a victim. Now it was time to learn the rules and become a player. If he could.

But what was the prize? If he could only figure that out, the rest would become simple.

Nine-tenths hidden, buried. Nine parts secret.

Perhaps that was the key.

Perhaps the game itself was a lie.

In the harsh surgical glare of their lamps, the door to the stairwell gaped open like a broken tooth. He remembered closing that door.

The rest of the mechs were here, shattered. There were deep gouges burned into the concrete floors and thick black smoke patterns on the walls. It was very silent.

"They hit us here, as soon as we came out. They'd been waiting all along, above us."

Glory stared at the destruction. In the light reflected from the walls her face was set and cold. She nodded. "A trap all the way," she said. "You walked right into it. Stupid."

"What choice did we have? They were above us. We had to get out."

She made a soft, clicking sound of disgust. "You should never have come in."

He turned away and walked to the door. The lower part of the last mech, the one he'd left to guard Frego, partially blocked the opening. The mech had followed its instructions and died fighting. He felt a wave of sadness. It was only a mech, but it had died well.

He bent over and pushed at the tangle of steel. It moved suddenly, with the screech of metal on stone, and shivers crawled up his spine.

The stairwell itself seemed smaller than he remembered it. Then he understood how the dark had made it seem larger. Now it was only a scarred concrete landing between the depths and the surface. He flashed his lamp down and saw flaky black patches. Frego's blood. He remembered laying Frego beside the wall, remembered his ruined face.

Had he lived after all?

But if he had died, why had they taken him? Not to cover anything up. They'd left the mechs. The trap had not been concealed.

And Hyarl Thomas had killed him. He stared down at Frego's blood and understood. Hyarl Thomas had thought him dead. Only Frego remained from the beginning, from the pawnshop and Garth and the artifact.

Glory shouldered past him into the stairwell and shone her light up the stairs. She grimaced. "What a mess."

"Maybe the trap was for Frego," Garry said slowly.

"What?"

"But why? What did Hyarl Thomas want from him? Who was Frego, Glory?" And he realized he didn't know Frego at all, either. He knew nobody, in the end.

"Frego was a Searcher," she said.

"Yes." He paused. "He was more than that, I think." Everybody was a mystery. Nobody was what they seemed. "But what was he?"

She stared at the bloody patches and made no reply.

"Hyarl Thomas knows," he said into the silence.

"Well, have you two been getting along?" Chasm was playing the organ of his voice like a demented virtuoso, halftones and grace notes dripping from his words like syrup.

It was the first time the odd little man had joined them for dinner in almost a week. Garry wondered what had kept him so busy. He had come to accept his own paranoia as a normal, even healthy thing. It wasn't hard to imagine everything in Chasm's household being centered on him.

"I don't know." He glanced at Glory, who winked. "Have we, Glory?"

"Like bosom buddies. Like brother and sister." She winked again and Garry felt his cheeks go warm. He remembered the stirrings in his crotch when he'd first seen her in her leathers. Maybe I am recovering, he thought. I used to have a hard-on all the time. She smiled a wide, crooked smile and Garry placed his knees together under the table. "That right, Garry?"

"Yeah. Brother and sister." He thought about that and blushed hotter.

"Good, good." Chasm nibbled at a crusty piece of something golden and pepper-flavored. His eyes flicked from one color to the next like a slide show. "I want you to be friends. I want us all to be friends." His eyes turned a clear, guileless blue.

"Oh sure. We're all friends here. You and me and Glory, just pals."

"Garry." Chasm squeezed a thick dollop of hurt out of his words, like a washerwoman twisting a rag. "Surely you understand I'm your friend."

Garry put his fork down. "Oh Chasm. Tell me where you got that video of Hyarl Thomas. Tell me about that again."

"ELINT. Electronics intelligence. Satellite surveillance."

"No. You're lying to me, my friend. Unless you expect me to believe Hyarl Thomas penetrated your most sacred place, your first contact, and then wandered out to wave at a passing spysat. You said you didn't even know whether he was downplanet. Wasn't it convenient for him to do that? Just after we landed, of course." Garry paused. The smell of gray meat in thick brown gravy on his plate made him feel sick. "Perhaps it was coincidence. You believe in coincidence, Chasm?"

Chasm slid a long look in Glory's direction. She ignored him.

"You should learn to trust people, Garry," he said at last.

"Sure. It's only gotten me killed once, so far."

Chasm winced. "You shouldn't have gone there."

"Then why didn't you stop me?"

"How could I?"

"You could have told the truth, you son of a bitch."

Glory looked up, her green eyes bright and alert. She seemed to be enjoying this. Chasm's eyes cycled to black. A danger signal, Garry thought.

"Garry, you sit at my table and eat my food and insult me." His voice was cold and flat.

"Yes. All of that, computer man. But none of it my doing. I've been a pawn. Pushed here and pulled there. By what, Chasm? By who? Do you know? I think you do."

"I don't know anything."

Garry rubbed his forehead hard. It seemed warm in the room. He felt sweat slick on his skin. "How did Hyarl Thomas get downplanet without somebody knowing? If your ELINT systems are good enough to catch his one short step outside that warren, they had to see his ship."

"Coincidence. Luck."

"Do you believe that?"

"It doesn't matter what I believe, Garry. It happened."

"Who does Thomas work for?"

"Glory told you. He works for himself. Free-lance."

"But he has worked for you before. That's right, isn't it? How did you get all that data in his file, Chasm? How long have you watched him? How long has he watched you?"

Chasm's black features dissolved into a welter of jittering red lines. He looked at his plate. "That is none of your business, Garry."

Garry pushed his chair back. "Of course not," he said. "And on that note, I think I'll be leaving."

"You should finish your meal, Garry. The chef—"

"I don't think you understand. I meant leaving this planet. Leaving Arius and Hyarl Thomas and you and whatever dirty game it is you're all playing. I'm done. I'm going home."

Glory spoke for the first time. "Home, Garry? Where is that?"

He felt unutterably tired. "I don't know. But it isn't here." He sighed. "H'hogoth, maybe." He thought of Hal, his AI, and wondered if the computer program still existed. "I'll try there first, at least."

He stood up. They watched him silently. "It's over," he said finally.

"I'm afraid not, Garry," Chasm said.

"Then I'm a prisoner," Garry said. He and Glory had returned to his rooms. His thin face was cold and withdrawn. "Should I just plan on staying here for the rest of my life?"

"Don't be an idiot," she said.

"Did you know about this?"

She shrugged.

He moved jerkily from one piece of ornate furniture to the next, touching a polished tabletop, letting his fingers rest on a bit of nubby upholstery. "Why am I here?"

"Chasm has some projections," she said.

"Oh? What is he projecting?"

"I can't tell you."

He paused. He drummed his fingertips on the shoulder of a huge cloisonné vase. "No, of course not. Nobody can tell me anything. Not my father, not Frego, not anybody. Maybe Hyarl Thomas is the only honest one. He only wants to kill me."

She had settled in a vast, overstuffed leather chair. Now she lit a cigarette and flicked ashes on a priceless Oriental carpet. A tiny housebot scurried over like a silver rat and snuffled at the embers. "Hyarl Thomas? You believe that? Then why aren't you dead?"

He stared at her. "But I was."

She exhaled and watched the smoke eddy. "Really?" Her rough voice went flat. "Then tell me. You saw the wreckage of your mechs. There were lasers. Heavy weapons. Even a fucking plasma beam. But good old Hyarl Thomas takes you out with a pocketknife. Does anything seem strange about that?"

"A knife kills. Death is death."

She snorted softly. "Not in this day and age, Garry. You told me you remembered the darkness coming down. It wasn't darkness. It was Chasm in a great big attack chopper with full emergency medical facilities. If you saw it coming in, you think Thomas didn't? There were any number of ways he could have snuffed you. Permanent ways, things the chopper couldn't begin to cope with. So what does he do? A nice clean surgical throat slashing. And then he's gone."

He listened to the scorn in her voice. She was right. It was one thing he hadn't considered. "Then what?" he said finally.

She flipped her cigarette butt out over the carpet and watched the housebot catch it neatly. "I don't know. Neither does Chasm. And that's why."

He thought about it. "I'm a prisoner for my own good, is that it?"

"Something like that."

He shook his head. "No, more than that. I don't buy into Chasm's altruism. I don't think that little man does things out of the goodness of his heart. If Thomas doesn't want to kill me, what does he want? And what was that charade at the building in the mountains about?"

"What do you think?"

It came to him then. The overwhelming fact of his own murder had clouded his memory of the incident. But now he picked his way through it, moment by moment. "There's only one thing that makes sense," he said at last.

"Go on."

"Thomas was proving a point. That he could kill me whenever he wants to. Despite whatever protection Chasm could offer. Is that it?"

She lit another cigarette.

"He was letting you know. I was his hostage, his pawn. Just as much as yours."

She listened to the slow, dead movement of his voice and was shaken. So young. And so old. "It's a possibility."

"And isn't it strange," he said. "After this you appear. What are you, Glory? My bodyguard?"

And now she grinned. "But of course, little buddy. What did you think I was? Your mother?"

"What do you mean, we wait?"

Chasm's interface room was as bright and antiseptic looking as ever. Chasm sat in his leather chair and regarded them with yellow-brown eyes. Cat eyes. His neon tattoos glittered and danced in red and gold patterns. "Garry." The little man sounded tired. "You seem to understand. Thomas wants something, but I don't know what. Your death was a message. Glory is my reply. If she can't protect you, then you cannot be protected. Now it's his move."

"This is great," Garry said. "I feel great. Where am I on your game board now? Do I get sacrificed if you want to take a more important piece?"

Chasm swiveled the chair away. "He will make a move. He has to."

"What are you playing for, Chasm? What is the game?"

Chasm ignored him. After a time he repeated, "He'll make a move."

"After me, you mean."

"I don't think so. He could have killed you before. But he didn't."

"So you bring in a high-powered bodyguard. Isn't that just an invitation? Have another try, my man? Take your best shot?"

"Garry, I'm not a monster."

"No. You're a good man with my best interests at heart. I understand."

"Garry. This has to be resolved. It can't be left hanging. Surely you can see? Eventually Thomas will kill you, if only to tidy up loose ends. The first time was a message. The next time might be a different, more permanent message. But it can end here, if we force him out. If he makes a move and it's the wrong one."

"Bait for the trap," Garry said. "I like that."

"What other bait do we have?" Chasm said.

Garry sat down on the floor and leaned his back against the wall. Bits and pieces and fragments. It was all he had. A huge amount of information, but none of it made sense. Yet he was certain he knew the answers. He had been given enough data, if he could only arrange it correctly.

He stared at the smooth leather back of Chasm's chair, at the small panel that housed the induction ring. A little time. He would certainly have enough of that.

He wished suddenly that he had Hal. He was certain his old friend could help him. But he was alone here, perched in the center of a trap he didn't understand.

Slowly Chasm's chair turned. The corona of fine, hair-like cables from his socket shimmered like silk threads. His face had gone perfectly black and his eyes were as transparent as water. Garry saw tiny red veins embedded there, and shivered.

"What?" he said.

"Thomas has made his move," Chasm said.

Garry's shoulders twitched without warning. "What . . . has he done?"

Glory entered the room silently and walked over to Garry. She didn't say anything. For all Chasm's reaction, she might not have been there at all.

"Coming into the system. Now. A lizard fleet. High H'hogoth has entered the game at last."

Chapter Sixteen

The tunnels were more extensive than he had dreamed. The entire crust of the planet was riddled with them. As the bullet car flowed like a bead of mercury through the dimly lit path carved in deep rock, Garry closed his eyes and stared at the inside of his skull.

Glory sat beside him. She smoked incessantly, chaining lights one from the last, and ignored him. Chasm sat in front, wrapped in the silence of his own thoughts.

"This world is like a fortress," Garry said at last.

Chasm's eyes changed color. It was his equivalent of a blink. "What?"

"I've been trying to figure out why everything centers here. Events conspired—were arranged—to bring me to Arius. Thomas came here. Frego wasn't surprised to find us headed this way. And now an entire H'hogothan war fleet shows up. On top of all that, Arius has at least one huge space terminal that seems deserted, and the planet itself is full of empty rooms. Everything about this world is mysterious. Why is that, Chasm?"

"All worlds are different. Arius is just a little more different than most."

"That's not an answer, Chasm. Tell me how Arius is different. Tell me why."

Chasm glanced at Glory. She lit a cigarette and blew smoke in his face. "Go on, Chasm. Tell him."

The little man squirmed uncomfortably in his padded seat. "Garry, I don't want say anything. Some of your questions have answers, but they aren't answers I want to give. Perhaps when we arrive . . ."

"Yes? Arrive where? Where are we going to hide from a fleet of angry lizards?"

A purple and gold crosshatch of fine neon appeared on

Chasm's black skin. He settled back into his seat. "A place where you can get answers, Garry. We have a little time yet. Time enough for that."

His voice was cool and distant. Garry laughed nervously. "You make it sound like heaven."

The big eyes slid through a prism of color. "As good a description as any," Chasm replied.

The car shot out of its tunnel onto the high flank of a huge mountain. Garry looked down and saw buildings like sugar cubes far below. And he had one of the oddest experiences of his young life.

The scene was still and perfect; the buildings shone in the morning sun like white jewels set on a bed of velvet green. He had seen them before. Hadn't he?

He couldn't remember.

He blinked and rubbed his cheek. Couldn't remember?

I remember everything, he thought.

But not this. Only the ghost of it, the *déjà vu*, the hint of familiarity but not its substance. "I feel dizzy," he muttered softly.

"What? Are you okay?" Glory stared at him through her perpetual cloud of blue smoke.

He shook his head. "Yeah. Just something . . . weird." But his mind was shivering. Something basic he hadn't even realized he trusted had been shaken. Could not remember.

What else couldn't he remember?

Not only could he not trust any other person, he couldn't even trust his own brain. The realization made him physically sick. His stomach churned. The morning blurred in and out of his vision.

Nothing could be trusted. Not even himself . . .

He licked his lips. His hands felt cold and shaky.

"Garry. What's the matter? You're pale as a fish belly."

"I'm . . . I'm okay. Just give me a minute. . . ."

He felt her fingers on his arm. He started to turn, to face her, and then an electric current jumped the gap between her flesh and his, and he felt a sudden warmth.

Real warmth, the kind he hadn't felt since Garth. It came over him in slow waves and soothed his fear. It was like a soft blanket on the inside of him. His eyes widened.

"What . . . ?"

Her green eyes stared into his, as if sharing some vast, unnameable secret. "Friendship," she said softly.

"Oh."

She took her hand away but the warmth remained awhile before slowly beginning to fade. The car descended the mountain toward the white buildings.

Garry had a sense of events rushing down the mountain with him. Converging at last on that bright spot of morning.

"What will happen?" he said at last.

She moved her shoulders. "Time will tell."

He felt a thrill of understanding. Yes. Even if he couldn't remember, time would tell. And it would tell him everything.

Strangely comforted by a sense of the ominously inevitable, Garry turned back to his window and watched their descent. The buildings were dotted haphazardly across the top of a long foothill that nuzzled up against the greater peak like a companionable dog.

The tracks on which they rode switchbacked down the side of the mountain, each turn revealing an even more spectacular view. Ranks of ice-capped stone giants marched into the blue distance.

Clouds lumbered overhead and caught the light from the ranges in an ever-changing symphony of brightness.

The tracks were an anomaly. Everything about the planet was hidden, protected, except this place and the huge spaceport where he and Frego had landed. But here the buildings were out in the open and this track was as exposed as a laid-open nerve. It was almost as if whatever resided here was fearless. In contrast to the secrecy of the rest of Arius, this place flaunted its existence. He savored the incongrutiy. Hiding from Hyarl Thomas beneath Chasm's granite shields but then, at the first sign of real attack—a lizard fleet—, scurrying for the safety of naked buildings on a mountaintop.

It only made sense in one way. This was a seat of power.

The tracks finally ended their drunkard's skip down the mountainside and shot straight as an arrow across a wide, long meadow. He saw clumps of brilliant wildflowers and stands of pine and what might have been oak. Then they fled silently into the shadows of vast buildings, and in those umbras he realized precisely how big this place was.

Their car slowed and stopped at last. He blinked. They rested beneath broad eaves of white stone that overhung a station platform capable of accommodating a hundred of their cars.

Chasm yawned. "Everybody out," he said. "We made it."

Their heels clicked on empty rock as they walked down the station platform. They walked almost a mile before they came to the end. Like everything else on Arius, this place was deserted and the sounds of their passage echoed vacantly. But there was a difference. Garry felt a power, almost a heat, and knew that here, at least, something resided. This place was functioning now, not waiting for long-departed residents. It was as if the people here were just around a corner or right up the street, and he kept turning to look behind himself. But the platform remained empty and they kept on walking.

"You people ever hear of transport systems?" Garry said. He was sweating mildly in the morning's sultry glow, and wondered just when he'd managed to get so out of shape. His old teacher, Shi-tzsu, would have been ashamed of him. He resolved to start his morning workouts again and then chuckled softly. Perhaps the lizards sweeping into the system would have an opinion about that.

An alabaster slab of marble rose clifflike in front of them, pierced by a great opening. Chasm didn't even slow, and Glory paused only to grind out a cigarette on the spotless floor and light another. Garry winced. It was somehow like profaning a place of worship. Then he decided that was what this place reminded him of. A temple, a place where a god might rest for a moment and hear the prayers of the faithful. He chuckled again. Mankind was predictable. All huge buildings made humans feel respectful. Kings and priests had known this since the first one piled up dirt and built an altar on top.

They crossed an arcade the size of a football field. Light blazed down from an arching dome of crystalline material. Garry looked up and tried to figure out what sort of architectural miracle had created that dome. It had to be a monomole of some kind, but the thought of the technology involved boggled his mind. In its way that dome was even more impressive than the building itself, for as far as he could tell, it was impossible.

"How did they build the dome?" he said.

Chasm paused. "Above?"

"Yes."

He shrugged. "I haven't the slightest idea. You can ask later," he said. His tone was vague and distracted.

"Ask who?"

"When we get there," Chasm said, and started walking again.

"You ever read *The Wizard of Oz*?" Garry asked Glory.

She laughed, and her husky croak made him feel good. "Oh yeah," she said. "Many times."

He nodded. He wondered what kind of mask the wizard who lived here had rigged for the suckers. Judging from all the prelude, it would be a wild one.

Smoke and mirrors, he thought. But the stone that hulked overhead was real, and if it fell, it would crush him. He stared at his feet as he walked. He didn't see the man who waited for them at the far side of the arcade until they had almost reached him. He wouldn't have understood the expression on the man's face either, any more than he comprehended his first words.

"It's about time," the man said. "And I mean that any way you care to take it."

Garry stared at the man, and this time the vertigo of not remembering slammed into him so powerfully he almost blacked out. He swayed slightly. Glory had him by the arm within an instant. He didn't even know it. All he could see was the man who stood there with a burglar's grin on his face, his gray eyes snapping with secret amusement so hallucinatory Garry wanted to laugh himself into hysteria, and know that he *knew* this man. Knew him and had absolutely no idea how or when.

Then he felt Glory's strong fingers bite into the meat of his arm and the man said, "Give it a rest, Garry. Just give it a rest."

He came back and it was just a man. He shook his head. "Okay," he said. "Let go. I'm fine."

Glory released him. "That's the palest fine I've ever seen, pal." But she moved away and lit yet another cigarette. Hundreds, Garry thought. She must smoke hundreds of cigarettes a day.

"Enough of this wonderful reunion," the man said. He had a big, hooked nose that gave his face a foxy look. His hair was cut short and was all of the colors that are usually called brown. "I've enjoyed it about as long as I can stand. Let's get out of this dump. Waste of space if you ask me." He glanced up at the crystal dome. "Ozzie likes skylights, though."

Glory laughed. "You old fraud," she said.

He grinned his absconder's grin again. "I learned from the best," he said.

Garry watched Chasm while the others snickered at each other. Chasm was absolutely still, with the kind of petrification that means utter respect or utter fear. Garry couldn't decide which it was in this case. There were no colors on Chasm's face, and his eyes were the same hue as his skin. A blend of coal and night. The phrase "black as treachery" scampered across Garry's mind.

"What's the matter?" Garry asked softly. He moved closer and touched Chasm's shoulder. The little man jerked like an electrified frog.

"What!"

"Let him alone," their new companion said. His voice was a clear, even tenor. "He'll be fine in a minute. He's just suffering from a terminal case of greed and awe. He'll get over it. Right, Chasm?"

Chasm didn't answer.

"Greed and awe?" Garry said. "Why?"

The new man chuckled. "Chasm's a religious man. Believes in God and heaven."

"I don't understand."

The man chuckled again. "This is heaven and I'm God. But you can call me Jack. Now let's get moving. I haven't had breakfast yet. Need a woman around the place. To do the cooking, maybe a little housework." He turned a sly, happy glance on Glory.

"You're still a swine, Jack," she said.

"Yeah. Isn't it nice that some things never change?"

Carved into the rock wall of the vast room was a series of openings, and once again Garry had a flicker of remembrance, as if for some reason those dark mouths were familiar. Had he come this way before? But how could he, and not remember?

His world tilted, but this time he was able to conceal his confusion. Focus, he told himself. He stared at the man who had joined them. It was odd. Were all the males on this planet small and scrawny? Chasm was no superman, but Jack was even more unprepossessing. And all this bull about being God. He didn't even have the grace to say "a god." No, it had to be God, the one and only. And heaven? This place was big and impressive, but it fit no heaven Garry had ever heard of.

Yet there was something about Jack. The wild whine of unheard laughter wrapped him like a fog, as if the entire universe were a joke only he could appreciate. And Chasm, who had seemed competent enough before, was obviously terrified of the man. What kind of power could cause that?

Jack said, "Glory. Have you been in touch?"

He half bowed toward the nearest opening and motioned the little group toward it. Glory moved first. Chasm still seemed to suffer from a lingering hint of paralysis, so Garry touched his elbow as he went past, and though the odd little man—not so odd as I supposed, Garry thought—jumped slightly, he followed immediately. His eyes were slowly fading from black to a dark purple, and in their slow transition resembled bruises.

"That's it," Garry said. "You can tell me later."

Chasm gave him a grateful glance and nodded slightly.

A few feet ahead, Jack had his arm around Glory's waist. As they walked, they talked softly, and Garry was struck by how familiar they seemed to each other. How easy and right their closeness seemed.

For a moment he felt bitter envy. He had nobody. There was no one in all the universe whom he could trust or love. Or even simply walk with, and touch, and hold.

He was utterly alone.

He and Chasm followed the other two into the tunnel. Far above and behind them, something flickered in the air. A bit of color. A tiny folding in the atmosphere. Perhaps only a trick of the light.

Only a scrap of color.

And laughter.

The tunnel they entered, which had seemed so dark in the blazing brightness beneath the skylight, was actually

well lit. The floor was made of some smooth, faintly
spongy material that gave slightly beneath their weight
and soaked up sound as well. The walls were of the same
material and everything was an iridescent gray, so Garry
had the disconcerting feeling of walking on the inside of
an oyster.

After a short distance the hall ended at a wide elevator
door. There was a single touchpad next to the door and
Jack wiped his fingers across it. He turned and grinned at
them.

"This looks familiar," Glory said.

Jack shrugged. The elevator door slid smoothly aside
and he motioned for them to enter. "Breakfast first," he
said. "You're hungry, aren't you, Chasm?"

Chasm nodded slightly, swallowed once, and stepped
inside.

The elevator did not seem to move. Garry stared at the
Oriental carpet on the floor and wondered why everyone
on the planet seemed so addicted to antique luxury.
Chasm's mountain stuffed with polished wood and gleaming metal. This vast temple of a building. And now an
elevator that didn't go anywhere with a priceless carpet
on the floor.

"Something busted?" he said.

Jack leaned against the wall and put his hands in the
pockets of his black denim jeans. He wore a T-shirt that
said, "Off The On Ram," and had a lightning-bolt sigil
beneath the words. "Don't worry, we'll get there."

"Where are we going?"

"You'll see."

Soundlessly the door opened. Jack bowed slightly. "Welcome to my humble abode," he said.

It was a big room, longer than it was wide, and two
stories tall. Big enough, but it didn't have the feel of
overwhelming size most of the other places on Arius had.
And it was cluttered.

"Looks lived in," Garry muttered to Chasm, who ignored him. Directly ahead was a large grouping of three
leather sofas arranged in a U shape around a scarred
wooden coffee table. There were other haphazard group-
ings of chairs and tables scattered about the big room.
Bookshelves were placed here and there along three walls.
The books were piled and stacked on the shelves; Garry
recognized the syndrome. His own bookshelves looked

the same way. It came from use. Books taken out, read, put back with no regard to order or classification. Working bookshelves.

But his books were antiques, and he had only a few. This man had thousands. And there was more. Despite the size of the place it seemed crammed, overstuffed. On every flat surface sat bowls, vases of dried flowers, metal gimcracks of every size. Ashtrays overflowed with butts. The walls were covered with an amazing variety of pictures. One caught his eye. It was a line drawing of a bird diving. The signature was a broad scrawl.

The cold remains of a half-eaten pizza rested on the coffee table. Jack plopped down on the sofa closest to the pizza and lit a cigarette.

Great, Garry thought. Another smokestack. I hope the ventilation works here.

The far wall was entirely windows from floor to ceiling, masked now by gray drapes that admitted a thin, diffuse light.

Jack saw Garry eyeing the drapes. "You want view?" he said, "Sure. Take a look." He paused. "Open, says me," he said. The drapes began to move.

Garry walked over to the windows. He stopped. Finally he said, "What is it? Where are we?"

"New Chicago," Jack said. "Ugly town. You like it?"

The room was at least fifty stories above the endless city spread out below. Great towers poked up from lesser spires, many of them taller than his own vantage point. The city was built on the edge of an endless body of gray water that spread to the horizon. Wisps of fog moved across the dully sparkling surface. Boats drove across the water, leaving long tracks like white feathers.

It was morning in the city. A bank of clouds across the water masked the sun, turned the light to a coppery color.

It was a breathtaking view. New Chicago. Garry had seen holos, read about it. He turned. "Great holo," he said. "Must have cost a fortune."

"Not a holo," Jack replied. "You want some coffee?"

Garry stared at the dead pizza and realized he was very hungry. "Yeah. That'd be great."

"And food," Jack said. "You like pizza?"

"For breakfast?"

"Sure."

Garry thought about all the healthy breakfasts Garth had insisted he eat, and felt faintly sinful. "If I can have a beer," he said.

"Beer and pizza for breakfast?" Jack grinned his thieving grin. "Garry, you're my kind of guy."

Glory came out of the kitchen carrying a silver tray on which sat a beautiful old silver coffee service. She put the tray on the coffee table. Garry thought it looked at home there, as if the same service had rested there many times before. In fact, Glory herself looked much at home; a part of the edgy tenseness that usually surrounded her had softened. Her smile was more frequent, and her green eyes glowed rather than glittered. She seemed amused by Chasm's behavior.

The little man sat rigidly on the sofa across from Jack. Every once in a while his eyes would cycle through a series of colors, so quickly that it was impossible to make out the colors themselves, but only an impression of kaleidoscopic change. He studiously avoided looking directly at Jack. The other man, in turn, ignored him completely.

"Blue Mountain," she said, indicating the coffee service. "Pour it yourself."

Garry glanced quizzically at Jack.

"Blue Mountain?" the older man replied. "A kind of Terran coffee. Grown in Jamaica and very good." He poured himself a mugful, sipped, and grinned. "I like my little luxuries."

Garry poured a cup for himself. The taste was just a bit thin at first, but then the richness of the blend took hold. "This is good."

Jack nodded. "Nice to see you have decent taste. Some people . . ."

Glory poured cream and sugar into her own mug. "Some people aren't hopeless snobs," she said.

"You don't have to ruin it in front of me. Why don't you drink that slop in the kitchen?"

"Why don't you see if you can insert your—"

Garry listened to the byplay. "You guys know each other, right?"

Glory nodded over the rim of her mug. "You could say that."

"A long time," Garry continued.

Now Jack grinned again. "Quite a while, yes. We were even married once, before we came to our senses."

Garry put his cup down on the table. "Why do I feel like I'm in some kind of joke that everybody knows the punch line to but me?"

Jack blinked. Then he nodded once, as if he approved of the question. "Because it's almost true. I think you've got a lot of the pieces, Garry. You should. Enough of them have been shoved in your way. What do you think is going on?"

Chasm said, "May I have a cup of that?"

Jack glanced at him. Jack's expression was bland, but the other man shriveled back into the sofa. "Pay attention, Chasm, old buddy. It's an interesting conversation."

Garry said slowly, "I think you're the missing force. The key I need to put the rest of it together. I know about the lizards, and something about the Search. Hyarl Thomas. The artifact. But I can't quite put it together. Something else is involved in the game." He paused. "The game that isn't a game. You are the key, aren't you?"

Jack drained his mug and poured another. His features seemed to turn inward. "The key? What an interesting phrase, Garry. You continue to surprise me. But, to answer your question, yes. You could say I'm the key. It is, after all, one of my names."

Garry felt icicles begin to chime at the base of his spine. "Will you tell me?" he said.

Jack nodded. "You thought I was kidding, but I wasn't. Welcome to heaven, Garry. This is where most of it began."

Chapter Seventeen

Jack drank another cup of coffee. He sighed as he drank, as if he hadn't tasted coffee in a long time. Then he leaned back and glanced at Glory, who perched on one arm of the sofa and stared down at him. "Go on," she said. "You love this kind of suspense crap."

Garry hadn't realized how strong the brew was. As he finished his second cup, tiny electric thrills chased each other up and down the skin of his arms. At least he thought it was the coffee.

He felt perfectly at home in this strange place. He didn't even think about the view of New Chicago that wasn't a hologram. If this was heaven, then maybe heaven was a place answers went. Or came from. Either way, he was content to wait.

Jack lit another cigarette. He grinned at Garry, and his laughing gray eyes sparkled happily. "I did it," he said. "A few hundred years ago. I didn't know what I was doing, of course, but I did it anyway."

"Your usual style," Glory said sourly.

"You did what?" Garry said.

Jack put his booted feet up on the coffee table, and Garry began to understand how the wood had gotten so scarred.

"Hyarl Thomas, for one thing. I did him."

Garry shook his head. "You're not making any sense. At least not to me."

"No, probably not. You have to understand the history, you see."

"So tell me the history."

Jack nodded. "Fair enough. It was at the end of the Matrix Wars. I was at loose ends. A little of this, a little of that. Playing around with some fairly esoteric gravity

180

theory and stumbled on the principle of the Wormhole Drive. Actually, Einstein and Rosen had enunciated the theory a long time before. What I did was more engineering than physics. Anyway, I built a probe. To test things out."

Garry blinked. In one paragraph Jack had raised a hundred questions, rewritten history, and obtained Garry's riveted attention.

"Right. So the probe didn't come back. I didn't expect it to. Classical theories indicated the probe went into the past. I wasn't sure how to handle that, but then the lizards came along and handled it for me. They sold us the timeband."

"Yeah. Quite a surprise."

"More than you know. I incorporated it immediately into my designs and sent another probe. This was done in secret. Guess what came back?"

Garry shook his head. "I don't know."

"The artifact, of course. The same block that ended up several years later on the floor of your pawnshop."

Garry saw it again, as clearly as if a video screen had replayed the scene on the inside of his eyelids. The rat-faced man, half-beaten to a pulp, panting and sweating as he hauled the cube through the front door of the Golden Ball.

"How the hell?" he said finally. "What happened? Where did the cube come from?"

"A black hole. A singularity."

Garry thought about it. He wished his physics were stronger. "That's impossible. Nothing comes out of a black hole."

"On the contrary. Everything does." And Jack's face assumed a magician's expression, a rabbit-out-of-the-hat leer. "That's the real joke. And like all good jokes, it's an old one. The cosmos has a sense of humor after all, and Steven Hawking was the first one to catch on."

New vistas opened in Garry's mind as the doors of his education slammed open. "Stephen Hawking. Major physicist. Perhaps the great one of twentieth-century Terra."

Jack nodded his approval. "At least you learned something in your studies. Anything else?"

"Hawking specialized in black-hole theory. Practically invented the things."

"Mm-hmm. Anything else?"

Garry thought for a moment. "Nothing real specific. I know some of the math. The basic stuff."

"Okay. Hawking came up with one very interesting bit. It never gets much publicity, because nobody really knows what to do with it, and it is very unsettling."

For a moment Garry found it strange to be discussing off-brand theories of a long-dead genius, but his interest was completely engaged. "Go on," he said.

"I'll keep it simple. You don't really need the math. Just follow this. All our black-hole theory teaches us that singularities operate under a kind of cosmic censorship. What goes in can never come out, and consequently we can never know what happens inside one. Even the Worm-hole Drive doesn't contradict that, because although we use the path of a singularity, we never come in contact with the actual interior. Our shields prevent it, and if they didn't, we would be destroyed."

"I follow so far," Garry said.

"Good. But then along comes quantum mechanics. Quantum effects violate the laws of cosmic censorship, and we find that black holes do evaporate. Some slowly and some more quickly, but all black holes evaporate."

"I don't quite understand the quantum effects involved, but I accept the thesis," Garry said.

"Good man. You'll run into it in your later schooling, if you go heavy on math and science. Anyway, take it one step further. *What* evaporates from a black hole?"

Garry riffled through everything he knew on the subject and came up blank. "I don't know."

Jack's grin was diabolical. "Anything, Garry. Anything at all can come out of a black hole. And we can never predict what it will be."

His head spun. It was as if the concept had been lurking inside his brain for a long time, but needed some-body else to put it into words. "Wait . . . a minute. That means . . ." He paused. "Causality doesn't exist, then. Because holes change the topology of space-time." He fell silent one more time, as the full horror of the joke sank in on him. "Then nothing is impossible," he said at last. "And we take a rational universe on faith. We have to. We have to believe in the universe, because there is nothing, nothing at all, that says it *has* to exist. Not if what you say is true."

He was stunned by the implications.

"It's worse," Jack said gently. "Not only *can* anything come out of a singularity, everything eventually *will*." His voice went soft and musing. "That's where the artifact came from. And it brought Hyarl Thomas with it."

Garry's eyes widened. He tilted his head back and stared at Jack. "But you said there was only the artifact. You mean it was some kind of transmitter machine?"

"In a way. It did transmit Hyarl Thomas, but not the way you think."

Garry waited. Jack evidently liked to spin out his tales.

"Okay. So you don't bite this time. You remember the scratches on the cube? Surely you noticed them?"

"Uh-huh."

"It took me a while, but I deciphered them. An equation."

"The scratches were an equation?"

"Right. And then—"

"You worked out the equation." Garry felt a surprising emotion rise in his chest. A wild anticipation. Messages from black holes! How strange was the universe? How strange could it be? *And why hadn't he heard of this before?* "What was it? The stardrive? Immortality? What?"

Jack's lips quivered slightly, as if he were suppressing a laugh. "I don't know. The value was a transcendental number."

Disappointment. He knew what transcendental numbers were—numbers not expressible in a finite number of terms. Infinite numbers, like the value of *pi,* or any logarithmic function. A bit of his feelings showed in his voice as he said, "Then the equation was meaningless?"

"Well, not exactly. It was an interesting equation, and I started working out the transcendental number itself. I don't know what the equation itself means. Just as a caveman might not have understood the value of *pi* as a constant. But as I worked out the number, a strange thing occurred. After a very long series of numbers—say, ten to the thirtieth power—the integer values disappeared, and a series of ones and zeroes began to show. Nothing else, just ones and zeros." Jack's eyes beamed brightly at him, waiting to see if he saw the significance.

But already that bursting feeling was back. "A code! A binary code hidden in an equation! Were you able to crack it? What did it say?" He was so excited the words tumbled out on top of each other, almost garbled.

"I cracked it," Jack said flatly. "The code wasn't designed to be hard to decipher. The real requirement was having computers and an awareness of numbering systems. You see the implications there?"

Garry forced his racing mind to slow, to consider the problem. Finally he got it. "Yeah, of course. The message could only be decoded by a civilization that had reached a particular level of sophistication. Mathematics, computers, that sort of thing."

Jack beamed proudly, almost as if Garry were a favorite son who had figured out a tough question. "That's it."

"So what did it say?"

"It was another kind of code. A genetic code."

Garry felt as if the top of his head were going to blow straight up. The immense complexity of the message. The source of it. And the message itself. But he understood. He breathed the words slowly, with a kind of awe. "Hyarl Thomas. It was his genetic code, wasn't it?"

"Bingo," Jack said.

"Oh my God."

"I don't think so, but we already decided anything was possible, didn't we? Anything at all?"

When he poured himself another cup of coffee, he noticed that his hand was shaking. So overwhelming was the wonder of Jack's story that he couldn't figure out why nobody else seemed affected. Glory lit cigarettes one after the other, and Chasm remained a black lump on the third sofa. Then he realized, and a thread of despair wormed into his soul.

"It's a joke, isn't it? I don't know why, but it's a joke. When you think about it, it's impossible. A message in a transcendental number. Ten to the thirtieth power out. That's impossible. No computers exist that could even decipher such a thing, and as for encoding it in the first place—there isn't enough time, let alone big enough machines—in all the universe." He paused. "Why are you doing this to me?"

Now Glory was looking at him. She had the same expression on her face as when she'd whispered the word "friendship" to him.

"I told you it wouldn't wash, Jack," she said softly. "He's too smart. Now you have to tell him the rest."

Jack looked grumpy. "I don't have to tell him anything."

Her rough voice went sharp. "Yes, you do."

"Why?"

"Because I said so."

Two sets of eyes, one gray, the other green, dueled for an instant. Garry was amazed when Jack was the first to lower his gaze. "Nasty, nasty," he said. He fell silent. Then, "It could be a mistake, you know."

"Anything could. But since even we don't understand . . ." Glory said.

Jack seemed to make up his mind all at once. "Okay," he said. "No, Garry, it's not a lie. Everything I told you is the truth. Just not all the truth."

Garry's armpits felt hot and greasy, but his forehead was clammy. His stomach lurched one way, then the other. True? But he'd spoken truth also. No such computers existed. Yet for some reason this bizarre story fascinated him as nothing had before in his life. "Tell me the rest," he said.

"The computers exist," Jack said. "One, at least. You studied the Matrix Wars."

Garry nodded. "I never really understood why they were called that," he said. "They were really religious conflicts, while Shigeinari Nakamura struggled to consolidate his control of Terra."

Glory and Jack glanced at each other. Garry couldn't understand the meaning of that enigmatic look, but it made him feel uneasy. These two shared too much information. They had too many secrets.

"The meatmatrices," Jack said.

"That would explain it," Garry replied, "if they really did exist. But there is no documentation. The existence of bioelectronic supercomputers is as much legend as anything else. Remember, the time of the Matrix Wars had a strong element of the antitechnological. It was the high-tech Lunar society that was considered the villain by the Terran forces."

"Does any of that seem odd to you?"

"In a way. It was an intensely technological era. But such things usually provoke a backlash."

"But we aren't on Terra now. Even if meatmatrices

didn't exist then, the potential certainly was there. Why have none been built since?"

It was a tougher question. Garry wasn't sure he had an answer. "Well, maybe the problems in building them were greater than had been supposed. In any event, there is the Ban. Meatmatrices are proscribed on every Terran world."

"Yes. But there are always rebels. Don't you suppose somebody would have tried to build one?"

Garry shook his head. "I don't have an answer. Unless there is some strong force, some outside entity enforcing the proscription . . ."

Jack smiled. "Yeah," he said. "Now you're getting it."

"You mean you've been the one behind the suppression of bioelectronic machines? But why?"

Jack stood up. He turned away from the group and wandered to the windows and looked at the neon city burning beneath him.

He stood with his hands clasped behind his back. The morning sun turned his face into a map of shadows and harsh lines. His voice was muffled as he replied. "I saw the implications of the Wormhole Drive immediately, of course. It isn't really a drive. Merely a method of shielding that allows normal matter to enter and exit a wormhole without being destroyed. The wormhole itself is the drive—and a time machine to boot. It takes us back in time, and the timeband, which is a different kind of time machine, brings us forward. At first I didn't see any necessity for the timeband. The wormhole was sufficient to reach other star systems, and even if they were in the past, they existed and could be used. None of this took into account possible other races." He paused and turned to look at them.

"Why the timeband? To protect themselves, of course. The lizards, like any self-respecting paranoid race, didn't want anybody messing around with their past. But there was a corollary. Obviously they retained the ability to mess around with ours. I couldn't tolerate that."

Garry tried to imagine the turbulence of those times. The lizards appeared literally out of nowhere and immediately imposed restrictions on Human ability to navigate the cosmos. They backed up the restrictions with a threat of irresistible force. Obey us or we will destroy your past.

Humanity, given the carrot of faster-than-light travel, and threatened with the stick of destruction, immediately capitulated.

"So what did you do?"

"Got out from under. Left Humanity. Came here to Arius and hid. And continued with my research."

"That still doesn't explain why meatmatrices were suppressed," Garry said.

"The lizards aren't the greatest computer whizzes in the galaxy. I didn't want them to understand the capabilities they were dealing with. And there were a couple of other things I wanted to remain hidden. From everybody, lizard and Human both. Given the big meats, somebody would have eventually stumbled on the same things I had. So I proscribed the meats. And I enforced it."

The little man's voice turned cold as he spoke the final words. Garry shivered. He tried to imagine the means of enforcement, and decided he didn't want to know.

Garry poured more coffee. It tasted dank and bitter. He made a face and put down the cup. "So, what? What now? You're telling me you have the only supercomputer in existence. And you keep it hidden. What have you done?"

"A few things," Jack said. "Nothing I want to discuss now."

"You think maybe the lizards have figured some of it out? Or maybe they sent a fleet to this backwater system just to say hello?"

"It's a problem," Jack said. "Nothing I can't handle."

"You seem pretty calm about it."

"Don't worry about the fleet, Garry. Worry about what brought them here in the first place."

"And what was that?"

"Hyarl Thomas. The lizards would never have figured out a reason to come here on their own. They had help. This is Thomas's work. I recognize his fine hand at work, and it stinks. He's moved against me at last. And I have to fight back. I have no other choice. He's out to destroy humanity itself!"

A bell chimed softly in the kitchen. "Breakfast is served," Glory announced. The tension slowly drained from the moment. Jack's face rearranged itself into a semblance of bland disinterest, and he returned to his sofa and sat down. He folded his hands in his lap and stared at them. He didn't look at Garry.

Glory disappeared into the kitchen and returned with two large sausage pizzas. The melted cheese on top steamed and bubbled, and suddenly Garry was ravenous. He picked up a slice with both hands, ignored the heat, and gingerly bit into the tip.

"Beer," he said a moment later, and Jack laughed.

"A great breakfast. About my all-time favorite."

Garry agreed silently and continued to eat.

"Why is Hyarl Thomas putting the skids to you now?" Garry said.

Jack's foxlike face brightened. "I don't know," he said. He seemed happy about the idea. "Maybe it's his origin."

"Out of a black hole. He came back with your probe," Garry said.

"In a manner of speaking," Jack replied. "My probe, dealing as it did with vast gravitational forces, was equipped with sensors to measure any change, no matter how minute, in total mass. When I checked the records of the probe, I discovered something a little wild. After the probe exited the wormhole in the distant past, there were some minor changes. But sometime on the trip to the present, the cube appeared. It was immediately noted, of course. But the mass of the probe didn't change in the wormhole, nor immediately after exit. It happened later." He sighed. "The truth is, I'm not even sure the wormhole had anything to do with it. But the probabilities are somewhat small that it didn't. Besides, when you add in the properties of the cube itself, it becomes even less possible that a black hole of some kind wasn't involved."

"What do you mean?"

"The cube. It's made of neutronium."

Garry's mouth dropped open. "That's absolutely impossible."

Now Jack's amusement became openly evident. "What was the saying? Believe three impossible things before breakfast? Well, you've just had two. Hyarl Thomas, and the cube itself. Want to try for the third?"

Chasm had not drunk any coffee or eaten the pizza.

Garry had almost forgotten he was there until the rich organ tones of his voice suddenly filled the room.

"I knew none of this," he said.

Jack looked at him, astonished, but Glory's green eyes gleamed expectantly, as if she'd been waiting for something like this.

"Chasm," Jack said. His clear voice somehow held a warning, but Chasm shook his head.

"You've told me none of this . . . history before. Yet I've done your work without question." He said the words slowly, with dignity. "You think it's because I desire the Joining, and perhaps that is part of it. But there's more, there always has been. I believed in what I could understand of your role in Human affairs. But this, this . . . endless manipulation. And Hyarl Thomas! He's an incredible threat. Yet you never told me. You even edited my own files. Thomas didn't first appear in a spaceport on Old Terra. He isn't even Human!"

"It was necessary—"

"My ass!"

"Chasm, that's enough."

The dark little man made a short, bitter gesture. "You could have trusted me."

Glory sighed. She reached over and touched Chasm on the shoulder. He looked up at her. "That isn't entirely Jack's fault," she said. "He can't trust anybody, that's true enough. But in this case, he was actually justified, for once."

Jack squinted his eyes and puffed out his cheeks. He looked like an angry squirrel. "Well, thanks for that."

"No problem, old man." Glory smiled sweetly. "Someone has to interpret your convoluted nastiness to the general public."

"Bitch," he said.

"That too," she replied.

Jack turned to Chasm. "Listen. I wish I could have told you. But the knowledge is incredibly dangerous. So dangerous that for the first time in my life I tried to ignore it. Tried to pretend that it would go away. Of course it didn't. Now things are finally coming to a head. And I'm not prepared. Secrecy is my only weapon. I'm not even sure it will be enough."

"You will tell me," Chasm said.

"Yes, I will tell you. But later. We have another problem now."

Chasm nodded. "I'll wait."

Garry had listened with rapt attention. He didn't understand all the overtones of the dispute, but he had the vague feeling that it concerned him in some way.

"So what's going on?" he said. "What about Hyarl Thomas. And that lizard fleet? And the artifact?"

Jack stared at him a moment, then turned away. Since meeting this man, Garry had never seen him waver from his mask of mocking, capable cynicism. But now, in the silver light of a mysterious morning, Jack no longer appeared so capable. The cynicism had fallen away. He only looked old. And tired.

"The game is like entropy. It only increases," Jack said at last.

"What do you mean?"

"There was another equation on the artifact," Jack said. "After my experience with Hyarl Thomas, I didn't dare to experiment further. Yet eventually Thomas himself forced me to it."

Weird little crawly things began to dance on Garry's flesh. "And the second equation?" he said at last.

"You," Jack replied.

Chapter Eighteen

He slept that night in a small bedroom off the main living room. The bedroom was simple—it reminded him of hotel quarters. Another anomaly amidst the richness of Arius.

Glory stuck her head through the door as he lay in darkness staring at the ceiling. "You asleep, Garry?"

"No."

"I didn't think so. You want to talk?"

He propped himself up on his pillow and stared at her. "That's all we've done is talk. Jack talks and talks. Spent the whole day talking."

She stepped into the room, her small, wiry figure a ghostly punctuation mark in the gloom. After a moment he felt the foot of his bed give beneath her weight.

"It's a lot, isn't it? To take in all at once."

He nodded to himself. Her rough voice was sympathetic, and without wishing to lower his defenses, he found himself responding to the sympathy. "It's crazy," he said.

She spoke softly, but there was a hard undercurrent to her words. "Is it? At least it's an explanation. It's more than you had before."

"And I should just trust Jack? Is that what you mean?"

"You don't have to trust him, but I don't think you have much choice in what you actually do. Whether you believe his explanations or not, Frego is still missing, Hyarl Thomas remains at large, and a lizard battle fleet will be taking up positions around Arius any minute now."

Yes. He'd tried to ignore all this. But the hard realities kept intruding. Whatever he thought of Jack's exegesis, it did explain the web of what had already happened.

"I still don't understand why the lizards are involved. And why would they come here?"

"They are threatened." She paused, as if debating whether to say more. He heard her inhale twice, but no words came. Another moment of silence. Then, "Consider this, Garry. If they are attacking now, in realtime, why aren't they also attacking all along the time line? They have the ability. They aren't limited by the timeband."

He hadn't even considered the possibility. But it made horrible sense. "Then why aren't we dead?"

He could almost see her smile. "Perhaps we are defending all along the time line."

The concept was breathtaking. He felt his heart pound in his chest. "Jack can do that?" he said at last.

"Why aren't we dead?"

"Yes," he said at last. "Why, indeed." And began to understand that he might really come out of this alive.

He woke up the next day tangled in a sweaty mass of sheets. His body smelled sour, and though he couldn't remember, he knew he'd dreamed bad dreams. There was a small bathroom off his cubicle and he used it. The hot water felt good on his skin. As he scrubbed, his fingers touched the faint welt of scar tissue that ringed his neck like a choker. The scar would eventually disappear, but he knew he would always feel it there. Until—when? He knew the answer. He would feel the scar as long as Hyarl Thomas lived.

Glory was in the main room drinking coffee and eating chocolate donuts. She had her booted feet on the coffee table and ignored him as he flopped down on the opposite sofa. He poured coffee, sipped, and reached for a donut.

"Morning."

She grunted. He ate his donut.

"You're real cheerful. Where's Jack?"

"He's not a morning person either," she said. Her voice was raspy and harsh, as if she'd stayed up all night smoking one cigarette after another. Maybe she had.

He regarded her thoughtfully. She was wound tight as new shoes. She exuded an invisible cloud of tension. Her black hair was a ragged mess. The only shred of calm about her was her eyes. They were green and empty. It was the placidity of death. He shivered.

"What's up for today?" he said. It sounded like a childish question to his ears, and he regretted it.

But she answered, after a moment's consideration. "I think we take a trip," she said, and stared at him. It was odd. Her eyes suddenly came alive and flamed like the sun behind arctic ice.

The big room was silent. Then, all at once, what seemed like a hundred clocks began to ring, buzz, chime. From a few even came small birds that chirped and whistled. His mouth fell open.

"What the hell . . . ?"

Her rough laugh echoed the sound of the clocks. "Jack's weird. Now you know how weird."

Garry shrugged. "He thinks he'd a god. That's bizarre enough." He reached for another donut. "What kind of trip?" The donut tasted slightly stale.

"Just . . . a trip. Why? I thought you wanted action."

"I'm a little tired," he said. "Go here, stay there. People moving me around, you know. All that crazy talk last night. You want me to make sense out of it? I can't. And now I'm going on a trip." He swallowed the last of the donut and washed it down with coffee. He raised his head and stared at her. "I'm done with it, that's all. You'll have to tell me from now on. I don't go blind anymore."

She blinked. "Wouldn't have it any other way, then, bucko."

A long silence. "Well?" he said.

She grinned. There was nothing happy about it. "Back," she said, "Of course. Where it all began."

He squinted. "Back?"

She swung her boots off the table and slapped the knees of her black leather jeans. "Back in time." She glanced at him. "I figured you to like the idea. Frego's there. And Hyarl Thomas."

He nodded. "Naturally," he said.

That night he went to sleep in darkness and dreamed. Again he swooped and swam through crystal air down to a great white dome. This time he recognized the place: it was Jack's castle. The glowing cloud filled the vast room. His smooth forward motion halted just at the boundary of the cloud. He stared into the universe of glowing motes and something stirred inside him.

It's not real, he thought suddenly. This is only a dream.

Dreams are information too, the cloud hummed at him.

I'm having a conversation with a cloud, he thought.

Come in, the cloud replied. There was no voice to the thought, only a long, plaintive welcome. Yet he understood. He felt himself move forward. Then it turned into a long fall, down and back forever into light.

He hung suspended in the twisting golden motes and he saw faces. Some he recognized, some not. There was Frego. Garth. Jack and Glory, and their features melted into each other. The face of an angel. And a Golden Man whose eyes were the palest of rubies.

There was no meaning to any of it. No message. Yet he knew he'd been here before. And just beyond that memory was another. A different place. He knew that place was even more important, if he could only recall it. But there was nothing.

The color blue.

Then he awoke and it was a new morning. Jack and Glory took him to a small room and told him to sit. There were four chairs.

Glory sat next to him. She patted his knee and grinned.

"Things are moving right along," she said. She seemed happy about it.

"This is a room," he told her. "It can't go back in time. Wormholes don't exist in planets."

Jack stepped out of the room. He waved once, just before the door shut.

"They don't?" Glory said.

The walls of the room began to flicker. They turned gray and resembled smoke. Things he couldn't watch trembled there.

He shook his head stubbornly. "No."

"Better watch that first step," she replied.

The room was utterly silent. It was like traveling in the ghost of a dream. After a time the surroundings lost their novelty and his thoughts turned inward. He'd purposely tried not to think about the most upsetting of Jack's revelations. His own genetic code had been found on an impossible hunk of neutronium magically retrieved from the noncausal swamp surrounding a singularity. He was a child of a black hole, and Hyarl Thomas was as much his family—perhaps even more—than his unknown mother or Garth Hamersmidt himself.

Where did I come from? he wondered. It was a tale more strange than any he could have imagined. Jack wasn't the secret player of the game, not really. There was somebody—some *thing* else involved—a player perhaps not even in time or space. Was it the Kurs'ggtha themselves? And who were *those* shadowy beings?

Did the entire universe dance to their unknown geometries?

In a sense Hyarl Thomas was his brother. Their genesis was the same. But the thought gave him no comfort. Human history and Human myth was littered with the enmity of brothers, from Cain and Abel to Thor and Loki.

He glanced over at Glory. She seemed sunk into a trance, the sharp bones of her face softened somehow. Her eyes were closed. Her head tilted forward slightly. The effect was almost one of prayer. She seemed so beautiful. He shook his head slightly and wondered who, or what she really was.

Brothers. Somehow doomed to destroy each other. In all the legends such brothers were fated to their ends from birth. He tried to avoid the obvious analogy, but the idea wouldn't leave him alone. Perhaps the creators of the artifact and hence himself and Thomas weren't gods, but their science was so far beyond anything Human they might as well be. Their science was indistinguishable from magic. Yet he and Thomas existed and now he felt the stirrings of that existence. A hunger. Somehow he would not be complete without Hyarl Thomas. He wondered if Thomas felt anything similar.

Then his thoughts made the mystic leap, the connection he'd waited for so long without even realizing. Hawking radiation, the curious stuff that was emitted from black holes at the boundary where time and space broke down. Pairs of particles created by the impossible gravity stresses on the event horizon. A particle and an antiparticle. Each doomed to join and destroy the other.

His hands began to shake. The equations that contained his codes and those of Hyarl Thomas. He knew their sum. He remembered it.

Remembered what he'd always known because the memory was written in his genes.

The equations were canceling.

Entropy was the measure of one, and its name was chaos. Order was the other. The game was the waltz of the universe.

The arrow of time was meaningless.

The end of the dance was death.

"We're here," Glory said. She lit a cigarette.

Garry looked up. The smoke that had walled them in was gone. The ordinary room had returned. He watched the curl of smoke from her cigarette rise slowly, then suddenly whirl and disperse into the pull of the air-conditioning currents.

He knew he'd traveled far, but felt as if his journey had only begun. But the journey was in his mind, and only he could walk that road. Step by step, he thought. This is the first.

"What?" Glory said.

"Huh? Nothing."

"You mumbled something." She stared closely at his face. "Are you okay?"

"You always ask that. I'm fine."

"And you always answer the same way." Her rough voice still bubbled with manic cheer. He wondered what was making her so happy. Something bloodthirsty, no doubt. He still wasn't sure he trusted his own intuitions, but he trusted this: that Glory loved a fight. People always enjoy things they're good at. He was glad she was on his side.

If she was.

He shook his head and felt the fog of thought begin to slide away. "You know what?"

She unbuckled herself from her chair and stood. "What?"

"I'm starving."

Her emerald eyes sparkled. "Pizza?"

"Burgers?"

"How about McDonald's?"

He removed his own straps. "They have one here?"

She grinned. "McDonald's is everywhere."

He had no idea what to expect when she opened the door to the room. Everything he knew suggested that a singularity large enough for a wormhole couldn't occupy a planetary space, so nothing should have changed. He should still be on Arius and Jack or Chasm ought to be waiting outside. But he knew it wouldn't be so and it wasn't. They stepped out into a long, curving hallway. Gray metal walls and a maroon carpet stretched in either direction. Glowstrips set into the ceiling cast a thin, shadowless light. The corridor seemed faintly familiar.

"Which way?"

She didn't answer. She walked toward the right as if she knew exactly where she was going. He shrugged and followed.

After a few moments he began to hear a distant roaring sound. It sounded like a great river rushing over submerged rock. The noise grew as they walked. The corridor made a sharp right turn and debouched suddenly into a vast open space.

Garry blinked. They had indeed traveled.

Thousands of people moved, walked, skipped, chattered, pointed, shouted, and bounced off each other. The noise level was deafening. Glory stopped.

He knew where he was, at least, if not exactly when. When he'd first seen it, the vast empty platform that orbited Arius had seemed incredibly huge. Now, choked with humanity, it shrank to crowded insufficiency.

"Where did they all come from?" he shouted.

Glory raised her shoulders. "Magic," she said. "Come on. McDonald's is this way."

He watched them leave the corridor and disappear into the crowd. His blue eyes were hooded. When the light hit his pupils, it seemed to bend in on itself, so that to catch his gaze was to begin to fall.

His face was enigmatic. His head moved once. The motion was almost imperceptible, but it might have been a nod of satisfaction.

The boy looked thin and tired, but he wasn't deceived. Nor did the woman dupe him. He knew what she was too.

His lips twitched slightly. He searched for them one more time before he faded back into the throng himself. It didn't matter. When the time came, the arrow of time would lead them to him.

He moved smoothly, with long strides. He moved like a dancer.

The thought pleased him.
Only a dancer could end the dance.

Inside the burger palace the crowd noise was muted.
As Garry munched a double order of fries he tried to get
answers from Glory. She wasn't making it easy.

"What is this place?"
"A burger joint."
"No, this satellite. It looks like the one orbiting Arius."
"It is."
"Then we didn't go back in time."
"The satellite has been here for a while."
He chewed a bit of potato. "More salt," he decided.
She passed a small packet to him. He broke it open and
shook it. "How long?"
She stared at him over her burger. "Several millen-
nia," she said at last.
"Millennia? How many is several?"
"Several."
"How come you don't want to talk to me?"
"Do you feel . . . different?"
The weird conversational shift startled him. "What?"
Then he thought about it. "I don't . . . wait a minute."
He'd noticed it even before he'd left the room, but hadn't
understood what it was. Now he could actually feel the
energy pouring into him. It fizzed and bubbled. It made
him feel lighter.
"I feel better," he said, and realized it was true.
"Stronger. More . . ." He couldn't quite express it.
"Stronger," he said again.
"Good."
He ate another french fry and reached for his own
double cheeseburger. "How come I feel that way? Why
do you know about it."
Her green glance was full of wicked glints. "You should
feel something," she said. "It's out there."
"What's out there?"
"Your singularity."
He probed the thought gingerly, with the mental equiv-
alent of a tongue into a sore tooth. "Mine?"
"Uh-huh." Her white teeth knifed sharply into the
edge of her burger. He stared at those teeth, fascinated.
She chewed and swallowed. "Yours." She licked her
fingers. "Welcome home."

*　　*　　*

There were people everywhere. Mostly they ignored him. Glory had disappeared into an endless series of "meetings," and left him free to roam as he pleased. He wandered the halls and corridors, stuck his nose into labs and storerooms, and stared in awe as swarms of liners disgorged hordes of new faces into the vast entryports of the satellite metropolis.

The flow seemed to move both ways. Not only did people arrive and almost immediately board shuttle boats downplanet, but laser-launched boxcars arrived back up on a second-by-second schedule. The satellite channeled this flow in both directions.

Where did all these people come from?

One day he stood outside the McDonald's, sucking a sick-sweet strawberry shake and marveling at the rise and fall of sound, a pounding roar that numbed his ears. He didn't even notice her until she yelled into his ear.

"A mess, isn't it?"

"What?"

She was about his age, maybe a little older. No more than twenty or so, barring any antiagathic treatment. But there was a freshness about her eyes, a happy shine, that seemed to preclude the darker wisdoms of age. She had straight brown hair that shone with dull golden highlights and covered her finely shaped skull like a short cap. Her nose was short and curved slightly. Her eyes were almost the same brown as her hair. And when she smiled at him, he forgot all of this, because a wide, warm sensation turned all his muscles into gooey pabulum.

"This." She was munching a french fry. He found that absolutely fascinating. "This mob. Sometimes I wonder how they ever get it straightened out."

"Uh . . ."

"What's the matter? You retarded? Can't talk or something?"

He felt like an idiot, and the rush of hot blood to his face made him feel even more stupid.

"Hey, you're blushing."

"Am not."

"It's cute."

Don't stutter, you nitwit, he told himself desperately. "Cute?"

"Sure. Boys don't blush very often. Means they still have the capacity for shame."

A remarkable statement, he thought. So profound. So . . . He inhaled. My brain is turning to mashed potatoes, he decided.

"You are the most beautiful girl I've ever seen in my life," he said out loud.

She stepped back, her eyes wide. He noticed the way her long thighs moved beneath the fabric of knee-length shorts. "My God, it speaks complete sentences." But then she smiled again, and all the sting went out of her words. "I'm sorry. That's about the nicest thing anybody's said to me in a long time. I shouldn't make fun of you."

Wordless, he shook his head.

She stuck out her right hand. "My name's Sharnita. Shar for short. What's yours?"

For one ridiculous moment he couldn't remember. "Uh." He shook his head. "Garry. That's it. My name's Garry. What's yours?"

She looked at him strangely. "I just told you."

"Right. Yeah. Uh-huh. You just did. It's uh . . ." He realized he was babbling.

"Shar, you idiot. You want to finish your shake inside? This mob scene gets to me after a while. I'm not used to it."

He knew that statement should have intrigued him. It opened all kinds of vistas. But there was only one vista he wanted to open just then, and the way was across the slick metal top of a McDonald's table. Besides, if she'd suggested a short walk, suitless, outside the walls of the station, he would have just as happily followed.

"So, Garry, how come you're hanging out in the front door of the local burger palace gawking at crowds?"

"Gawking? I'm not gawking." Somehow he had to say something impressive. But he knew his disadvantage, and it was the same one all tourists had with locals. There was only one way to trump such chauvinism. "I'm from High H'hogotha. Center of the Confederacy. Why would I gawk at some backwater immigration satellite?"

She put down her french fries and stared at him with something he hoped was dawning respect. "High H'hogoth? Wait a minute. Garry. You aren't Garry Hamersmidt, are you?"

Did everybody know something about him? How many spies could there be? But he nodded. If she was a spy, maybe her job was to seduce him. If not, he would suggest it.

"And you came in with Glory. Wow. What's she like? I've always wanted to meet her."

"Glory? You're interested in her?"

She lifted a french fry to her perfect lips. "Why? Oh. You didn't think it was you, did you?"

His spirits plummeted right toward his toes. But then she grinned and he was dizzied by his sudden rise.

"Well, maybe a little bit," she said.

His palms felt moist. "How come," he said slowly, "everybody seems to know me?"

"What? You mean all those thousands of people wandering around out there have been coming up and saying hello?"

He glanced toward the door. Outside, crowds still surged past in faceless intensity. "Well, not exactly. But you did."

"And you hope it might be because I crave your masculine body, I bet."

He felt his face go up in flames again.

"That's okay," she said. "It's not that bad. A body, I mean."

His lips moved, but nothing came out. And she laughed.

"Garry, I'm sorry. I know about you 'cause you're kind of a celebrity. With certain people." She licked her lips. He was mesmerized. "I'm a regular. I live here on the station. Those people out there are just passing through. I doubt if any of them even know you exist. But the regulars . . ." Her voice trailed off. Distance opened in her brown eyes. "Anybody who shows up with Glory is news."

Caution slowly penetrated the pink fog that had turned his brain into cotton candy. Why was Glory such an event for these people?

"How come?" he said at last. "Why's Glory such a big deal?"

She blinked. "Glory? But don't you know? She's one of the founders."

He stared intently at the tabletop. "What's a founder, and why is it important?"

She examined his face. "You really don't know?"

"Huh-uh."

"This station has been here thousands of years. Glory is the first founder to visit since it was built."

He still didn't quite catch it. "So?"

Her brown eyes widened slightly. He thought it might even be fear. "The founder's visit. Our legends say it's the beginning."

He felt tendrils of hidden meaning swirl around him. Her voice had gone chilly, and now her fear was in the open. Her fear tightened him up like a spring.

"The beginning of what?"

"The end," she said. "And you must be a part of it."

Chapter Nineteen

On the surface of the planet spinning slowly beneath the station things finally began to move. Dawn cut like a knife across the great white complex that had been prepared millennia before and eons in the future. Beneath the crystal dome in tanks full of golden, milky liquid, the seeds were injected.

These vats were made of glittering steel. Set into the steel frames were windows behind which viscous fluid swirled in slow, mysterious movement.

There were four seeds. Each seed contained a computer less than a micron on a side, and each computer housed the entire complexity of information needed to build the flesh matrix. The liquid was milky because of the sheer number of assembler motes needed to do the actual building.

Slowly atoms began to accrete to the seed itself. A molecule was formed. Other molecules, each precisely tailored to the master blueprint encoded in the seed, joined the first. Eventually—slowly, by certain standards, infinitely faster by others—the molecules formed a clump the size of a bit of dust. Four such dust bits appeared. They seemed like tiny shards of white light within the moving fluid.

Around the vats technicians checked readouts and watched gross processes. The actions in the vats were far too minute and quick for true human interaction, so incredibly efficient process-control monitoring systems provided the interface.

More molecules accreted as the dust fragments grew. Now dots that resembled microscopic tadpoles trembled in the thick suspension. Thousands of assemblers rushed to the construction sites, each one performing a single,

simple task. The milky fluid changed color slightly, shifting from warm gold to a lighter color as new raw materi-
als were pumped into the vats.

The tadpoles began to retrace the patterns that were a
dance already millions of years old. Eventually forms
took shape from the chaotic void. The technicians were
used to the process. Awe was not a part of their emotional library. They barely noticed the forms taking patterns in the amniotic fluid.

The evolutionary gavotte continued. Finally, the four
figures began to move. Fingers twitched. Leg muscles
contracted and relaxed. Eyelids slid open and fell shut
again.

At the end hearts began to pump. The amplified sound
echoed in the great chamber like a distant marching beat.
Lips stretched and hyperoxygenated liquid invaded lungs.
The organisms had reached completion.

After a time the milky liquid was pumped away. Thick,
ropy streams of it fell from naked shoulders and flowed
down freshly made skin.

The figures coughed, spitting up more of the fluid from
lungs now able to handle oxygen directly. The sides of
the vats dropped down. The figures turned and stared at
each other. Then they stepped forward out of the tanks.

The woman said, "This is cutting it pretty fine."

The man, who was shorter than she, replied, "We have
enough time."

The angel, who was seven feet tall and whose hair was
the color of the sun at dusk, said, "It all depends on the
boy. If we are wrong . . ."

And the Golden Man whose eyes were faded rubies
nodded slowly. "If we are wrong it doesn't matter. We
have no choice. But the boy is a mystery even to himself.
His secrets are the gamble."

The man replied, "We have always gambled with
secrets."

And the woman laughed.

Trailing bits of slime the color of ancient precious
coins, the four walked across white stone floors toward
darker openings. The technicians ignored them.

The founders had arrived.

"Tell me about Glory," Shar said.

Garry leaned back against the thick pillows that lined

benches on three sides of the small observation room at one of the outer wings of the station. Shar had brought him here. "It's my own secret place," she'd said. "Hardly anybody comes here. I can get away from the crowds."

Now, as he gazed down on the cloud-covered splendor of Arius, he couldn't think of anything he wanted to do more. How long had it been since he'd been able to relax, to be just seventeen, to chase a girl?

He shrugged. "She's okay," he said. "For an older woman."

Shar's thin-boned, haunting features shifted slightly. "Don't get me wrong," she said. "It's not a religion or anything. But Glory—all the founders—are very important to us."

Garry tried to think of Glory as Shar obviously did. A very important, perhaps even mythical person. But all he could see was a thin, intense woman who smoked too much and cracked jokes that had very sharp edges to them.

It was an opening, though. Anything to continue this conversation, this moment. He decided he could spend the next ten years or so staring into Shar's deep brown eyes.

"I don't understand. Who—what—exactly are the founders?"

"You mean you really don't know?"

"Huh-uh."

"That's strange." Her voice was musing. "You mean you didn't come in from Arius Prime?"

He thought about the odd, deserted planet far in the future. "I don't know. It's somewhere in the future from here. I guess." He realized suddenly that he had only Glory's word for the location of this place in time.

But Shar nodded thoughtfully. "That's where Prime is supposed to be. Right on the leading edge."

Sometimes it seemed everybody spoke a different language than he spoke. He understood the words but not the meaning.

"Leading edge?"

"Of history," Shar said. "Prime is at the furthest limit forward. I've read about it. Lizards and primitive Humans and the Confederacy. It seems like a strange place."

Primitive Humans? And this girl seemed to regard the whole of Garry's universe with a kind of condescension,

the same kind of feelings he reserved for prespaceflight
Terra. But how could that be? "It can get kinda strange,
I guess. But it's interesting."

She nodded. "I bet. This station gets so boring sometimes. At first, when the crowds began to arrive, I thought
it would be better. More fun. But everybody is on the
way to somewhere else, and nobody stays around long
enough to really get to know. You're the first. Are you
gonna stick around a while?"

"I don't know," he said. And realized he didn't. For
the first time the reality of his position held emotional
weight. He'd been moved and maneuvered from one
place to another, but after Garth's death his essential
rootlessness had made the manipulation seem trivial. If
you have nowhere to go, it doesn't matter where you end
up. Now, though, as he watched the light shift across
Shar's high cheekbones, he knew he wanted to stop.
Perhaps even put down a root or two. At that thought,
an analytical part of himself noted the obscene pun and
he blushed without realizing it.

"What?" Shar said.

"Huh?"

"You're doing it again. Blushing."

"Oh."

She moved closer to him on the pillows, until her
elbow just brushed against his shoulder. He held himself
still, afraid of frightening her away. Sexual mores, he
understood, were dependent on a host of things, and he
didn't understand the rules here. Not yet. But he wanted
to find out.

"I hope I will," he said after a moment. "Stick around,
I mean. I like it here."

Her voice moved around him like a soft fog. "I hope
so too," she said. "But if Glory has other plans, then
you'll go."

He thought he heard a hint of sadness. "What do you
mean?" he said. "I can do what I want."

"Not with Glory," she said. "Not with a founder."

There it was again. "Who the hell are the founders?"
he said, exasperated. "Glory's only a woman. And she
smokes too much."

But Shar seemed upset with his tone. "Garry, the
founders are everything. They created this, all of it."

He still didn't understand. "This station?"

She was silent for a few seconds. Then she took a deep breath. He felt her press closer to him. "The Human race," she said. "The real one." She paused. "What you call the Kurs'ggtha."

Frego moaned in his sleep. The short, scarred man was having a bad dream. His lips moved and the muscles in his back bunched and relaxed. After a time his face went slack and his eyelids ceased to flutter.

The tall man whose eyes bent light into darkness watched him silently. He felt nothing that resembled human emotions. The forces that drove him came from a colder place. To him the human heart was a pump.

But Frego had his uses. It was why he still lived. Why the little man had been repaired and carefully stored, here on the Schwartzkild boundary where all things began and all things ended.

Hyarl Thomas smiled. Such facial expressions had been hard to learn at first, but he'd persevered. Now muscle memory took care of it for him. That duplicity had been necessary at the beginning, when he hadn't understood the matrix in which he found himself. Now he did, and realized that the fleshy envelope was merely an algorithm for the greater pattern of this universe.

He remembered no more than Garry Hamersmidt of his true origins, of the place he had been before. But he'd been awake and aware far longer, and while he didn't understand the source of the drives that moved him, he understood the particulars quite well.

Patterns existed to be broken. Order was but the aberration of a moment, and where order persisted, destruction would surely come.

He stepped from the small room where Frego dreamed bad dreams. Softly he closed the door. He could feel the unimaginable, curling in on itself beyond the fragile boundaries of his ship.

He smiled once again. Destruction would indeed come to this pattern, this aberration of lizard and humanity. He knew it would, for it had already arrived.

As he thought about it, his lips stretched into a long, metallic laugh. The bright manipulators of order had made a mistake. They had called him into being first. The boy was too young.

Not that it mattered.

Even in the spinning arrow of time, entropy could not be denied.

The boy would come, if only to save that bit of order dreaming terrible dreams in a cell on the edge of causality. Frego was bait.

I am the trap, Hyarl Thomas thought with contentment, and glided on.

The word clicked into the mosaic of Garry's understanding like a key into a lock. "The Kurs'ggtha," he said, when his astonishment had faded enough to let him speak.

She felt the emotion in his voice and turned toward him. Her face was only a few inches from his own. He could smell her breath. It was sweet.

"Yes. You knew, didn't you?"

Numbly he shook his head.

"Oh God, I'm sorry."

"Hey, no. It doesn't bother me."

"That's not what I meant. If you came in with Glory and you didn't know . . . if she didn't tell you . . ."

"Slow down." He reached up and touched her cheek, felt the soft smoothness there, like warm feathers. Her eyes slid away from his. She jerked her head back from his fingers.

"You don't understand. Maybe I'm not supposed to tell you. The founders have reasons for everything they do. Who knows what damage I might have done?"

He was pulled two ways. Her distress twisted at him and he was willing to do anything to make her feel better. Say anything. But to do so would be to acquiesce to yet another strand of the web that bound him in mystery. Everybody kept secrets from him. Now Shar regretted telling him a truth, and the only way he could soothe her was to create a lie himself.

He didn't hesitate.

"It's okay, Shar. Don't worry about it. Don't tell me anything more, and I'll forget everything I've already heard. Is that okay?" And he reached out and took her chin gently between thumb and forefinger and tugged her face closer to his. "Please?"

The wildness went out of her eyes. All he could see were her lips moving closer to his. He sighed and pulled her down.

"Okay," she said at last.

He watched the shifting spectacle of Arius sliding its endless spiral below him, the coruscating glitter of its clouds stippling their room with shadow, with light. Shar nestled silent in his arms. One of her fingers rested on his chin. His head was tilted so his cheekbone touched the soft down of her hair. It was very quiet. He could hear her breathing slowly, in tune with the rise and fall of his own chest.

He had never been happier in his life.

Something had melted inside him, a seed, a dark husk, and now new things bloomed from the shattered remnants of the old.

I love you, he mouthed silently. There were no words spoken but somehow she seemed to hear. She moved slightly against him. He felt the movement in every pore of his body, accepted it with every cell of his mind.

The part of him he sometimes hated stood back and hooted catcalls. Stupid, that part said. Love. It's sex and you're a child. You don't even know this girl. Glands and solitude and ejaculation. Not love.

Her finger tapped his chin lightly and the bad part went away. He was glad. Later, perhaps, he might have to face that alter ego and lay those questions to rest. Later. For now the light, the touch, the closeness was enough.

For Garry was certain of one thing. He was beginning to understand the dance, and this girl was part of it. Such things as fate and doom did exist. The universe suffered from both. But there was a balance, and the weight was love.

He couldn't foretell the future—who could?—but he knew one thing. She was a part of him now, and whatever might yet happen, that wouldn't change.

He would always remember. Of course. He never forgot anything.

"You awake?"

"Yeah."

"My arm's going to sleep."

She laughed. "That's pretty romantic."

He grinned in reply. There was an ease to their words, a comfort he'd been unable to imagine. Could it only have been the sex? He refused to believe that. "I'm a romantic kind of guy. Don't you think?"

She kissed his fingertips. "Oh yeah. And your arm goes to sleep."

A sudden thought widened his eyes. "Hey. Does this place have a lock on the door?"

"Yes."

"Well?"

"It isn't locked, if that's what you mean. Why? Did you think I brought you here to rape you? Planned ahead, me the scheming woman?"

He felt silly. "No, of course not. But what if someone . . . ?"

"Finds us? Why? Are you ashamed?"

He shook his head. What if somebody came in? Who did he know, besides Glory, who would only be amused, and Frego, who was missing? Jack and Chasm were in the future. There was one other, but if *he* came into the room, embarrassment would be the least of their problems.

So his thoughts turned to Hyarl Thomas and he felt suddenly colder. He became aware of Shar's weight, of the numb tingling in his arm, and of the pattern of the shadows. He took a deep breath and let it leak out slowly.

"Tell me about the Kurs'ggtha," he said.

The timbre of her voice changed slightly. "Is that it? A quick roll, and the young lady reveals everything?" Her tone was bantering, but there was an undercurrent of seriousness beneath her words. He spoke to the deeper current, with a wisdom beyond his years.

"Logically, it wouldn't matter," he told her. "If Glory is as powerful as you seem to think, she would be aware of us. So if she hasn't intervened, then it must be okay with her whatever you say." He paused. "But that's logic, and I'm not going to press it. I meant what I said before. But let me tell you a story. When I'm done, then you decide. And I'll abide by whatever decision you make."

A tiny silence stretched between the end of his words and the beginning of hers. Then, "All right."

And he told her everything.

It was, he thought, the least he could do.

Shar said, "The quickest way I can show you about the Kurs'ggtha is a fast history."

They held hands as she spoke the verbal codes that activated a small monitor screen concealed in the wall of the observation cubicle. A slice of metal moved aside to reveal the screen, which lit up with a white flare of light before settling into smooth, seamless blue. The color made Garry's memory itch. Before he could even try to scratch, Shar spoke again.

The screen jumped to a blade-sharp view of Arius, seen from some distance away. Perhaps even from this station itself.

"This was the beginning," Shar said. "The founders had a problem with Prime. It was in the lizard universe, what to us here is the future. The founders were afraid of the lizards, frightened of their power over humanity with the Wormhole Drive. So they used their own drive to come here. All the way back to a younger planet, and a time before the lizards had crawled up out of their own swamps."

Garry stared at the shining planet. His mind twisted slowly around the paradox. The lizards threatened Human history, and so the founders went deeper and earlier, to a time before lizard history. How long ago? How far back had they gone? Where—when—was he now?

The picture on the screen changed. Now they flashed lower, though the cloud cover, and rushed to the needle points of a towering range. Finally a white city appeared on the flanks of one stone giant. Garry recognized the city.

"I know that place" he said.

"Yeah," she replied softly. "The founders built it in a day, it's said."

"That's impossible," he replied. He remembered the huge stones, the long, sweeping marble paths, the great crystal dome. All that in a single day? He dismissed the notion as legend.

"No. Garry, don't you understand yet? This is the future of mankind. Here, now, in the past. What you think of, your present, is the past to us. A few hundred years before your birth, man went back. We've been here a long time, going forward from you. To us, your time is ancient history. We've gone far beyond it."

It took him a moment to straighten out the weird flip-flops she described, but finally he understood. Humanity had been here eons, moving forward from the jumping-off place of his future. He was the one out of place, out of time. He was the primitive.

The majesty of the concept was startling. How far could humanity have gone, with thousands of centuries to evolve?

"What's it like, then?" he asked. "What have we become?"

His voice trembled slightly.

She spoke more code. Slowly a picture grew upon the screen. It was a golden cloud, but unlike any cloud he'd ever seen before. The cloud hovered—no, *hung*—across the top of a barren, rocky landscape. Above the cloud burned a sun the color of molten pewter. Tiny lights danced and flitted above the cloud, separate from it, like mindless fireflies. The cloud itself was thick and viscous, halfway between vapor and honey. Its lower parts clung to the rock, dripped from it, rolled down and filled cracks and valleys with clotted light.

"What is it?" he asked.

"Mankind," she replied. "One of us, at least. Those who have given up bodies. They have the potential for bodies, of course. But they exist in the cloud, are the cloud. Incredibly small . . ." Her voice was touched with wonder. "The cloud is the sum of trillions of intelligences."

"I've never heard—"

"This is the future, Garry." The screen shifted again. Now he saw a world of low buildings. The buildings were full of odd, streamlined metal tanks. They seemed to be culture vats of some kind. Interspersed among the tanks were low, hulking shapes he thought might be computers, although he didn't recognize the design.

"What is it?" he asked. "Some kind of information processing center?"

"Meatmatrices," she told him.

He remembered his conversation with Jack. "Then they aren't proscribed here."

"Of course not." She sounded surprised by the idea. "Why would they be?"

He didn't try to explain. "Why so many?" he asked.

"The matrices house intelligence," she replied. "Human intelligence, machine intelligence, and every conceivable blend of the two. They exist in a world called the metamatrix."

He tried to imagine what she was talking about, but he

failed. After a time the picture faded and what appeared to be a graphic star map of part of the local galactic arm appeared.

Colors moved across the arm, red, blue, green, until most of the screen was marked off by areas of different hue. An immense number of stars were delineated.

"What's this?" he asked.

"Human space," she replied. "The Human space of now. Of the time before the lizards. Each color represents a different kind of humanity. The total is what we are now." She sighed. "The culture whose remnants will one day be found by spacefaring lizards, the race they—and you—will call the Kurs'ggtha."

And so, staring at a screen that revealed secrets he could never have imagined, he finally understood. This was the future of man, hidden in his own past. Man split and sundered to chase a hundred possibilities, yet joined by a chain that stretched to the farthest boundaries of heredity.

The Confederacy was but a dot on that vast map.

And now a puny lizard fleet, attacking a tiny part of a far future history, endangered it all.

Hyarl Thomas had called that fleet.

Only his destruction would could save man's future.

And only Garry could destroy him.

He shivered, and pulled Shar close. He felt so lucky, to have this little time with her, before the end.

Chapter Twenty

He felt warmed by her. That was it. He lay in the silent darkness of his room, half sensing the movement, the interplay of great forces around him, and thought about her.

His first instinct was to quantify, to enumerate each moment of their encounter, to understand her intellectually. But that would be a mistake. Rather, he decided, it was better to simply give in, to relax and bathe himself in the warm tides of emotion.

She warmed him. He had been so cold. Ever since the murder of his father, his world had become faster and more frigid, as if that moment of hot violence had released a deep vein of ice in his soul. His emotions had slowed, had become solid and frigid with fear. Nothing stayed the same long enough for him to encompass it. His life had become headlong movement, only pausing to instill more terror. He had become a pawn on a great field of ice, and he was dying from the cold.

She warmed him.

How could he possibly be falling in love? What a spurious emotion. Yet she had held him, and he had held her, and her warmth had broken the chilly claws of his life. Was there something in him, perhaps on a cellular level, that demanded such relief?

The sex had been real. He had not had enough experience to make comparisons, so the movements, the quick holdings and unfoldings, stood by themselves, complete and beautiful. He recalled the thin film of sweat across the bridge of her nose. The way her eyes slid shut at certain moments. The texture of her skin, the feel of her belly against his.

Her toes had curled against the thick pads of his feet, and she'd squeezed him until he could hardly breathe.

He rolled his fingers into hard fists and felt his nails bite into his palms. Love? It was a ridiculous thought. He had no idea if he would survive. Until now he had barely cared. He'd simply wanted it to end. But now he was weaker, because of her. He cared now. He wanted to see her again.

Love was weakness.

But she warmed him.

In the darkness his lips moved around a soft, hungry sound and he rolled over on his stomach.

He closed his eyes and willed sleep to come. He wanted the night over so he could be with her again. For the first time since this madness had begun, dawn held a promise of hope.

Sharnita.

Shar.

The four rode a laser-driven pillar of fire to the station. They threaded through the surging mobs toward the quarters already prepared for them, rooms kept always ready though they might not use them for centuries at a time. As they pushed and shoved through the crowds they gloried in the physical; the stretch and pull of muscle, the firing of neurons, the push and shove of *bodies*.

They experienced bodies so rarely.

"Like old times," the angel said. His voice was cheerful.

"You got a lousy memory," the short man said. "I don't remember old times being all that wonderful." He sounded sour and tense.

The woman said nothing. She simply flashed her ferocious smile in every direction, like a searchlight made of knives. People fell back from her grin without even realizing it.

The Golden Man was also silent. His ruby eyes glittered palely as his body moved with machinelike precison. He never seemed to touch anybody, though people crowded around him like ants.

In the silence of their rooms they relaxed, each in ways that seemed most appropriate, or desired. After a while they met in a larger room, one lined with the shoals of an endless wave of technology.

The man said, "We're here. Now what?"

The angel said, "What we planned. Is there any reason to deviate?"

"We are now defending a stretch of five hundred years. The lizards must be completely shocked. They couldn't have anticipated such an event. They will be slow to regroup. And when they do, even they have to reach the obvious conclusion."

"Which is?" the woman said. She examined her black fingernails with great care.

"That Arius is a phenomenon that must be extinguished. That Arius is the threat they have always feared. The nightmare from the darkest part of the wormhole." The Golden Man's voice was as flat and empty as the endless grinding of a machine.

"So what will they do?" the little man asked.

"The obvious. The lizards are not a devious race, only a paranoid one. They will go back, or try to, until they find a moment of weakness. Then they will concentrate their fleets and destroy the planet."

"Simple," the woman said. "We always knew we might have to do it. We destroy them."

The little man shook his head. "Not the answer. The lizards aren't the problem. They are only a tool. The problem is Hyarl Thomas."

"Then destroy him," the woman said.

"Yes . . ." the man replied. He made a slight motion with one hand, and a huge monitor screen brightened on one wall. On the screen Garry Hamersmidt was just waking up and rubbing his eyes and wondering how long it would take to find Shar again.

"Bring the girl here," the Golden Man said. Beneath the clear timbre of his voice was the endless metal whirling of saws and ruined bone.

He didn't know it, but he had all the symptoms. He ate his breakfast without tasting it. He had to look twice at the controls of his shower to figure out whether the water was warm or cold. He brushed his teeth but forgot toothpaste. His socks didn't match, but he didn't notice until he saw himself in a mirror.

"Stupid," he said to himself. He kept glancing at his nailtale. She'd said not to call until nine o'clock.

He didn't know why. Why not eight, or ten? Her family? Did she even have one?

He knew so little about her. And he didn't care. In the

night his surrender had become complete. He'd become selfish. He only wanted her.

It was almost time. Precisely as his nailtale announced nine o'clock, he punched in the number she'd given him. And waited.

No answer. No recording, no message, nothing.

He sat on the edge of his bed and stared at the wall.

What had happened?

He was discovering the terrible intricacies of love, and he was alone.

He threw a pillow across the room and waited.

He found her at last, as afternoon thinned into evening. He hadn't eaten lunch. The thought of food made him sick. Instead he pushed his way through the crowds, never pausing to notice a single face. Or rather, he saw her face many times, but when he stopped, or called, or shoved frantically through the bodies, it was always a stranger.

He found her address, a single door down a long corridor indistinguishable from his own. He rang three different times, and each time an anonymous doorbot took his message. I was here. I called. I'm waiting. *Where are you?*

By four o'clock he was back in his own room, alone with his thoughts. What did I do? Was it me? Is it her? What happened?

He'd been chasing that tail-eating snake of words for over an hour when his comm-center chimed.

"What? Hello!"

"Jeez, Garry, what's the matter? You sound out of breath."

He'd tripped over the corner of his bed in a headlong lunge for the phone, and now he rubbed a badly bruised elbow. "Where have you been?"

In the screen her face tightened. "Hey, wait a minute, buddy. You sound like you've got a problem there."

He forced himself to speak calmly. "I'm sorry. You said to call at nine. I was worried."

She blinked. "I did? I forgot. I apologize."

He stared at her eyes. He took a deep breath. "Listen, forget it. How about dinner. Someplace nice. I'll buy."

The skin at the corners of her eyes crinkled slightly, and he thought she was about to smile. But she seemed to consider the question seriously. "I don't know . . ."

"Aw, come on, Shar. Please?"

She smiled. "Okay. What time?"

"Now. Ten minutes. When?"

She giggled. It was a musical sound. "About seven, I think. I've got some stuff to do. You want to meet me?"

"Whatever you want."

"Okay. The Neon Chicken. You'll have to make reservations. It's expensive. But you said someplace nice."

He nodded. "About seven. I'll be there."

"See you," she said. She started to turn away from the screen. Then she paused and touched her fingers to her lips and blew him a kiss.

Shakily he raised his own hand. The screen went blank.

He turned away from the screen and stood absolutely still for a moment. Then he jumped straight up into the air.

She wore something thin and white that ended above her knees and clung to her body when she moved. He couldn't take his eyes off her.

The waiters of the Neon Chicken were Humans who had stropped their hauteur to a fine edge, but he used the chip Glory had given him to bribe the maître d' for a good table, and now busboys and captains swarmed around them like lizard real estate salesmen smelling money.

She ordered, because he was lost in the five-page menu. At one point she startled him when she turned to a busboy and said, "Hey, Harry. Long time no see."

The practiced facade of grandeur cracked on the boy's face and he grinned. "Shar. How you doing?"

Later she grinned. "I went to school with him. He makes a young fortune fleecing tourists. I bet he never thought he'd see me in here."

"What? Am I a tourist, ripe for the shearing?"

"Huh-uh. You're with me. That's why I spoke to good old Harry. To let him know that this is pleasure, not business."

"Business? Exactly what kind of business are you in, Shar?"

"I'm not sure I like the tone of that question, Garry."

He stared at his silverware in confusion. "I'm sorry. I didn't mean anything. It's just that I know so little about you."

She thought about it. "It's okay. Nothing I'm ashamed

of. I've been escorting folks around the station. Some of these guests are brass of one kind or another. They stay over for a few days. I show them around, is all."

"You bring them here?"

"Sometimes."

"And . . ." He couldn't help it. "Anything else?"

She raised her face and stared at him levelly. Her brown eyes were calm. "Do you mean anything in particular?"

He felt his cheeks go hot. "Uh." After a moment he looked away.

"Garry, let's get something straight. I like you, and we certainly got along okay yesterday. But I'm not your girlfriend or anything. You don't have a claim on me, don't have any reason for jealousy. Get it out of your skull. We're friends. You understand?"

I'm acting like an idiot, he thought as he choked back an angry reply. "Yes. I get it." He was almost able to keep the bitterness out of his voice.

She ignored it. "Good. We'll get along just fine, then."

The rest of the meal was mildly strained, but afterward he walked her to the door. Just before she went inside she paused and turned to him.

"Thanks for a great evening, Garry. I loved it."

And I love you, he wanted to say, but instead he kissed her.

She was gone in an instant.

He went back to his room. He had had sex with her only a day before, but a single kiss had left him with an erection. His head was full of the smell of her.

From another place eyes the color of faded rubies watched him. They narrowed in approval.

The boy was well and truly hooked. Now to reel him in.

Like shooting fish in a barrel, the Golden Man thought. And if he'd been capable of emotions, he might even have felt sorry for him.

"We are playing with fire," the short man said.

The four were gathered in their meeting room, and their voices were shadowed by the clicks and hums and sighs of their machines. The power that connected them to their real world was almost unimaginable. They tapped the force of gravity where it turned into the lightless kernels of the black holes merely to maintain those connections. They had been alive, in one sense or another, for a very long time.

The angel said, "We knew it was a risk all along. But if he can be activated—if the *Human* part of him can be activated . . ."

The woman shook her head. Her shaggy black hair bounced in the dim light. "He's Human enough." She lit a cigarette. "I was close to him. I know."

"You don't know anything," the man said. "Those codes were a complete mystery. I would never have allowed his creation, except for—"

She exhaled sharply. "Except you'd already fucked up with Thomas. So what? It's done. Now we make the best of it. He'll do okay."

The man's voice went sharp and sarcastic. "What's that, mother love talking? You thought it was a joke at the time."

"Fuck off. So I carried him to term. That was your idea too."

He shrugged. "At least his zygote had human genes. Thomas is one hundred percent strange. And look at what we got with him."

"I told you we shouldn't have grown him in the first place," the angel said. "We didn't know enough."

"What's the matter?" the man replied. "No sense of adventure?"

"None of this is germane," the Golden Man said. "What's done is done. We have to deal with the problem now."

The little man sighed and leaned back in his chair. They sat around a large steel table, polished so brightly that their features were reflected up into their clear, empty eyes. "You're right, of course. Although you don't have to be so fucking rational about it. What do you think? You've been keeping track. Do we have a shot, or not?"

The Golden Man seemed to sink into himself. His eyes turned gray, then white, then totally empty. His body slumped, as if he'd left it for a moment. Then the moment passed, and the body straightened again.

"I ran a series of phaged logics. The questions that eat the questions. Probability gets all fucked up down on the quantum level. Which is where we're working anyway. But it still seems like the best idea is confrontation. Put

them all together, the boy and Thomas and the a[...]
Then see what happens. The kid's either Human en[...]
or he's not. I don't see how our problems can ge[...]
worse."

The short man nodded. "What I thought. Othe[...]
we have to wipe out the entire race of lizards. An[...]
have no idea what that might do to the time line[...]
wouldn't affect us. I don't think. But what it might [...]
the Human half of the Confederacy. Not to mention [...]
still have Thomas to deal with."

"What's the matter?" the woman said. "You don't [...]
playing God?"

"I don't know. Do you?"

She lit another cigarette. "Fuck off, Jack," she sai[...]

Forever after, the scene would be etched on his me[...]
ory. He awoke early, filled with buoyant, almost hyste[...]
cal anticipation. He whistled in the shower, laughi[...]
when the water bubbled on his lips. He dressed quick[...]
and then realized he had no place to go. She was busy [...]
the morning, she'd said, and would call him in the afte[...]
noon. The room was too small to contain him. He pace[...]
for a few seconds, then realized he was hungry. H[...]
decided to go out for breakfast.

As he walked quickly down his corridor, feeling th[...]
muscles move in his legs, savoring the roll of his shoulders, he felt somehow larger. Filled to overflowing with
emotions he barely understood. Hyarl Thomas had faded
into a dim, distant specter. He hadn't thought of Garth
for at least a day. Even Glory, his most recent companion, seemed faded and unattractive in the blazing light of
Sharnita's glow.

As usual, the main concourse was a throbbing mass of
people. He paused a moment and stared at the crowd. So
many people. They seemed normal enough. He could
even imagine this mob chattering and laughing in the
streets and plazas of High H'hogoth.

Yet, if Shar was telling him the truth, they were sol-
diers. They passed through here in their limitless streams
bound from one time to another, from the worlds of the
past to the ships of the future, where they guarded a
single planet against a lizard fleet five centuries long.

The sound of all these people was a dull, rising roar,
their individual voices submerged in a surf of sound.

tifact.
ough,
t any

rwise
d we
s. It
lo to
we'd

like

m-
eri-
ng
ly,
in
r-
ed
le

d in every kind of clothing and were of
or. He tried to imagine the planets they
Some were giants, roped with muscle,
bouncing strides, as if the station gravity
ing. Others were thin as sticks. Some had
altered in one way or another. He saw
lash of gill slits and wondered how these
rid atmosphere. Or not altered—he still
d to the sheer size of humanity's garden
time of it. These strange ones were the
ration descendants, no more altered than
izen of their planets.

hands in his pockets and leaned back against
small alcove and watched them, glorying in
lities. This was what the Confederacy was
ard. This polyglot multitude was but a slice of
otential Worlds, the Human Worlds, hoped to

ppreciated for the first time the wisdom of the
They had moved humanity back to freedom,
ould spread and grow without the shadow of
. Here man prospered without a shadow poised
e line, like a knife against a vein.

e paradox. He tried to unravel the unholy com-
ty of it. Mankind's future was in his past, yet the
this time was in the future. Man was still threat-
How could the universe allow it?

en he realized that the universe didn't care. The
rmholes were real, were explained by arcane physical
aws, were even necessary to the form of the universe
itself. And the universe cared nothing for paradox. If a
man went back in time and killed his grandfather, perhaps the man would never exist. Perhaps any man, perhaps any kind of life, even a race, a species, was only
probability, like the quantum particles that made up the
universe. Perhaps there was no paradox at all, only possibility. No matter. The strong force would still glue atoms
together, the electroweak would stretch its ghostly fingers, and the curve of space called gravity would still turn
in on itself in the places of perfect darkness.

Whether the spinning balls that circled the stars carried
any particular mote of life was irrelevant to the great
clock of infinity as it ticked toward the point at the end of
time. What cared man of the paradoxes of bacteria?

Chapter Twenty-one

He found it when he was packing a few things for the trip. He'd almost forgotten he had it, but the heavy, elongated weight buried beneath underwear and socks resisted his fingertips and reminded him. Slowly he drew it out and stared at it. Its carved horn handle was rubbed smooth in places. Slowly he opened the blade. There was still a tiny rust-colored spot at the very tip of the point. He stared at the smooth edge of the blade and remembered the first time he'd met Frego. So long ago.

He'd brought it with him from Arius Prime, far in the future. Far in his own past. He sighed and folded up the blade into the handle and put the knife away.

He wondered if Frego was still alive. Glory had taken him from his room to another room and showed him the bloody rag wrapped around a gnarled finger.

"Like some kind of stupid gangster video," she'd said. "I gave Thomas more credit."

But he was already ruined by the terrible meeting with Shar—he couldn't forget the scorn in her brown eyes—and the faint strips of white at the base of the ruined finger, where bits of tendon gleamed like liquid bone, made the room whirl. He bent over suddenly and vomited on the floor. The slow, heaving cramps jerked him again and again, until there was nothing left but the tears running down his face.

"Frego," Glory had said patiently after he told her about Shar. "She's only a girl. Frego saved your life. You owe him."

He sat in his empty bedroom and imagined that Shar was calling him on the comm right now, but nothing happened. Eventually he put the knife away and finished packing.

But for Hyarl Thomas none of this would have happened. Thomas was his nemesis. He would have to face him again.

There was no other way.

"I know you," he said to the Golden Man when he saw him seated across the round table from him. The Golden Man nodded faintly, his eyes washed with pink, but made no reply. Garry stared at the others in the room. Jack, his face pinched and enigmatic, sat to the right. The Golden Man was next to him, and a tall, thin young man with hair like molten steel wool was at the other end. Glory sat next to the young man, an ashtray piled with butts in front of her.

"You know Jack," Glory said. "That one"—she pointed at the Golden Man—"is Bill. And this one is Wizard."

The tall young man grinned, and Garry thought suddenly that he might be able to like him. Under other circumstances. "Like the Wizard of Oz?" he said.

Wizard's grin widened. "Exactly," he said.

"Where's Chasm? If this is old-home week," Garry said.

Glory stubbed out her cigarette. "He's not . . . one of us."

"So what are you?"

"The founders," Glory replied.

"Ah." Garry stared at their silent faces. They seemed human enough. They breathed and smoked cigarettes and smiled and ate pizza—there was the wreckage of several half-eaten meals scattered across the top of the table. Papers and napkins and empty beer cans. "The founders. You didn't come here for a picnic, I guess?"

Jack shook his head. "Not exactly."

"Well." Garry watched the Golden Man. What was his name again? Bill. Just plain Bill. "I don't think I'm pleased to meet you."

"Makes sense," Jack admitted. "Most people aren't."

Garry didn't say anything.

"Okay" Jack said. He paused. He placed his hands out, palms up, on the tabletop. "I think you deserve a few answers."

"I don't *deserve* anything," Garry said.

"All right, then. We *owe* you some answers. Better?"

Garry stared at him silently.

Jack tapped his fingertips lightly, nervously. "We may even owe you an apology. I don't know. Our concerns have been larger, perhaps, than the safety of a single boy."

Garry felt the skin on his face tighten. "It's a question of viewpoint," he said. "Whether the boy's, or those who claim a larger vision."

Glory chuckled. "Yeah, come on, Jack. He's got you. Old men always find young lives less valuable. It's one of the reasons war is such a popular sport with the aged."

Jack glanced at her. "Not me. We. Remember?"

She turned to Garry. Her voice was rough and cheerful. "That's right, buddy. Me too. You were doomed from birth, and I played as much a part as anybody. Maybe more."

"Would you people please quit fucking around and tell me what's going on?"

"Ask your questions," the Golden Man said.

"Sure. You and your Search have been stage-managing my life. Even I can see that. And I can understand it, in a way, if what you told me about my origin is true. Genetic maps carved on a chunk of neutronium. But why? Even now, none of this looks real organized. Okay, so you set up some kind of major confrontation with Hyarl Thomas. But it seems to me like he had as much to do with it as you. In fact, I don't see you doing much about him at all. Am I right?"

Jack shrugged. "It's worse than that. Thomas may be manipulating us. We don't know. He screws up every probability projection we make."

"Ah. Yeah. So you ignore him and go ahead with me. What do you get with your projections about me, then?"

Jack looked at the Golden Man. "Bill?" he said.

"Same thing," the Golden Man replied. "Gibberish. Nothing. We don't know what will happen."

"Then *why*?"

"We have no choice," Jack said at last. "The projections *are* clear about one thing. If Thomas continues as he has been, the future Confederacy will be destroyed. Humanity will never rise on Earth, and our civilization here, the Kurs'ggtha, will never exist. Screw the paradoxes involved. It will still happen."

Garry stared at the tabletop. He thought about the look on Shar's face, the scorn, when the fat man pushed him away. "What if I told you I don't give a fuck at all?" he said.

Into the silence Jack said, "Neutronium."

"What?"

"The artifact, Garry. You've ignored it, but think about it now." He raised one hand slightly, and a large screen on the wall behind him lit up. It displayed a picture of the artifact, the silvery cube about half a meter on a side. Garry stared at the screen, remembering the first time he'd seen the cube, recalling the terror of the rat-faced man who'd brought it to him. Who'd brought, as inexorably, Hyarl Thomas.

"I haven't thought about it much because it's impossible," Garry said at last. "For that thing to be neutronium, its mass would have to equal that of a medium-sized asteroid. About fifty kilometers in diameter. You wouldn't be able to haul something like that around on a cart. Not in this universe."

Oz grinned. "Precisely," he said. "Not in this universe."

"But it's real," Jack said. "It is neutronium. And it doesn't weigh anything like what it should. It is, in fact, impossible. Just like you say. Yet it exists. And Hyarl Thomas has it."

Garry stared silently at Jack's face. The little man seemed to be urging him to something, expecting something from him.

"What do you want me to say?"

"Where did it come from?" Jack said.

"A black hole. You told me."

"Yes, but why? How?"

"You told me it didn't matter. That anything could come from a singularity. Anything at all."

Jack's shoulders slumped. "Okay. It wasn't a fair question. I just hoped . . ."

"We want to put everything together," Glory said. "It's all we can think of. A gigantic gamble. That somehow you and Thomas and the artifact are all connected. And that those three factors add up to something that might solve our situation."

Finally he got it. A slow feeling of wonder began to suffuse him. He felt the bubbling warmth of emotion fill his skull until it spilled out. He laughed.

"What's the joke?" Jack said. His voice was almost bitter.

"You call yourself gods," Garry said finally, when he was able to breathe again. "But you believe in God."

Glory nodded. "Of course. In the beginning was the singularity."

"So what does that make me?"

She rubbed her lips. Then she lit a cigarette. "Got me, kid. That's what we want to find out."

Later, Garry said, "Does it bother anybody, sending me out alone to face Thomas? I mean, he's already killed me once."

"You'll have help," Jack said.

"Who? Chasm?"

"No," Glory said. "The best we've got."

"Who's that?"

"Us," she said gloomily.

The ship was huge. Garry's stateroom alone was the size of a small house, and furnished with appointments more befitting a castle.

"You may have noticed," Glory told him, "that we have a fondness for the finer things."

"You eat a lot of pizza," he replied.

"It's one of the finer things. And silver trays don't hurt it a bit."

Departure had been uneventful. He rested for a while and tried not to think about Shar. It was like trying not to think about an elephant. His attention kept returning to that moment when she'd rejected him. But why had she done it? Was their relationship just a casual thing to her? He couldn't believe it. Didn't want to believe it.

It had happened. It was real. Had she somehow sensed his essential differentness? The pall of strangeness he lived with every day?

He shook his head and leaned back on a thick leather sofa and closed his eyes. Somehow it was his fault. Something he'd done, said. Why hadn't he just left her alone, waited until later, mentioned the fat man in passing.

Why had he made a fool of himself?

He whiled away the next few hours with such pleasant thoughts. He decided his mood for Hyarl Thomas should be appropriately suicidal.

I'm only Human, he thought. It wasn't a comforting notion.

"That trick with the girl, it was a little rough, don't you think?" Glory said.

Jack was occupied with a steaming cup of coffee. He placed the heavy mug on the low table in front of him and frowned. "You know, you seem to get more squeamish, the older you get."

"And you seem to get nastier," she replied. "He's pretty fucked up about it."

"Fucked up," Jack mused. "The Human condition, most of the time. And wasn't that the idea? We don't know what he is, after all. So we try to make him as Human as we can, tie him down, so to speak. And what's more Human than a broken heart?"

"Like I said," she answered, blowing a cloud of blue smoke. "Nasty."

"You take something away, you make it more valuable. We took his father. We hid his mother. We let his friend get taken. And we stole his lover. All that Human misery, focused on Hyarl Thomas. I wonder if he knows how hard we worked?"

"You better pray he never finds out," Glory said. "I don't think he'd much thank us for it."

"You gotta do," Jack said, "what you gotta do."

"Hell of a way to run a universe."

"We aren't running it. That's the problem."

"I wonder," Glory said.

"You want a beer?"

"What?" Garry looked across the vast domed room. Glory was at least a hundred yards away, dwarfed by distance. A faint blue haze surrounded her. She was smoking incessantly, lighting one cigarette from the ember of the last, and throwing the butts on the floor. Amazingly, the smoldering stubs immediately went out. Magic, Garry supposed sourly.

"A Budweiser? You want one?"

They were alone in the huge chamber. She'd brought him up earlier, but he'd had nothing to say to her.

"Yeah. I guess."

"I'm not a waitress. You want one, come on over." She had a crystal ice bucket the size of a trash can near her feet. It was full of beer cans. He guessed she was emptying one every fifteen minutes.

The light in the room had an amber cast to it, shadowed and sinister. Overhead, reminding him of Jack's playpen on Arius Prime, curved a clear canopy. Outside was darkness. No stars.

"Sit," she said, and patted an empty space on the sofa that was only moderately dusted with cigarette ash.

He sighed and plopped down, raising a small cloud, which held for a moment, then drifted with invisible currents toward a distant vent. "I don't think I like you very much," he said.

"Drink a beer, you'll feel better. Besides, it's sour grapes."

"Beer? I thought it was wine."

The corner of her thin smile twitched slightly in response. "Your attitude, buddy."

"So what's my attitude supposed to be? Thrilled? Happy to even be in the presence of the mighty founders?"

"Mm. You're developing a taste for sarcasm. That might be interesting."

"God knows, I want to be interesting."

"The best way to handle sarcasm is not to overdo it. Lightly does the trick."

He popped a Budweiser and raised it to his lips. The tart, malty taste was cool on his throat. Despite himself, he chugged half the can before he put it down.

"I didn't have a choice about doing this, did I?"

"What do you think?" she said.

Overhead, something empty swirled against the endless black. It was more a hint, a thought, than any visual effect. He glanced up. "Wherever this is, it doesn't look very appetizing."

She shrugged. "We're hopping the tubes," she said. "Not a normal procedure."

He blinked. "You mind explaining?"

She crumpled a can and tossed it in the general direction of a small pile of other empties. "One wormhole into another. You notice the timeband hasn't been used once?"

He had, but the idea hadn't really registered. "So?"

"We're going back. We can't go all the way back, but far enough."

"All the way back to where? Jeez, Glory, you are the most cryptic frigging woman sometimes."

This brought a real smile. "Really? You think so? Jack says I'm transparent. But then he's known me longer."

He shook his head. "Goddammit, would you answer my question. For once?"

She reached out and patted his knee lightly. He stared at her fingers and she removed them. "This universe begins with a singularity. A big one. Actually, if you do the math right, the singularity doesn't exist. Hawking again. He proposed a no-boundary universe, that is, if viewed from the perspective of imaginary time. In imaginary time, time and space are the same. There are no beginnings or endings, and the universe simply is. Of course, that doesn't describe what we see in our universe, the universe of space-time, but Bill hasn't been able to knock any holes in Hawking's original ideas. So it just may be the way we look at things. What we call real may only be a reflection of imaginary time, which is the underlying, deep principle of the universe. You follow?"

"You kidding?" He finished the rest of the beer. "Why are you telling me these things? I haven't touched on any of this stuff in school."

She paused before lighting another cigarette. Her thin face was thoughtful. She stared at him for a moment. "Your genetic structure isn't entirely Human. Surely you realize that."

He reached for another beer. "You haven't let me forget. Codes scratched on impossible neutronium." He stopped. "Hey. Maybe it isn't impossible neutronium. Maybe it's just imaginary neutronium, from your imaginary time." He opened the can and grinned.

"Are you making a joke?"

"Sure, I . . ." He swallowed some beer, but this time didn't really taste it. Overhead, midnight eddied slowly, a great dark soup of emptiness. Something inside his skull responded to her words, to the viscid movement of the black. Something almost . . . remembered. "I don't know," he said at last. His voice was soft and distant. "Am I?"

She'd straightened up slightly, her green eyes beginning to glow, but now she slumped back. "Garry, you're so fucking ordinary. It's enough to drive me crazy."

He considered that. "How did you expect me to be?"

"We don't *know*!" She flipped her cigarette viciously, watched it shed sparks all along its parabola to the floor.

"That's what's so frustrating. You're like any other seventeen-year-old kid. And we expect you to rescue Humanity. Sometimes I think we are crazy."

"Yeah," he said at last. "Me too." He glanced at her, saw the lines cut into the skin around her eyes. "Don't worry," he said. "It'll work out."

He didn't know why he said it.

But he thought it might be true.

Abruptly she stood up. "I gotta get out of here," she said. She held her cigarette between her teeth in a smoky grimace and ran both hands through her ragged black hair. "Out there. It makes me nervous." Her green eyes flicked up at the strange, colorless, starless night beyond the crystal dome. "This is all new to me. I thought I'd done just about everything, but . . ." She shook her head suddenly. "I wish we knew what he was. I wish this didn't have to be."

He stared at her silently. He felt tired, but not exhausted. He could feel everything converging on this spot, this time. "Isn't this what you wanted?" he said.

"No. I didn't want it. I only accepted that it had to happen."

He thought about the difference. She inhaled suddenly, then turned away. The sound of her boots on the carpet was soft and precise. Swish, swish.

Garth, Frego, the Golden Girl. Hyarl Thomas. Something cellular, built into the most basic structure of his body, cried out for completion. A joining. An end.

"I want it!" he called after her.

She didn't reply. After a moment she was gone, and he was alone under the dark. He opened another beer and drank, his eyes hooded. The past rushed up and hovered over him.

Hyarl Thomas was waiting. That was fine. He'd waited a long time. A little more wouldn't hurt.

At least he already knew what it was like to die.

Chapter Twenty-two

He sat for a long time drinking beer. The great chamber around him soaked up sound, so that he felt like a tiny island in the darkness. Occasionally he looked up and watched space curdle and eddy around the incredible shields of the vast ship. He knew the ship was huge, and yet against the endless reach of the universe it was less than an atom.

He drank and listened to his thoughts spin.

There were five empties on the floor around him when he noticed that the room was growing brighter. His gaze rose. Was it his imagination? No, the darkness was no longer dark. A faint wraith of deep, deep red drifted lazily through the black, like the most ethereal Christmas ribbon. He blinked. What was it?

They had been going back, ever backward in time, leapfrogging through a never-ending series of wormholes. How many years now? Millions? No, certainly billions. The universe was still young, perhaps fifteen of those billion years, but that was a long, long time. Yet everything had an end, and a beginning. Perhaps in imaginary time, as Glory said, the universe simply existed, without edges or boundaries. But Humans didn't live in imaginary time, and for them the beginning and the end were the same. Singularities. The two black holes that were Alpha and Omega. The universe itself was merely the breathing between the two.

They must be very early now, so distant in the past perhaps even the galaxies themselves had not yet formed. He reached down and picked up his sixth beer and held the can without opening it, his fingers lightly sliding over the cold, wet surface. What had he learned in elementary physics? He fumbled for a moment through the ordered files of his memory and came up with a few references. All the action from the Big Bang occurred mostly in the first minutes, primarily in the first tiniest fractions of a second. The galaxies themselves didn't begin to coalesce until what was called the moment of recombination, when free electrons combined with protons to form the first true atoms, and the overwhelming number of photons that had interacted until that moment were free to move at last. He tried to imagine what that instant had been like; before, the universe had been incredibly hot, but dark. Light—photons—couldn't move very far. The entire universe had been like the interior of a sun. Then the temperature had dropped below three thousand Kelvin, and the universe had become transparent. That was the true instant reflected in all human creation legends when something said, "Let there be light."

Of course, in the real universe, it was only the laws of the quanta and the atoms that spoke the words. The universe was a clock ticking on the face of its own rules.

Yet it must be an awesome sight. Yes. He looked up again. The deep, dark red was growing brighter, more crimson. And spreading. He wondered what the ambient temperature beyond the shields was now. Hot, he guessed, and growing hotter.

The time at the beginning of time was looming closer. That, and the creature even stranger than himself. Hyarl Thomas waited for him, in the moment of all creation.

He swallowed his beer in two quick gulps and let the can fall to the floor. He belched. Then he stood up. The founders were somewhere on the ship. He went to find them. They should know.

He was beginning to hear the whispery call of his own destiny.

There would be great light before the dark.

"Pizza's okay, but you ever heard of too much of a good thing?" Jack said sourly.

"You made up the menu," Glory replied.

He shrugged. "I wasn't feeling very original."

"What's the matter with pizza?" Oz asked. His young face glowed with pleasure. Amber tints chased themselves across the surface of his eyes.

"Use a body more often," Jack said. "You get tired of things."

The Golden Man didn't say anything. He chewed mechanically. His eyes were the color of watery blood, and somber.

The great domed chamber had been remodeled in Garry's short absence. Now the floor was of some soft, black, faintly yielding material. The walls were deep burgundy, and their rich texture seemed to absorb light. Only the crystal dome overhead was the same. Some trick of shielding polarized the unbearable glare of the universe outside, cranking down the intensity of the white blaze so that the people inside weren't blinded by the light. Even so the illumination was harsh and even. There were no shadows because the light came from everywhere. It even seemed to permeate the ship itself, so that Garry imagined he could see into its structure, read the atomic lattices that were the only true matter in this time.

"What do you think will happen now?" he said. He'd bitten off the tip of a slice of pizza and chewed slowly. His eyes had darkened until they gleamed flat and opaque as marbles.

"I don't know," Jack said. "We've gone beyond the capabilities of the drive, and probably beyond even the limits of the wormholes themselves. This era is too far before even the protogalaxies." He looked up at the incandescence. "I don't know what's pulling us back, or when it will stop."

Garry swallowed. "I do."

The Golden Man showed his first sign of interest in the conversation. "What?"

"Hyarl Thomas is," Garry said. "He wants us in his playground."

"How do you know?"

"Can't you feel it?" Garry asked.

Glory looked at Jack. Her eyes narrowed slightly. "Feel what?"

He tried to find words that would explain the bizarre sensations he'd been enduring for at least an hour. The slow, sucking call that summoned even his own molecular structures. It felt as if his body were trying to collapse in on itself.

"He's calling me," he said at last. "He doesn't care about you at all. It's me he wants."

Jack's voice was curious. "Do you know why?"

Garry puzzled over it. "The artifact. It's got something to do with the artifact."

Jack waited. His mouth was slightly open. "That's it? You don't know anything more?"

Garry shook his head. He reached for another slice of pizza. "It doesn't matter," he said.

"Why?" Glory asked.

"We'll find out soon enough. We're almost there."

The Golden Man raised his head. In the stark sheets of white light his pale ruby eyes had faded into near transparency. Garry shivered. He was frightened of Hyarl Thomas, but the strange vacuum that seemed to surround the Golden Man held echoes of the same chill vacancy. There was something of the machine about both men.

"He's coming," the Golden Man said.

As if his words were a signal, the universal radiance that had surrounded them was suddenly extinguished. Garry sat in utter and complete darkness. "What happened?" he said.

Jack's voice answered him. "We've passed the point of transparency. The space around us is hotter now, over the cutoff level of three thousand Kelvin. Photons can't penetrate. We're actually entering the period of the Big Bang."

As Garry's eyes slowly adjusted to the heat of this strange new light, he saw that each of the founders was surrounded by a faint, ghostly radiance. Their outlines shimmered, so that their bodies were like holes in the dark itself.

"How do you know he's coming?" he asked the Golden Man.

"He's already impinging on my space," the Golden Man replied.

"What does that mean?"

He heard Glory suck hard, then exhale. A tiny red dot glowed at the end of her cigarette. "We don't entirely operate in realtime," she said.

Garry paused. There were so many questions. Glory's

voice had been slow and nervous. Were these people frightened too?

"What's that supposed to mean?"

Again the soft, rushing sound of her inhalations. "What you see, Garry. Us. It's not real."

He made a soft snorting sound. "You're as real as I am."

"We use bodies," she replied. A short chuckle. "We're the ultimate body snatchers. When we need one, we build it. But us, ourselves, our personalities, those exist . . . somewhere else."

He chewed on it. "How can that be?"

She sighed. "It happened a long time ago. Ancient history. But it's true. We live in something called the metamatrix, with occasional sidetrips to somewhere else. A place that's Human, but not very understandable."

He shook his head. The soft white T-shirt he was wearing was soaked with sweat. His armpits itched. "You're all crazy. This is all crazy. Hyarl Thomas is coming. Doesn't that mean anything to you?"

The Golden Man's voice sliced into the silence like a saw cutting cheese. The sound of it made Garry's spine ache. "It means everything, Garry. We've planned for this moment almost three hundred years. Do you think all of this is coincidence? We knew what Thomas was the moment he appeared. An anomaly. A universal anomaly, in fact. His existence was impossible. The artifact that contained his genetic code was impossible. And you are impossible. Three impossibilities all wrapped up in one package. We had to do something."

Jack chimed in, sounding morose. "What we did was dictated by what Hyarl Thomas did. He's been attacking us—we four, and Humanity itself, which in a way we represent. This assault by the lizards is only the latest, and most blatant effort on his part. But we've known he was our enemy for a long time."

Garry thought about the resources these founders seemed to command. The planets, the vast civilizations of the past, the incredible computer power. "Why didn't you kill him?" he said at last.

"Because," Glory replied, "we couldn't."

Outside the crystal dome it remained absolutely dark,

a color so absent of light and yet suffused with intimations of such great heat that it was hard to look at. Jack finally polarized the dome and brought up the interior lights.

The Golden Man had sunk into a kind of wide-eyed slumber. He seemed oblivious to the rest of them, almost in a trance. Jack stared at his feet. Oz stared at Glory. And Glory watched Garry with intent fascination, as if waiting for him to do something startling, miraculous.

"What?" Garry said.

She blew him a kiss. "Just waiting, sweetheart."

"For what? You think I'm gonna blow up or something?"

"I don't know." An amused expression twisted her faint smile. "You feel something like that coming on?"

He exhaled and felt a tingling in the tips of his fingers. Nerves, he told himself. "Fuck you."

"You think *that* will help?"

He couldn't stop himself. He grinned. "That *always* helps."

Hyarl Thomas appeared at the dark fringed edge of the great chamber. The artifact was at his feet. His eyes were empty rippling pools.

The Golden Man blinked. "He's here," he said.

In that moment something peculiar began to happen in the blank, black soup that surrounded their ship. Garry felt a sudden shrinking, as if space itself, or whatever passed for space, underwent compression, folded in on itself. He sensed movement, intricate and complete. He understood that they had passed a sort of barrier. They had entered Hyarl Thomas's domain.

And mine? he wondered suddenly.

"Silly people," Hyarl Thomas said. "But you brought him. At least something went right."

He stepped away from the shadows, and it was as if a video screen flickered and became clear. Garry stared at him. Thomas had a high forehead, clear and unlined. It set off the electric blue crackle of his eyes. He was smiling. His teeth seemed impossibly huge and white behind the thin line of his lips. Again, Garry was conscious of the ageless quality about the man; he looked thirty, but he might have been any age. His short blond hair was like spun platinum, almost silver. Long muscles rubbed slowly against each other as he moved.

His suit was impeccable. His hands were empty.

He was one against their many.

Then why does he make my stomach feel like it's full of ice cubes? Garry wondered.

Thomas flashed the barracuda smile in his direction and Garry looked away. "Well, Garry," Thomas said. "Do you feel anything yet?"

"What should I feel?"

"Your healing," Thomas told him. "The thing that makes you whole."

Garry started to speak, but it was Oz, surprisingly, who broke in, his voice quick and brittle. "Don't say anything, Garry," he said.

Slowly, Thomas turned his gaze on the tall young man. "Ah. The angel speaks. Do you speak for all, or for yourself?" Thomas's voice was light and mocking. There was a slow cool laziness to it, as if he had all the time in the world. Perhaps he did, Garry thought.

Oz moved his lips, but Jack raised a finger and the younger man fell silent. "We created you," Jack said.

Thomas laughed. It was a short, barking sound, almost a cough. "You? You built me. This body. But created me? You only call yourself a god. Don't be presumptuous."

Jack shook his head. "Without what we did, you don't exist. A few scratches on some bizarre metal. Nothing more."

"And do I owe you, then? Is that what you're saying?" He laughed again and moved forward. Now he was almost to them. He seemed to tower over the seated group. His eyes flicked from one to the next, touching lightly. Garry thought of whips.

"It's not a matter of owing," Jack said. "It's about control, isn't it?" His voice was old and rough and tired, but his back was straight. He seemed entirely unafraid.

Thomas stared at him. "You know more than I thought. Or is that it? Do you know, or are you only guessing?"

"We've had three hundred years to guess, Thomas," Jack replied.

Thomas nodded. "Was it enough? What do you guess, little man who wants to be a god?"

Jack winced. Perhaps he was regretting his casual use of that bit of self-description. Garry couldn't decide. Jack seemed shrunken and despairing in the pitiless glaze of Thomas's scorn. He licked his lips. Then he glanced at Garry and Garry blinked. Something, some final secret, lay hidden in Jack's eyes. But Garry couldn't even begin to imagine what it might be.

"If the rate of expansion at the beginning of time had varied by more than one part in ten thousand million million," Jack said slowly, "this universe would not now exist. It would have collapsed."

Garry's mouth opened slightly. He felt the air move across his cheeks. He was lost. What was Jack talking about?

Hyarl Thomas stepped back. Not far, but a single small movement that seemed like a hammer blow in the stasis of the room. The Golden Man smiled.

"What?" Garry said.

Hyarl Thomas turned on him. Now Garry saw it. There was an absolute fury behind the blankness of Thomas's eyes. The man was enraged. But about what? Yet the anger was so strong, so palpable, that Garry involuntarily raised both his hands.

"It's nothing," Thomas said. "The old man babbles. He's insane, Garry. Didn't you know that? Think about it. Think about living inside a computer for centuries. Think about how Human he is. How Human *any* of them are."

"I don't know," Garry said. "What you mean. What do you want with me? Are you the one? Or is it them?" He looked at Jack, at Glory. Her eyes were an emerald blaze, but otherwise she seemed distracted. The Golden Man was staring blankly at the crystal dome. He seemed entirely uninterested in the conversation. Oz tapped his thumb and little finger together and stared at the quick, spastic movement.

"What do you want from me?" Garry said at last.

"Me?" Thomas said. He turned slightly and moved his hand. A gesture that led the eye. Garry saw the artifact, still in the shadows, cool and silvery. "Not me," Thomas said. "Never me. But you knew that. You've always known. If you just remembered."

*   *   *

A sort of irresistible pressure was building in Garry's skull. He closed his eyes. He wished that somehow, if he opened them, everything would be different. Changed back to what it was before, when he was still a child. When he worked in a pawnshop and had a father named Garth.

But it wouldn't be so. Something essential had been burned away, never to be remade. He had passed a marker, a chit on the path to adulthood. He could never return. When he opened his eyes, time would not have run backward. The arrow of time pointed ahead, and could not be denied.

He would have to face Hyarl Thomas. Whatever he was, whatever he represented. And the artifact.

"All right," he said. He opened his eyes and saw them watching him. Then the power took him and he stepped forward. A glint of vacant ferocity surfaced in the flatness of Hyarl Thomas's eyes, but even he, startled, moved out of Garry's path.

"Yes," Thomas said. "Go to it, the artifact. I am there, waiting. Go to it."

Garry nodded. Something about the squat, heavy chunk of metal was wrong. The room blurred about him, then cleared. It was as if the universe itself had flickered.

Outside the ship and inside his head symmetries were beginning to form.

"Come to me," Hyarl Thomas said.

"Yes," Garry told him.

The ship itself, barricaded behind shields of unreal complexity, shuddered. Garry didn't notice. Nor was he aware that in the sliver of that instant many things occurred.

They had moved to the very beginning of the Big Bang, the first few seconds of the life of the universe. In quick succession they penetrated to the fusion area, when the universe itself was a hydrogen bomb. Then to the first second, and the eras of the leptons and the hadrons. They passed through a time when the stuff of the universe weighed about a thousand tons per cubic centimeter.

The shudder that Garry didn't notice was caused by the sudden shrinkage of the universe, a reversal of the original inflationary period, when space expanded millions of times in picoseconds, becoming smooth and uniform in the process. And finally, less than 10^{-15} seconds into the birth, the electroweak forces knitted themselves into symmetry and the fields of matter and energy became unified.

Ahead waited only infinite mass, infinite curvature, and infinite temperature: the singularity.

The black hole.

Garry took another step.

They entered and were lost forever.

Chapter Twenty-three

He floated. He did not have a name.

There was no space. There was no time. There was no thing but that perhaps to be.

Perhaps.

All was potential.

The Planck distance covered him like a blanket.

He opened his eyes and saw a silver cube.

He regarded it.

He moved toward it.

Hyarl Thomas appeared between him and the cube. He recognized a relationship that didn't involve distance. Hyarl Thomas wasn't really between him and the cube, for there was no between.

He moved again.

"No," Hyarl Thomas said. "It ends now. Before the beginning. I've waited long enough."

Garry stared at the knife in Hyarl Thomas's hand. "What is my name?" Garry said.

Thomas smiled. "You have no name. You are the nameless one."

The cube glittered.

Remember. You can remember.

Garry stopped. The thought had come from deep inside him, yet it was not truly a part of him. It was a message, from himself to himself.

"No," Hyarl Thomas said.

Remember.

Hyarl Thomas snarled. The knife in his hand blazed like a nova. But he paused. A dim light appeared. It thickened, solidified. Garry saw four figures. They faced each other in a circle. Each clasped the hand of another. Their forms were outlined with fire.

"What?" Garry said.

Hyarl Thomas moved his hands. One held the knife. Lightning flashed from the other, striking at the circle.

Garry was frozen.

The circle wavered, then steadied. A strong blue glow appeared above the circle, spinning madly. The glow steadied. It was like a star. Then, from the very center of the circle came a sword. It shone with the same glow that illumined the star. Slowly, like a great fish rising to the surface, the sword pierced the star.

Hyarl Thomas screamed.

The sound of his scream was a wave upon the nothingness, a convulsion that shattered nonexistence. Somehow the circle had something to do with his memory. The group—did he recognize them?—was a part of him too. A Human part. How he knew that, he couldn't understand, but he did. He felt a sharp, sad pang, for he knew the circle couldn't stand against what Hyarl Thomas was in this place. Yet the circle had done its part. Jack had called himself the Key, and even in Jack's utter destruction, the hidden locks that bound memory were slowly being unloosed.

Good-bye, friends, Garry thought.

The circle wavered, shimmered, collapsed.

A ripple, a cry.

Gone.

Hyarl Thomas laughed. "Humans," he said. He turned to Garry. "Come, brother. It's time."

Garry looked down at what he held. Frego's knife glimmered in his hand. On the tip of the blade was a tiny dot of red.

Human blood.

Human.

The knife shimmered with blue radiance.

Remember . . .

The artifact held them. In this place they had no form. Garry understood that much. They were symbols, dancing before each other, orbiting the artifact like tiny moons. A red light flared in Thomas's eyes. He grinned.

"Did you think you'd avoid me forever?" he said.

"No," Garry replied, astonished at how strong his own voice was.

Thomas seemed surprised. His eyebrows rose slightly. "They thought they used me," he said. "They think you are their answer, their salvation." He paused. "They are idiots. They understand nothing."

Garry thought about Jack, about Glory and Oz and the Golden Man. Weird, bizarre, but Human. He felt much closer to them than to this terrible apparition who called him brother.

The weight of the knife was solid in his hand. Slow, curling licks of blue fire fell from its edge. It looked like Frego's weapon, but even so it was something more. Somehow the sword created by the circle had transmogrified, became a part of the blade. Garry lifted the knife slightly, and realized it had been humanity's final gift to him.

"Yes, they armed you," Thomas said. His voice crackled with cold. "Do you think it's enough?" He feinted with his own blade and Garry jerked back. Somehow the artifact remained between them.

Thomas relaxed into a seasoned knife fighter's crouch. His grin was a rictus of loathing. "They created two of us," he said at last. "And only one can use the artifact. You see how stupid?"

Garry shook his head. "There were two equations. Maybe it was meant that way."

"It was meant this way," Thomas told him. "They were manipulated all along. So we could meet. Only one of us can survive here." The gelid undercurrent of laughter beneath his words left no doubt about his expectation of the outcome.

"Why are you so certain?" Garry asked.

Thomas giggled. "I killed you once. I can do it again."

"But you didn't. I live. I didn't die."

Thomas paused, his face alert and careful. "A chance. An accident."

"Perhaps," Garry said slowly, "there are no accidents." He reached out and placed his free hand on the surface of the artifact. The metal felt warm and greasy and—something else.

Thomas nodded. "You understand more than I thought," he said. He placed his own hand on the gleaming cube. Garry felt a jolt of power run up his arm. "But no matter. You don't know enough. You never knew enough."

Waves of arcane current coursed between Garry's right hand and his left, between the knife and the artifact, between the sword and the stone. He shuddered beneath the forces unleashed in that balance and felt chromosomal doors creak painfully open.

Thomas's eyes were pools of fire.

"I always knew," Garry said softly. "I just didn't remember."

The older man hissed. White fire began to cascade around them.

Thomas's hand moved in a quick blinding motion and Garry felt his throat open. Thomas made a low, wolfish sound and drew his blade back for a final strike. Garry stared at him through a haze of his own blood. And Thomas paused.

"I should savor this, you know," Thomas said.

Garry felt his breath sigh through the rent in his throat. A spray of red colored the exhalation. Long, chilly fingers crept suddenly up his legs, into his chest. His knees went wobbly. His knife turned slow and heavy in his hand.

"Only one of us. Me."

Garry shook his head. His blood dripped on the artifact. Each single drop sizzled for a moment, then disappeared. It was as if the metal itself were soaking up his essence.

And now, finally, giving back.

A wave of vigor roared from the stone into Garry's fingers. Thomas must have felt something, because he looked down. Some of the unholy light drained from his eyes, even as his skin went gray and older.

"No," Thomas said.

"Yes," Garry told him. Their eyes locked. "Only one of us. But I'm the right one. The stone knows."

Slowly, Thomas forced his knife hand up. Gouts of crimson incandescence fell from the blade and spattered the artifact, but the movement was slow. Muscles suddenly popped out in high relief, tendons straining along the man's jaw. His face turned into a skull then, and for a moment Garry felt his own concentration waver.

One final time he reached down inside himself, where the memories hid. The memories now slowly coming into the open. Stuff he'd been born with because the memories far predated his own birth. And the new ones, the carefully cultured memories that were the Human part of him, the unexpected part.

The part Thomas hadn't counted on.

Garry watched him through a mist of his own blood. He held Frego's knife in his hand and felt the faint thread that extended out and away to places unimaginably distant, places in a time and space perhaps never to be.

Felt Garth. Felt Frego. Felt them all, poor Chasm, Jack, Glory of the green eyes, felt all the trillions of living souls, the bizarre arrangements of molecules and neurons and synapses that made up the puzzle of intelligence.

Of life and love and laughter.

Remembered Shar.

Hyarl Thomas drove his blade forward a final time.

"I'm human," Garry said, and raised Frego's knife and plunged it into his brother's throat.

The artifact began to sing.

Garry stared at Thomas's face. Thomas had crumbled to his knees. Garry held the hilt of the knife. Its blade was buried beneath Thomas's chin. "No," Thomas said. His voice bubbled.

"I'm Human," Garry said again.

Thomas's eyes bulged. His lips worked. Blood leaked from the edge of his mouth. "Not Human," he said. "Something else. Like me."

Garry felt unutterably sad. Somewhere the artifact continued its song, a long paean that rose and fell. Thomas tried to smile. "Too late. You still don't know."

Garry shook his head. "You're wrong," he said. He let go of the knife. "I just remembered."

The light went out of Thomas's eyes. He tried one more time to say something, but it was too late. Dark fluid gushed between his teeth. The knife in his throat flared.

Then he was gone.

The artifact sang him good-bye.

In the endless fabric of nothingness a ripple appeared. It appeared by chance. It was the work of quantum laws. It was a universe.

Garry's touch on the artifact felt warm. Its shape began to change. Slowly it grew around him, a great shining lattice. The lattice cradled him like an egg, soothed him. Took away the fear. Healed his eternal wound. It was an imaginary construct in an imaginary place, but it was real. Somewhere, Garry knew, it was real. Tiny crackles of luminescence began to emanate from the emptiness between the spars of the lattice. The light felt sharp and prickly on his skin. He could imagine that light penetrating him, traveling the nervous paths, filling him up like a transparent bowl.

And he remembered. It was sudden, as if a door had been unlocked and flung wide. One moment his past was a cloud. Then his memory stretched back, ever back, to the matrix of his chromosomal etching. He closed his eyes and let the flood take him up.

A philosopher once wondered how man could ever comprehend the workings of the universe. It was vast, so complicated. But compared to the complexity of the Human brain the universe itself was a simple toy. The possible connections between the neurons, the many-pathed dance of them, dwarfed even the number of atoms that existed in fifteen thousand million light-years of space. Life was a creation of the universe and intelligence its mirror. The son could understand the father. It was almost as if the universe itself demanded such a thing, needed those minds to appreciate the wonderful sweep of creation.

Garry sighed. He was the message and the messenger. And now he understood. A part of him retained the memory of his recent life. He remembered the first light, when his head penetrated the space between his mother's legs and gazed out on reality for the first time.

He chuckled. He recognized those legs. Glory had kept her secret well, but all secrets fall in the end. Mother, he thought sadly. How strange you are.

Now he appreciated the dance. How hard they'd all schemed, plotted, and connived to bring him to this inevitable point where he had to come anyway.

Hyarl Thomas should have known better. He thought he'd set it all in motion years before, when he'd manipulated the founders into taking action against him. He'd understood then the only action they could take—create the being hidden in the second equation. Create Garry.

Create me, he thought.

The lattice that circled him like a ball had become a globe of white fire. The strange metal that had made it was gone now, changed into its natural state in this place.

Impossible neutronium, Garry thought, and grinned. Of course it was impossible in the universe he'd just left. It had, in fact, never existed there. The artifact the founders had seen and tried to use was merely a reflection of something that could only exist here, in the heart of the singularity, where causality was random and the only true things were potentiality and possibility.

Yet it was doing its job. The light flared and eddied and washed him in its cool glow. Soon it would be ready. It was a tool, nothing more, merely a bag of tricks for his own hands. He was a builder. His creators, the true ones, had understood. A builder needs hammer and nails and perhaps a saw.

For a moment as he drifted, waiting for the time, he thought about the creators. For his memory extended far beyond the moment of his conception. They had been thorough, those beings who sought to rectify their error. The map of his genes was a greater code, and he was tapped into something racial that was not truly his own. For he remembered the creators themselves, great shadowy beings who moved slowly and thought long cool thoughts in a place so different from the human universe as to be beyond comprehension. That place had been different, with different laws. The software of the meta-universe was of different programming. Yet they had their singularities. They even created such things. And they had created one by mistake, and poisoned it, and, driven by their own peculiar sense of guilt and retribution, had sought to fix it.

They were lizards. Nothing that any denizen of High H'hogotha would recognize as kin, but lizards anyway. The essence of lizard.

Garry wondered what horrendous mistake had polluted the singularity with that essence, so that a new universe was forever biased in favor of the slow, cold growth of their offspring. For a moment he recalled his old teacher and the idea that humanity was an impossible accident.

The teacher had no idea of the truth.

Yet the actions of a comet had given the greater race an opening. They needed tools to fix the mistake and, like all good workmen, had used whatever came to hand. They weren't biased in favor of humanity, only against the error that had placed their own seed in control of a new universe.

Perhaps, in some sense, they were even altruistic.

Garry wondered if they could see him now. Then he shook his head. It didn't matter. They could never come here, not even through the gate of the Primal Singularity. They could only send their messages, and hope.

He shivered. There was no temperature in this place and yet his bones ached with cold. He tried to summon up the warmth of Hyarl Thomas's blood on his hands, and failed. Thomas hadn't understood either. Which wasn't strange. He had only part of the story. He couldn't remember what wasn't there in the first place.

Although he'd had clues. He'd thought he understood.

He had been able, in some extent, to tap the power of the artifact. Some basic part of him had known about the metauniverse and the unimaginable beings who lived there. But he'd thought he was an invasion, a messenger to prepare the way. He'd thought the artifact was a gate. And he'd thought, in the poverty of his incompletion, that Garry himself was the key to the gate.

Garry shook his head. So many wrongs to try to make a right. Now he saw the founders for what they were, ancient computer intelligences, gone far beyond their original humanity yet still trying to protect the gene pool from which they'd risen like technological fish to unseen bait.

And I was afraid, he told himself. So afraid. But why not? I didn't know. I didn't remember. I was only Human.

So sad, those words. Only Human.

Even the metalizards could not have planned on that. They sent the message, but the receivers had misread it. The two equations went together, were parts of a single whole. Yet only half had been created. And when the other half was finally built, it was flawed. The Human codes were added too, and the result was a bastard. No wonder Hyarl Thomas had frightened him. His brother, his *other half,* was entirely alien to him.

He remembered the astonished look in Thomas's eyes. Oh yes, brother, even if I didn't remember, my genes knew. Only in death was there life, and even then, only in the singularity at the beginning of time.

Thomas had been right after all. The death of one of them had been necessary. He'd only selected the wrong death. That was all.

Garry paused. The burning globe around him had steadied and subsided. He no longer felt its cool heat. Now it pulsed like a heart.

He sighed and closed his eyes again. It will be a Human universe this time, he thought. After a time he stretched out his hands and began to work.

I wonder what will happen to me? he thought.

And then he realized. Whatever I want to happen.

He felt the working of the metauniverse above him straining to break through.

Somewhere mass coalesced. Eventually there was enough mass in the metauniverse and the space of that universe began to feel the strain. Finally, what passed for light in that place was no longer able to escape the metasingularity.

The ripple spread.

Garry sang to the artifact and it sang back to him.

Nothingness split wide open, but in a very precise way. Garry felt the tolerances caress him like a ghostly wind. One part in ten thousand million million.

It had to be right.

It had to be Human.

And it would be, for that was his function. He held it all within himself, every detail. He held the artifact within him, the blueprint for what was to come. And he held more; all that he had learned, all that had been programmed into him by Jack and Glory and the rest. Every moment, every item, part, portion, trait, and peculiarity of that which was Human. Everything. Because he never forgot anything.

As the lights of the exploding singularity flared around him, he remembered something Albert Einstein had once said. "God does not play dice with the universe."

And Stephen Hawking's reply: "Yes. He does. And sometimes throws them where they cannot be seen."

In the beginning, the Singularity moved upon the Void. Three hundred thousand years or so later, there was Light.

Epilogue

He stood outside the door and listened. A faint smile touched his face. The voices were familiar. They were arguing about something. He sighed and pushed the door open. They were gathered around a table, all the familiar faces. Frego and Chasm. Jack. Glory. Oz and the Golden Man.

At first nobody noticed his entrance. Then Jack looked up.

He seemed puzzled at first, but then his foxy features cleared. "Kid, you're in the wrong place. Go away."

Garry stared at him one long moment, knowing it would be his last glimpse of those who helped to order humanity's future. Humanity in a universe finally built for them.

"Sorry," he said at last. "I must have taken a wrong turn."

He moved back through the door, but Glory's voice stopped him. "Kid, have we ever met? There's something . . ." Her rough voice trailed off.

"No," Garry said, and closed the door. "Not in this universe."

He stood for a few seconds, until the hum of voices resumed. Finally he nodded to himself. An imbalance had been healed. There was an inevitability now. Humanity had triumphed and would never know. The battle had been hidden forever.

He thought about the lizards who had never been. Not in this universe, at least. The strange bits of chance that governed evolutionary winners. The lizards had lost those dice rolls here, so thoroughly they had never even existed. But he would remember the squat towers, the heavy stone of High H'hogotha. He remembered everything.

Yet it was all right. The lizards ruled another universe, and the contamination of this one had only been a mistake. A mistake they had fixed.

He stared at the door a moment longer. In his hand was a tiny bit of metal. All that was left of the artifact. It held a secret too. He thought a moment, then knelt and placed the bit of metal on the floor. Someone would find it. He thought perhaps the Golden Man would be able to figure it out. There was a way to exceed the speed of light.

Now there was.

It had only been a minor adjustment. Now there were twenty-six dimensions where before only eight had curled in on each point.

The model would show the way. They didn't need him any longer. Just as the founders had puzzled out the first message, they would figure out this second one. He wondered what they would feel as they contemplated the endless string of black holes, each dumping from one universe into another. Snakes, he thought. The worm that eats its tale.

In the end and at the beginning there is only the breathing of the singularities. And we are the pause between.

He stared one final second at the door, at the key to the drive on the floor. Let Jack be a god. He wanted it.

He grinned, and turned, and walked away.

"Yes?" she said. Her brown eyes were puzzled.

He felt his joined parts quiver with the ache of it all. It was time to disappear, to sink back into the family he'd made his own.

She peered around the edge of the door, waiting for him to speak. But he couldn't. He simply watched her.

"Do I know you?" she said at last.

He nodded his head. "Yes."

She opened the door a crack wider. "Where do I know you from? I don't remember. . . ."

He smiled gently. "I do," he said.

About the Author

W.T. Quick was born in Muncie, Indiana, and now lives in San Francisco. He was educated at the Hill School and Indiana University. He is fond of single-malt scotch and writing about the near-infinite possibilities of technology. He is not fond of Senator William Proxmire or cats. He has been publishing science fiction since 1979 and intends to continue.